Acclaim for
Heidi McLaughlin

"Heidi McLaughlin has done it again! Sexy, sweet, and full of heart, THIRD BASE is a winner!"   —Melissa Brown, author of *Wife Number Seven*

"If you're looking for a book with a baseball-playing bad boy with a reputation for living outside the box, and a love story to melt even the coldest of hearts, THIRD BASE is going to be your ticket."

          —Ashley Suzanne, author of the Destined series

"THIRD BASE hits the reading sweet spot. A must-read for any baseball and romance fans."   —Carey Heywood, author of *Him*

"THIRD BASE is sexy, witty, and pulls you in from the first page. You'll get lost in Ethan and Daisy, and never want their story to end."

          —S. Moose, author of *Offbeat*

"Heidi McLaughlin never disappoints."

          —Nicole Jacquelyn, author of *Unbreak My Heart*, on *Blow*

"McLaughlin will have you frantically turning pages."

          —Jay Crownover, *New York Times* bestselling author, on *Save Me*

"When it comes to crafting a story that leaves you breathless, no one does it better than Heidi McLaughlin."

          —Rachel Harris, *New York Times* bestselling author, on *Save Me*

"Heidi McLaughlin has once again delivered a heart stopping masterpiece."

          —K. L. Grayson, bestselling author, on *Save Me*

THIRD BASE

HEIDI McLAUGHLIN

FOREVER

NEW YORK   BOSTON

Copyright © 2016 by Heidi McLaughlin
Excerpt from *Home Run* Copyright © 2016 by Heidi McLaughlin

Cover photograph by Claudio Marinesco. Cover image © Shutterstock. Cover design by Elizabeth Turner. Cover copyright © 2016 by Hachette Book Group, Inc.

Forever
Hachette Book Group
1290 Avenue of the Americas
New York, NY 10104
forever-romance.com
twitter.com/foreverromance

Originally published in ebook by Forever in June 2016.

First Trade Edition: April 2017

Forever is an imprint of Grand Central Publishing.
The Forever name and logo are trademarks of Hachette Book Group, Inc.

The publisher is not responsible for websites (or their content) that are not owned by the publisher.

The Hachette Speakers Bureau provides a wide range of authors for speaking events. To find out more, go to www.hachettespeakersbureau.com or call (866) 376-6591.

Library of Congress Cataloging-in-Publication Data

Names: McLaughlin, Heidi (Romance fiction writer), author.
Title: Third base / Heidi McLaughlin.
Description: First trade edition. | New York : Forever, 2017. | Series: The boys of summer ; 1
Identifiers: LCCN 2016037248| ISBN 9781455598236 (softcover) | ISBN 9781478970118 (audio download) | ISBN 9781478919162 (audio cd)
Subjects: LCSH: Man-woman relationships—Fiction. | Baseball players—Fiction. | BISAC: FICTION / Romance / Contemporary. | FICTION / Contemporary Women. | GSAFD: Love stories.
Classification: LCC PS3613.C57535 T48 2017 | DDC 813/.6—dc23 LC record available at https://lccn.loc.gov/2016037248

ISBN: 978-1-4555-9823-6 (trade pbk.), 978-1-4555-9824-3 (ebook)

Printed in the United States of America

LSC-C

10 9 8 7 6 5 4 3 2 1

To Dad,
Because of you this book is possible.
Thank you for always teaching me the importance of knowing
the game, not just being a fan.
How many ballparks do we have left?

THIRD BASE

BOSTON RENEGADES

Three weeks in and the Boston Renegades are sitting at nine and five. Not too shabby, considering pitching hasn't been as predicted, with the guys giving up 68 runs with only 73 batted in. If the BoRes intend to make the wild card race, they'll need to figure it out quickly, especially with an out-of-town stretch that could hurt them.

GOSSIP WIRE

It's being rumored that center fielder Steve Bainbridge will retire at the end of the season. If this is true, that could pave the way for Triple-A player Cooper Bailey to move up. I wouldn't be surprised if GM Ryan Stone makes the move to keep the BoRes a younger team.

Ethan Davenport, a second-year starter, is already spouting off about how he's going to win the American League batting title this year. Personally, I think it's far too early to make that assessment. Last year he was a shoo-in for Rookie of the Year until he got caught with a college coed who was, at the time, underage. Aside from his off-field antics, the nose-picking third baseman who tweets out his home address on social media has a lot of growing up to do if he's planning on securing any titles in the future. Who is stupid enough to tweet out his home address?

The BoRes return next week for a seven-game home stretch! Let's hope they can hammer out some wins in the early part of the season.

The BoRe Blogger

ONE

"Why do you read that shit?"

Steve Bainbridge, center fielder for my team, the Boston Renegades, throws a ball at me, causing me to drop my phone so I can catch it. I'd rather replace a cracked screen on my phone than take a ball to the face. Having a busted lip or a black eye isn't my idea of a good time. He picks it up before I can and scrolls through the blog post I had been reading. The BoRe Blogger hates me and I can't figure out why.

"Well, at least you're not being called out for retirement three weeks into the season." Bainbridge hands me my phone and sighs. This is my second season in the league and he's been a mentor to me. Toward the end of last season, I had a lot going for me until I messed up one night. Bainbridge was there to help get my ass out of hot water before our general manager, Ryan Stone, could kick me off the team. The incident in question? I bought some drinks for a minor who was celebrating her birthday. She was in the bar. Apparently she had snuck in, but because I'm a Major League baseball player, the district attorney thought he'd try to make an example out of me. Thankfully, the Renegades have a stellar legal team and I was able to get away with a few hours of community service.

Hard lesson learned. In fact, I've had to learn a few over the past year—for instance, tweeting out my address isn't the smartest thing to do. Women of all ages show up wearing next to nothing, and when your mom answers the door...let's just say there are things even she shouldn't see.

"Are you done at the end of the season?" We prepare our whole lives for moments like this without even realizing it. Like when your best friend moves away, or the seniors on your team graduate. It's really no different when someone retires or gets traded. Retirement is harder to deal with because guys usually move back to their hometown or their wife's hometown and you don't see them as often. At least with a trade, the next time you play that team, you can hang out.

"My wife...she gave me an ultimatum. I quit or she walks with the kids."

"Oh."

"Nothing for you to worry about, kid," he says, as he walks down the stairs and through the dugout, disappearing down the tunnel. Just a handful of the guys on the team have wives. It's a low statistic, according the BoRe Blogger, citing the fact that our general manager is rebuilding a team with young talent that can last a few years. I think our GM wants to win and is doing everything he can to make sure it happens. It has nothing to do with age or marital status.

I pick up my glove and one of the loose balls sitting by my feet and toss the ball into the stands. We have two home games before we hit the road for six away and then back home for three before we get a day off. It's the start of the season and I'm already looking forward to a day off.

Before each home game, a young fan, along with his or her family, is chosen to be our guest for the game. Not only do they gain early access to the ballpark for a tour, but if a few of us are here early, we'll come out and throw the ball around for a little while so they can watch. The fan becomes our honorary bat boy or girl for the game, going home with a ton of selfies with the players, autographs, and souvenirs.

Tonight's fan is a girl with pigtails and a thousand-watt smile. Her Renegades hat sits on top of her head, barely hanging on. Her face lights up when she catches the ball easily in her glove and she waves at me before turning to her parents with excitement. Being good to your fans is something my college coach instilled in me after every single game. It didn't matter what test we had in the morning, what the weather was, how tired we were, or whether we got our asses beat—we'd stay to sign autographs and take pictures until the last fan left. Our boss, Ryan, feels the same way. He says fans make or break you, and he's right. That's why the BoRe Blogger gets under my skin so much. I don't know who he is, but I'd like to meet him to find out what his beef is with me.

Reporters line the wall outside our clubhouse, waiting for an interview. The media is allowed in the clubhouse until batting practice begins. Cal Diamond, our manager, has a list of guys who will talk each day, even though the media tries to get audio clips from everyone. I've yet to be chosen. I try not to let it bother me, but it does. I know I'm young and say stupid shit sometimes, but I don't do it to be harmful to the team. My mouth just works faster than my brain. It's something my agent says I need to work on. Stone says he's looking for someone to come in and give us all some media training. In the meantime, I usually visit the trainer or go into our lounge before batting practice, which is off-limits to the media.

They call my name. I wave and smile like I've been instructed to do and enter the clubhouse. It's chaos in here, but it's expected on game day. The Renegades are high energy, unlike some of the other teams out there. I've heard rumors that some clubhouses are quiet zones, the "Zen" zone. We tried that once last year, and most of us fell asleep before the game started.

The idea was quickly nixed, and since then the clubhouse has been a mecca for craziness.

On any given day, this room is filled with towel snapping, raunchy jokes, and guys running around bare-assed with only their jockstraps on. The one rule we have in here: no women, no wives, no girlfriends, etc....Not because we walk around naked, but because we're disgusting and our antics will give a bad impression. We want the women to remember us for what we do on the field, not the shit in here. Besides, the wives have a pretty stellar lounge that they can hang in until the game starts.

I change quickly, slipping on my long-sleeved jacket before heading back onto the field for warm-ups. It's still downright cold in Boston. There are a few cheers as we start coming out of the dugout as season ticket holders arrive early. Kids line every available space in hope of getting a high five or snagging a fly ball from batting practice. After a while, you start to recognize the same faces. I look for one in particular that I've been looking at since the midway point of last season. She usually sits parallel to third base, behind the enemy. When I look over in between plays, I swear she's staring at me. I can't always tell, though, because she wears her Renegades hat low and I can't see her eyes.

She's always in a black-and-white BoRe baseball shirt with her long hair pulled back. I've noticed that she changes the color from blond to brown depending on the season, but it's always long. She's always in the same seat for every home game, which leads me to believe she's a season ticket holder, even though, by all accounts, she seems too young to be able to afford tickets this close to the field. It also hasn't escaped my notice that the seat next to her is always empty. It should also be noted that I look for her each time I walk out of the dugout and walk to home plate, or when I finish warming up between innings. There's just something about her that keeps me interested, even though I don't know her name or anything about her.

What I *do* know and like is how she's at every home game, wearing her

Renegades gear. I really like that she's a baseball fan, but more important, that she never brings a guy with her, leading me to believe she's single. I also like that she's a mystery—I know finding out who she is wouldn't be hard. I could send an usher to get her or ask the office who the seats belong to. One of these days I'll hit up the usher, because asking the front office seems like a bad idea. I don't want the ladies teasing me, and even though they're nice and motherly, they'll tease the crap out of me for showing interest in someone.

As soon as I step out onto the track, I'm looking in her direction. Her seat is still empty, but it's early. We have two hours before the first pitch. I won't start to worry yet. I've grown accustomed to having her there, even though I know in the back of my mind I'm making up most of the subtle looks I get from her.

"Looking for your girlfriend?" Travis Kidd, our left fielder, slaps me on my ass as he walks by. He turns and makes a lewd gesture with his hand and mouth. I throw a ball at his head, but he dodges it easily and starts laughing as he walks toward center field for warm-ups.

Each game, we meet out in center field to stretch for fifteen minutes as a team before breaking off for individual warm-ups. By team, I mean mostly starters and a few of the pitchers who will be working tonight. The rest of the guys linger in the clubhouse until it's time to work on individual stuff.

"I don't know what you're talking about," I say as I catch up with him. He puts his arm around me and makes stupid eyes at me.

"I see you looking at her, grabbing your meat diddler in between batters."

"There are *thousands* of people in the stands. I could be looking at anyone. Besides, every time I look back, you're touching your schlong dangler, so don't even think about giving me any shit."

He shrugs. "I see her looking at you, too."

"Really?" I ask, pausing midstride.

"Nope, but you just affirmed my suspicions that you're into her."

I shake my head and push him away. He stumbles a few steps before righting himself. "Ask her out," he says, in his infinite wisdom.

"Nah, it'll just be more fuel for the BoRe Blogger, and Stone is already annoyed with me. He doesn't need a reason to trade me."

Kidd bellows out a laugh, bending over and holding his stomach. I'm not sure why it's so funny—the thought of me being traded—but you don't see me laughing.

"Dude, even if you started dating the fan, Stone isn't going to trade you." He puts his arm around me and turns me toward the stands. "More than half the people in the stands are wearing your jersey. You're his young rising star, and aside from screwing up last year, which really wasn't your fault, you're the golden ticket."

Growing up, I knew I wanted to play baseball. I didn't care who drafted me, but I knew that once I had a team, that's where I wanted to stay. I worked my ass off in high school, earning a Division One scholarship to Oregon State. My junior year, we won the national championship, and from then on, I knew nothing was out of my reach.

"I want to be the next Derek Jeter." I imagine legions of fans standing and cheering for me as I tip my hat to them in thanks.

"No, you don't. You want to be Ethan Davenport. Be you, no one else."

He slaps me on the shoulder with his glove, leaving me to look out over the stadium. People file in as the smell of hot dogs and popcorn moves through the air. Their laughter mixes with the music, creating a happy ambience. Without even thinking, my eyes travel over to where I'll spend half the night. I'm out too far to see, but everything tells me that the first seat in row C, section sixty-five is occupied.

It's game night at Lowery Field and the Boston Renegades are about to take on the Baltimore Orioles.

TWO

After the national anthem, we take the field. Kids are standing up and dancing, trying to get on the Jumbotron. I remember trying to do the same thing when I was a kid and my dad would take me to the Seattle Mariners games. I always tried to get on, or get a high five from the Mariner Moose. Small moments like that can make a kid's night at the ballpark. Catching a home run or a foul ball is the icing on the cake.

As I'm jogging to third, I let my eyes wander to the fans. She's there with her ball cap on; the seat next to her is still empty. The slight movement of her head has me thinking that she's watching me. I purposely walk over to the Orioles' dugout and talk to one of my buddies from college, Justin Shaw. He's a relief pitcher, and I'll likely be facing him tonight.

"Shaw," I say as I quickly glance over the top of the dugout and our eyes meet. I smile, and she turns away, but not before I see a slight grin. Justin comes out of the dugout and we bro hug—something I probably should've done before the game, but she wasn't sitting there then.

"Don't strike me out later, okay?"

"No promises, Davenport."

Shaw walks with me to third before he trots off to catch up with the other pitchers heading to the bullpen. Before I take my first grounder, I look back just once to catch her staring. Maybe I should ask an usher to bring her to the lounge after the game or ask the front office who owns those seats. However, asking the front office either means waiting another day or waiting until I get the nerve up to go in there. I make a mental note to grab an usher during the seventh-inning stretch. There's a good chance she'll blow me off, but I won't know until I try.

The first to bat for the Orioles is a lefty. I'm poised and ready for anything that comes my way. He swings, undercutting the ball, which flies up high in foul territory. I take three steps forward and four to the side, waving my hands to let everyone know I've got this. The ball lands in the pocket and my right hand comes over automatically, closing my glove. I take the ball out of my glove and, instead of throwing it to Jasper Jacobson, our catcher, who is waiting for it, I toss it into the stands at the girl who has caught my attention. She yelps in surprise, but snatches it like a pro. I wink and motion to Kidd that we have one out, even though I know he's aware of that fact.

I'm trying not to pay attention to what's going on around me, but as soon as I catch a glimpse of a replay of me throwing the ball to the girl on the Jumbotron, I stop and watch. When the camera focuses on her face, I find myself trying to memorize her features so that when I see her later tonight, hopefully, I won't get caught staring. From what I can see, even with her hat pulled down, she's beautiful, and seeing her getting shy on screen just tells me that I need to know her.

When the inning is over, Kidd runs by me, slapping me on the ass. "You better hope she's a penis lover," he says, laughing all the way into the dugout. I don't have time to mess around with him or listen to the other guys giving me shit about what I did. Besides, it's not like they've never thrown a ball into the stands. So what if I purposely aimed it at a female who also happens to be cute? In my defense, I didn't know she was pretty until after I gave her the ball. I did it because she was staring at me and I wanted a reaction. Now I've got it.

Our first and third base coaches head out to the field just as the Orioles pitcher finishes his warm-up. Up first is Kayden Cross, six-year starter and first baseman. He's recently come through a broken engagement that has hit him fairly hard. He's a good example of someone who can't separate his personal life from work. They had met in the front office and after they got serious, she quit. I guess she didn't like being taken care of, because she took a job in California before breaking it off with him. This happened during spring training while we were in Florida. When he came home, she was gone.

Cross goes down swinging, putting me on deck. Up next is Preston Meyers, right fielder and seasoned veteran. His picture flashes on the Jumbotron, much to the delight of the fans. He's been a fan favorite for as long as I can remember. He's been in the league just over ten years and shows no signs of slowing down. I step out onto the track and into the on-deck circle. I adjust and readjust my batting gloves and my helmet before taking my practice swings. Each one is timed with the pitcher.

Meyers hits a blooper over the shortstop's head, putting him on first. Those hits are bitches and hard to catch. Infielders can't backpedal fast enough and the outfielders can't get there in time. I hate them. My name is called as my walkup song plays, "Down and Out" by Tantric. My picture, along with my stats, is plastered all over the Jumbotron, and cheers ring out across the stadium. After one year, I feel like this is home...like Boston is home. The fans of Boston treat you as if you're part of their family. I love walking the streets downtown and running into fans, especially the little ones.

I'm trying not to look, but my eyes seek her out anyway. She's looking in my direction, leaning her arms on the dugout in front of her. With one last glance, I step into the batter's box with one foot, keeping my left out until I'm ready to take the pitch. I adjust my batting gloves, step in fully, and then adjust the sleeve on my shirt before settling the bat at my shoulder, ready to swing. The first pitch is a ball. I step out, clear the dirt in front of me, and readjust my batting gloves. I'm consciously trying not to adjust my cup right now even though it's sitting slightly awkwardly. As it is, I'll be all over the BoRe Blogger's page tomorrow since I gave the third base cutie the ball. I don't want to read how many times I touched myself, too.

I know I'm swinging as soon as I see the ball. My lower half starts to swing as I keep my eye on the center of the ball. The fastball is spinning its way to the plate, and as soon as I feel my bat connect with the white leather, I'm pushing my swing out. I drop the bat and watch the ball fly deep over left field. Meyers is holding at first, waiting for our first base coach, Shawn Smith, to give him the okay. I'm halfway to first when I hear Smith yell, "Home run!" and the fireworks go off. It doesn't matter how many times I hear them, I still jump when the first boom happens.

Smith gives me a high five as I touch first. My pace is a slow jog as I round each base, getting another high five when I get to third. I want to look over, but I don't. Not this time.

———————◆———————

I look at the scoreboard from the on-deck circle. It's the bottom of the ninth with two outs. Unless we go on some miraculous run, the game is over and we've lost, giving us our second loss in a row.

The Orioles' coach calls for a time-out and approaches the mound. This gives Meyers, our right fielder, the opportunity to talk to me. Actually, it gives me the ability to stare at the girl who has held my attention all night. After my home run, I thought I could focus on the game, but each time I came up to bat or went out to the field, I was looking to see if she was staring…and she was, which really stroked my ego.

I meet Meyers halfway between the on-deck circle and home plate. Usually, we'd stand back or talk to the third base coach, but there's no coming back from this defeat. When I reach him I can tell he's frustrated; we all are. We're a far better team than what our record shows. Even though it's still very early, our expectations are much higher, and with the road trip coming up, we have got to get out of this funk, fast...before it's too late.

"This ump is calling shit." Meyers kicks the dirt around his feet.

"Has been all night." On any given night it's either in your favor or not. Some umpires come into a game with a chip on their shoulder. *They* remember everything, and they don't let you forget it. People say once the game is over, it's over. Umpires don't feel that way.

"Play ball!" the umpire yells.

Meyers goes back to home plate and settles in for what could be his last pitch. If he gets on base, I'm up. If he strikes out, my night is over. I rest my bat on my shoulder and watch—not Meyers, but the girl in the hat. She's leaning forward, resting her elbows on the dugout. I had every intention of finding an usher during the seventh inning, but lost my nerve. I don't know how that would be received if Diamond were to find out, and short of going into the stands the second the game is over, I'm running out of options.

It's a swing and a foul ball for Meyers, still giving me hope. The girl hasn't moved, and something tells me that she's focused on me. I should be focused on the game, but I'm not.

I lean over to the usher who stands by the field and whisper, "There's a girl in section sixty-five, row C, seat one. I'd like to talk to her after the game."

He nods and says something into his really cool CIA walkie-talkie-type thing. When I first arrived at the park, I asked if I could play with it. I was told no. It was a total buzzkill. I asked my agent to get me one, and he told me to grow up...Not one of my finer moments.

Meyers goes down swinging, and just like that, the game's over. We lost

8–3. I wait for Meyers to walk by before returning to the dugout, but not without one last look at the girl in row C. Another usher is walking down the aisle toward her. I climb down the stairs and pause where she can't see me. The usher approaches her and talks wildly with his hands. She looks around, reaches for her bag, and follows him up the steps. I can only hope she'll be in the lounge when I get there.

Right now I'm thankful I'm not allowed to give interviews yet, because it means I can shower and get upstairs more quickly. The reporters call my name, asking about my home run. They know I'm not allowed to speak with them, but they try anyway. I keep my head down, my classic move after we've lost, and rush into the clubhouse. There will be no postgame meeting; Diamond will save that for tomorrow.

I shower quickly and slip into jeans and a T-shirt. My hair is still wet and dripping down onto my shirt, but I don't want my third base girl waiting too long. I take the back stairs two at a time and enter the lounge. This is where the wives and girlfriends hang out, and now that I think about it, it's probably not the best place to have sent her. It's like vulture prey in here for new girlfriends…not that she's my girlfriend. I just want to know her name.

As soon as I enter the hallway, I find her sitting outside the door. She stands up when she hears me coming and keeps her hands behind her back, watching me closely. I come to a halt in front of her, and all I can see is the top of her hat. She's about a foot shorter than me. I like that.

"I wanted to apologize for giving you the ball." I keep my hands clasped to avoid the nervous twitch I have. The last thing I want to do is scare her away.

"Oh…do you want it back?" Her voice is soft, sweet, and completely Boston. Hearing her speak makes me feel like I have something to look forward to, like I'm home.

"What? No, I thought I embarrassed you…It's just…"

My knees go weak when she looks at me. Her light-green eyes are the color of sea glass and she has a dimple that complements her smile. I find myself wanting to rub my thumb over it so I can feel it.

"You didn't embarrass me. It was nice."

"What's your name?" I ask, needing to know, because calling her "third base girl" or "girl in row C" isn't going to cut it.

"Daisy."

Daisy, I repeat in my head so I don't forget. Daisy...like the flowers that my mother loves.

"I'm Ethan," I stupidly tell her, but I feel like I should introduce myself. "Wanna get out of here and grab some dinner?"

She eyes me, and then the ground, making me wait what feels like an eternity for her answer.

THREE

Being a professional athlete affords you some liberties. By liberties I mean I'm invited to A-list parties, I can get into packed nightclubs, reservations that are hard to get suddenly become available when I need them, and women… I've had no issues getting dates or even the occasional hookup when I want it. I even have a friend back home whom I see during road trips. However, standing here and waiting for an answer on whether she'd like to join me for dinner is killing me slowly. It's just dinner, which I need to eat, and preferably soon.

I'm going to assume she's contemplating what it could be like to leave this building with me. The reporters are likely still outside, along with the fans, although with today's loss, the latter might have actually gone home instead of celebrating in the pubs across the street.

"Look," I say as she raises her head to look at me. I want to rip her hat off so I can see her fully, so I can take in what I'm sure is one of the most beautiful women I've ever seen, but she's hiding from me. "It's cool if you don't want to go to dinner. Technically, I just got off work and I'm starving, so I kind of need to eat."

"It's not that." Her green eyes shimmer even with the harsh overhead lighting. Voices echo down the hall, making my time with her limited. I don't want to be teased or risk one of the guys making some comment about her that will have her running scared. I lean back slightly to look down the hall. There are three or four teammates at the end who are heading this way.

"Let me walk you out and you can decide on the way down." I motion for her to turn around and walk toward the door, keeping my hands clenched in fists and securely in my pocket. I can feel the nerves working overtime, making my fingers twitch like crazy.

Having a nervous tic could be considered disastrous in the romance department. Anytime I'm nervous, it shows. And it has been used against me before. Not to mention that the element of surprise is gone when I'm trying to do something romantic and my damn fingers move on their own accord. The only time they're calm is when I'm up to bat.

Daisy picks up her bag and slings it over her shoulder, the strap lying perfectly between her breasts. I shouldn't stare, but they're right there and it's sort of hard not to. I swallow hard and try to think of granny panties and toothless women.

"Which door leads outside?" she asks. I look at her questioningly before pointing to the one on the right-hand side. How she knew there was a door that went directly outside is beyond me, unless she's been up here before. If I get the opportunity, I'm going to ask her. Plus a slew of other things like: Why is the seat next to her always empty, and does she have a boyfriend or not?

Daisy moves toward the door, and I reach out to push it open, allowing my arm to brush along her side. The hairs on my arm stand up, along with a set of goose bumps for good measure. I've only ever felt that once before, and that was with Sarah when we first started dating. Sarah was my high school sweetheart. I went to college in Corvallis, Oregon, she in Seattle, Washington. The distance was four hours, but that's not what broke us up. It was her schedule and my baseball. Being a sports medicine student takes up a lot of time, and I was focused on baseball. We remain pretty close to this day and see each other when the team travels to Seattle for games.

When we get to the bottom of the stairs, Daisy pauses. I can't tell if she's thinking of an escape plan or thinking about what dinner would be like with me. For all I know, she's planning dessert, and I have to admit that I wouldn't be put off by the notion.

"Are you sure you want to go to dinner with me?"

I sort of blanch at her with furrowed brows. Did she really just ask that ludicrous question? I asked *her* to dinner. Clearly, I want to go.

"Why wouldn't I?"

As she looks down, I follow the general direction of her eyes. Her feet do this odd bendy thing two or three times, then stop. She sighs and grabs the strap of her bag. "I'm dressed like a fan," she says, as if this is an issue for me. I briefly appraise her attire: skinny jeans, Chucks, and a BoRe baseball tee. I happen to think chicks in jerseys or baseball tees are hot, and even more so if I'm interested in them and they're wearing my name on their backs.

"I don't care how you're dressed. Look at me. My hair is wet and the neck of my shirt is soaked. I don't have a jacket so I'm going to freeze, yet I really want to take you to dinner. That is, if you want to go."

I have never in my life worked so hard for a dinner companion. I'm not saying I'm a smooth talker, but shit, getting her to agree is like taking candy from my three-year-old niece.

"I'll go, but on two conditions."

"What are those?" I ask, holding back a smile.

"That we go someplace casual because I look like this, and that we go dutch. I don't want this to seem like a date."

I pretend to think about her conditions, even though I know I'll agree to them. I'm not going to force anything on her. I want to spend some time with her so I can figure out why I'm so intent on looking at her during games. I can't help but smile, and seeing her smile in return even though she's shy gives me a surge of confidence.

"I have no problem meeting your conditions. Shall we?" I push the door open so she has no other choice but to brush by me. The same feeling I had before is back, and I'm not sure how I feel about it. As soon as we're outside, the cold April air hits me hard. I shiver and pull my phone out of my pocket, bringing up my restaurant app to find the nearest place with minimal waiting. I don't want to embarrass her by using my status to get us a table, at least not tonight. I think back to her two conditions and settle on Tasty Burger. It's casual, close, and affordable.

"Do you need to move your car or anything?"

She shakes her head. "I took the T."

I'd like to do that, especially with traffic, but I'd never make it to the ballpark with all the fans on the train. It'd be fun to ride for the day, though.

It doesn't take us long to get to where we're going. Being the gentleman that I am, I open the door for her, this time standing back so she can walk in without touching me. I don't want her to think I'm doing that on purpose, even though I am. I follow her to the counter and keep my head down slightly. She orders and pays, stepping aside for me to order. I never look fully at the cashier until it's time to pay.

The cashier's eyes gleam as she hangs on every word that I say. Her dreamlike state is comical; it is the same expression she has when any of us walk in to order.

I reach into my back pocket, and then my other, feeling around for my wallet. Shit. I left it in my locker. I search my front pocket, hoping for a credit card or at least a twenty-dollar bill. I have nothing.

"Shit," I mumble, running my fingers through my now cold hair. "Um…"

I look at Daisy, who is shaking her head. "I'll be right back," I tell her and the clerk. I can make it to the stadium and back in under ten minutes if I run.

"Wait." Daisy reaches out and grabs hold of my wrist. I freeze midstep and look down at where her hand is gripping my arm. My arm turns warm and my heart speeds up. The longer I let her hold on to me, the warmer I get. The heat is radiating up my arm and weighing on me like a ton of bricks. I should pull away, but I'm enjoying the way I feel right now.

"I can pay for you," she says, as if it's no big deal. Except it is to me, and I feel like a complete shit for forgetting my wallet.

"No, Daisy. I'll be right back."

"Ethan, please." The way my name rolls off her lips sends shock waves right to my groin. I moan internally, trying to keep the thought of her spread out on my blue sheets out of my mind. I have to tell myself she's not a conquest, but someone I've been eye flirting with.

"Okay, but breakfast is on me."

She narrows her eyes as she lets go of my arm, and I realize my blunder almost immediately. I didn't mean it like *that*, although I'm not opposed to taking her back to my place. However, the look on her face tells me she's on lockdown and I just blew any chance I had.

I decide to let her wait for our food while I gather the necessities and find us a spot in the back. This isn't a big place, by any means, but sitting in the back makes me feel a bit more comfortable. It means there are fewer people to walk by and ask me for an autograph.

My phone chimes, and I pull it out to see my Twitter notifications going crazy. I don't even want to know what they say, but my curiosity gets the best of me, as it typically does each and every time.

Lisa @LisaBst—3m

@TheRealEthanD is at Tasty Burger with a date!!

The number of retweets and comments are ridiculous. I'm thankful there isn't a picture of Daisy, because I've already embarrassed her enough, but this is sure to make the BoRe's blog report tomorrow. I don't even want to imagine what the headline will be. This is the last thing I wanted, especially for Daisy, and I can only hope she's not following me on Twitter. Before I can even pocket my phone, the tweet from the BoRe Blogger shows up.

BoRe Blogger @BoReRenBlog—15sec
@TheRealEthanD care to offer a statement?
EDavenport @TheRealEthanD—5 sec
@BoReRenBlog call my agent!

I pocket my phone when Daisy sets the tray down on the table. She sits across from me, but doesn't look up to meet my eyes. I pick up a few fries and stuff them into my mouth.

"About my breakfast comment, I didn't mean it like that."

Daisy looks up, and I can't tell if I'm hurting her more or not. I shake my head and put my hands up.

"I'm going to be blunt, okay?"

"Okay."

"Here goes...I've been watching you for a while. You wear the same couple of outfits to every game. You have killer seats, but you always sit alone. I've seen you look at me and I've thought about talking to you many times. Today, I finally grew a set and asked you...sort of. My comment up there, you can take it either way, because I'm game for both..I didn't expect you to pay for my dinner, so I owe you something in return. I said breakfast because it's the next meal, unless you count ice cream, but it's too damn cold for ice cream. If you want to think I'm asking you to come back to my place, you can think that, too, because I think you're fucking beautiful and I really want to get to know you better. And if we did that tonight, it'd lead, once again, to—the next meal of the day—breakfast."

I say my piece and wait for some type of reaction. A slow smile starts to form and lights up her eyes, and then she laughs, breaking any tension I'm feeling. My left hand starts to twitch, so I slide it under my leg to keep her from seeing it. I pick at my food, waiting for her to say something, anything.

"I'll have breakfast with you, but I'm not going back to your place."

"Fair enough, we can go to yours." I wink and get a fry in my face. She covers her mouth as she laughs, and I want to reach over the table and pull her hand away. I want to see all of her face when she laughs. I want to hold her hand and see if I feel the same radiation of heat I did earlier.

"I can meet you someplace," she says before slipping a fry between her lips. I try not to gawk, but it's no use. Now that I have her up close, staring is the only thing I want to do.

"Or we can stay up all night and talk."

"You have a game tomorrow. You need your sleep." It's in this moment that I've probably fallen in love with her and don't even know it. The fact that she has so much concern for my well-being means so much to me.

FOUR

"How long have you been a fan of baseball?" I reach across our small table and take one of her fries. She eyes me skeptically. I can't tell if she's about to slap me or shove the rest of her fries into my face. Either way, I'll take whatever she wants to dish out, because both actions constitute emotion, and that would mean I'm getting to her.

"Still hungry?"

I want to respond with "duh" but that seems very childish and inappropriate. I pull my hand back and wipe my fingers on my napkin. "Sorry," I say and offer a sheepish shrug. "I'm used to finishing my niece's food."

"How old is she?"

"She's three."

"Does she live here?" Daisy pushes the rest of her fries toward me. She's a woman after my own heart. Of course, I dig right in and avoid the question. I hold my finger up while I chew and try to swallow without choking myself.

"She lives in Seattle with my sister and my parents."

"Where's her dad?"

I suck down the rest of my soda and fight the urge to burp. *That* would not make a very good first impression, and I'm really trying to impress this girl. I should've paid more attention last year, but I was too wrapped up in being a rookie and being so stupid that I didn't notice people around me.

"He's in the Army. Right now he's deployed, which is why my sister and niece live with my parents. My mom can help out while my sister works."

"I bet you're excited to go home."

I nod and pull out my phone—not only to show her a picture, but also to count the days until we're in Seattle to play. My notifications are crazy. I have a few texts from my dad and even more from Jasper Jacobson, our catcher and my closest friend on the team. I also have message from Cooper Bailey, who plays for our Triple-A club, and Sarah. I clear the screen and bring up my photos, handing my phone over to Daisy. My hand starts to shake, and before I can pull my phone away, Daisy is holding it still so she can see my blond-haired, blue-eyed niece with a dirty face, grinning from ear to ear.

"What's her name?"

"Shea." I cock my eyebrow as her expression changes, and there's a hint of recognition. I like that the name means something to her, which reminds me that she's dodged my question about being a fan.

"As in the ballpark?"

I nod and pull my phone toward me. "We're a huge baseball family. I was happy she was a girl because my brother-in-law wanted to name her Catfish and I think my sister would've killed him."

"Shea's a pretty name for a pretty baby."

"Yep, twenty-five days and I'll get to see her." I try not to sound nostalgic. I miss my family. It can be lonely out here without them. I think that is what gets most of us in trouble. The nights like tonight when we've lost and we're wallowing. If I hadn't asked the usher to get Daisy, I'd be either at the bar drinking away my sorrows or picking up some chick for a night of fun.

"So back to my question—how long have you been a baseball fan?"

"Hmm…all my life, I guess. My grandpa loves the game and loves the Renegades. I grew up watching every game either on TV or in the park."

"You have amazing seats, even if they *are* behind the enemy."

Daisy laughs. "Well, my grandfather is very vocal and always felt he could scare the other team back into the clubhouse with his mouth." She speaks about her grandfather with pride and a lot of admiration. I know I just met her tonight, but I can tell that she's definitely a grandpa's girl. It hasn't escaped my attention that she hasn't mentioned her parents or any siblings.

"How come he doesn't come with you?" I lay the question out there and am met with silence. She looks at her wrist, which I notice is void of a watch or bracelet, before reaching for her bag.

"I should go. It's late." She stands, avoiding my question, and slips her bag over her shoulder. I want to kick myself for seemingly crossing the line when all I was trying to do was get to know her a bit better.

"Wait," I say as I stand and reach for her. There's an awkward silence and stare-down, until I drop my hand to my side. "I know it's late, so let me walk you." Even though the station is right outside the door, I'd feel better walking her to the train and making sure she gets on. Honestly, I really want to drive her home or just take her back to my place, since we're supposed to have breakfast.

"You don't have to."

"I know I don't. I want to." I come to her side and set my hand gently on her back. My touch is feather light for fear that I'll scare her.

The cold wind is brutal against my bare arms, and I'm thankful I'm close to the stadium so that I can run back in and grab my stuff. Daisy shivers, folding her arms over each other and rubbing her hands up and down to create friction.

"I can't let you freeze." I grab her hand and pull her down the street. Just holding her hand is warming me, and it's starting to freak me out. I'm not into that weird voodoo shit, but I'm starting to think she's a witch or something from the way my body reacts when I touch her.

"I'll be fine." Her protests fall on deaf ears as I reach the players' door and enter my code. We're technically allowed to come and go as we please, but they really prefer us not to return after a game. Luckily for me, or for us, the cleaning and grounds crews are still here.

I take Daisy down the hall and into the clubhouse. The lights are still on, and it stinks like sweat and other shit. I walk to my locker and grab the stuff I need. When I turn around, Daisy is lost in her own world. She's running her fingers along the lockers, our nameplates, and over the plaques we have hanging up. Some of the greats have their names engraved there, reminding us of everything they'd accomplished and built before we were even a thought in our parents' minds.

"When the usher came and got me, I thought I was in trouble. He told me that you wanted to meet me, and I didn't believe him at first, but when you showed up, I thought, 'Wow, he's true to his word.' Then you asked me to dinner, which I had to pay for"—she pauses and winks at me—"and I had a good time, but being in here…I've always dreamed of walking into the clubhouse on game day and wondered what it was like."

"Well, it doesn't smell like this, that's for sure." I run my hand through my hair and grimace because it stinks like something died in here. She laughs and shakes her head. Daisy walks over and stands in front of me. I've never really been attracted to girls who are much shorter than me, because of the whole having to bend down to kiss them thing, but there's something special about Daisy. I'm not sure what that something is yet, but I'm hoping to find out.

"Thanks for bringing me here."

In this moment, I wish I've known her longer than a couple of hours, or that we were hammered, because I'd really like to kiss her. Instead, I say,

"You're welcome." Except it comes out as a whisper, and suddenly the room is a sauna and she's licking her lips and I'm licking mine. We both step together at the same time, our chests matching a rhythmic breathing pattern. Our heads tilt in opposite directions, lining us up perfectly. One of us needs to close the gap and I want it to be her . . . There's something sexy about a woman who makes the first move, who goes after what she wants. I want Daisy to press what I'm assuming will be the softest set of lips I've ever encountered against mine. I want to feel the wetness of her tongue coat my lips, asking for me to meet her halfway in what's surely going to be an explosive first kiss.

"Don't forget to tell her about your pecker fungus, Davenport."

We both jump back and I'm muttering "Motherfucker" as she turns tomato red. If I didn't embarrass her earlier, I have now.

"Fuck you, Kidd." I pick up a piece of clothing and throw it at him. "What are you doing here?"

"I could ask you the same thing." He waggles his eyebrows and looks at Daisy, who has her eyes focused on the ground.

"We were just leaving." I don't want to get into why I'm back here because I'll never hear the end of it. I grab my jacket and sweatshirt and motion for Daisy to follow me out. She's right on my heels, bumping into me when I stop to turn around.

I catch her in my arms as she falls into my chest, using the situation to my advantage so I can feel her against me. It's a dirty trick, but I never said I played clean. She's the first one to pull away, adjusting her hat as she does.

"Here," I say, handing her my sweatshirt. "I've kept you out late and I don't want you to freeze because of me." It's going to be huge on her, but seeing her wearing something with my name on it will be worth it.

Daisy takes off her hat and tries to hide her messy hair. "It's okay. My hair looks crazy when I take my hat off."

She squints and sort of shakes her head. I guess I wasn't supposed to say anything about how her hair looks. How the hell am I supposed to know that? My mother raised me to be honest and say what's on my mind. I guess this is one of those times when media training will come in handy.

As soon as she pulls my sweatshirt over her head, I'm eyeing her backside. I'm not looking at her ass, but at my name and number spread across her back. There's no bigger rush for an athlete than seeing your name on the back of someone you like. This is a player-issued sweatshirt and not available for our fans to buy. The minute she walks out of here people are going to assume she's my girlfriend. Panic should set in. My palms should be itching and my heart racing at the thought of being labeled with a girlfriend, except none of those things happen.

Instead, I picture her in my jersey and nothing else, with her long hair free from any binding ties and her bare feet walking across my hardwood floors. The warmth of the afternoon sun beams through my window as she kneels on my black leather couch next to me. She's the only woman I can imagine in my place, and while that thought should scare the shit out of me, it doesn't.

There's a devil sitting on my shoulder whispering into my ear. He's telling me that I need to do everything in my power to get Daisy back to my place. The angel on the other side is telling me to walk her home, or as far as she'll let me, and get her number. The devil is telling me to bang the shit out of her, and I like that idea, except I have a feeling that once I have a taste, I'm going to be a greedy bastard and want more. And something tells me that waiting for her might be worth it.

"You look really sex—cute in my sweatshirt." I pull on the side a little; it's bulky and I don't even come close to touching her, but it makes me feel connected. Her eyes go from me to the shirt and back to me. The black fabric against her blond hair and green eyes makes her pale skin stand out.

"I really should go."

I nod, agreeing with her, even though I don't want this night to be over.

I wish tomorrow were an off day; we could spend all night talking, or just keeping each other company. Taking her hand, I realize how small hers is in comparison to mine. I hold them up together, examining them, before I drop our arms to our sides and start down the hall. Walking with her like this feels as natural as baseball does—only baseball doesn't make me horny, and she's definitely causing a reaction in my nether region.

BOSTON RENEGADES

Well...well...well...it seems Mr. Davenport has found himself a "friend." There will be more on that in a minute.

Today's loss hurt, especially after Davenport set a 2-run shot into the bleachers. Renegade fans thought for sure that after Saturday's loss, we wouldn't see our guys drop back-to-back games.

The Orioles, on the other hand, shelled starting pitcher Max Tadashi, bringing in early relief, who didn't fare much better.

Steve Bainbridge looks like the rumors of his impending retirement or trade are starting to get to him, as he looked stiff and out of sorts, committing 2 errors on the night.

The Renegades are home Monday night with Hawk Sinclair taking the mound. The fans hope to see a better showing than the previous night.

GOSSIP WIRE

This year is shaping up to be entertaining and this section might become my favorite part! I, the BoRe Blogger, often receive tips about the players. Some pan out to be juicy details and others fizzle. Last night's tweet from a patron at the Tasty Burger, in particular, turned out to be a gem.

Yesterday during the game, fans were shocked and some elated to watch Davenport openly flirt with a Renegade fan. I suppose we should be happy that she is a fan of our beloved Boston team and *not* the Yankees, where our wonderful general manager, Ryan Stone, joined us from. Davenport gave this fan the first foul ball of the game—is there a significance? I'm not sure.

What I *am* sure about is this: Davenport asked an usher to retrieve the fan and have her meet him somewhere...the wives' club maybe? From there we know, thanks to the Tasty Burger's customer, that they went to dinner. Now, I don't know about you, but I'm thinking Ethan Davenport can afford someplace better...but that's just me.

I, of course, asked Davenport for a comment, but all I got was "Call my agent." My sources tell me that Davenport's newest conquest left the stadium with him well after eleven wearing his team sweatshirt. Now if that doesn't say "hookup" or, at the very least, mean there's some kind of romance going on...I don't know what does.

The BoRe Blogger

FIVE

One thing I learned last night about Daisy is that she's stubborn. When we arrived at the train station, I asked for her number. She actually balked until I reminded her that we were supposed to be having breakfast in the morning. When she tried to tell me breakfast wasn't necessary, I told her she could either let me take her or I could make sure she gets every foul ball I catch so everyone can see her face on the Jumbotron. Once she realized that I wasn't giving up, she finally relented and gave me her number.

Now I'm sitting outside the restaurant she chose, waiting for her to get here. We're close to Boston University. It never occurred to me to find out what Daisy does. I guess I assumed she works, but now that I think about it, I've seen her at afternoon games before. So unless she has a flexible work schedule, she's most likely a student.

I pull out my phone and scroll through my notifications. My Twitter is going crazy with the new BoRe Blogger post that went live at five a.m. I'd really like to find this guy and pound his face into the bricks along the Freedom Trail. He doesn't know jack shit about me, yet he runs his mouth behind the cloak of the Internet, never showing his face or telling us his identity. In my book that's a coward. The shit he wrote about last night makes my time with Daisy feel cheapened. If I didn't think he'd misconstrue my words, I'd give him the interview he so desperately wants…All we need is a dark alley with no witnesses.

I spot Daisy walking down the street and take a moment to watch her. She's focused on her phone and is wearing her earbuds, making herself completely oblivious to her surroundings. I have the sudden urge to yell at her and show her how much danger she's putting herself in right now, but also to protect her by making sure she's being driven from her house to every single destination she needs to get to.

Thinking like that is only going to get me in trouble. I doubt Daisy wants me as a knight in shining armor. Her shoulder bag is in the same spot as yesterday, but this time she's carrying another bag, and I'm really hoping it's not my sweatshirt. There's a part of me that doesn't want it back, that wants to see her in it again, but getting a fine for not having my uniform isn't really my cup of tea.

When she's closer, I get out of my SUV and wait for her at the rear of it. I rest against the back with my hands in my pockets. As she steps into the parking lot, she looks up. Even from this distance I can see her smile. I have no choice but to return one as well. It's automatic, whether I want to or not.

"Good morning," I say, reaching out and moving a windblown strand of hair away from her face. I know I've caught her off guard when her lips part. Hell, I've caught myself off guard, but it feels good to touch her. I wish we had shared a kiss last night, because the urge to kiss her now is at the forefront of my thoughts. I'd give anything to be able to cup her delicate face in my hands and to press my lips against hers.

"Sorry I'm late. I missed my train."

"It's okay. You know I could've come to pick you up."

She looks away, fumbling with her phone. "It doesn't look busy; we should be able to get a table right away."

She deflects my statement about picking her up. Maybe that's a hint, and I shouldn't ask about anything that has to do with where she lives. Either that or I'm being friend-zoned. I've never been friend-zoned before, and I'm not sure I'm going to like it here.

Daisy pushes the bag in her hand toward me. "Your sweatshirt," she explains.

"Thanks." I take the bag and push off my car so I can put it in the back-seat. My luggage for our six-day road trip is in back and ready to be trans-ported by Renegades staff. The timing really can't be any worse, especially when I'm trying to get to know someone. Not that any time between Feb-ruary and October will ever be convenient. I get the impression that Daisy is different from the others. It's hard to put my finger on why. Maybe it's the thrill or the fact that she doesn't give a rat's ass about who I am.

Daisy is by my side when I shut the car door. Her being there gives me a glimmer of hope, although I don't know why I'm worried about whether she's into me or not. If not, I'll move on, no big deal. Thing is, though, I want to test the waters and see where this could go. I know that means spending time together, which I don't have, but with creative scheduling, and some flexibility on her part, we can see each other a lot. She's the first woman who has held my attention longer than one night, even if she doesn't know I've been watching her from the field.

I place my hand on her shoulder and open the door, guiding her in. She tells the hostess "Two" and follows her to where we're going to sit. The booth—if that's what it can be called—is small and does not accommodate my six-foot-two frame.

"Good game last night," the hostess says as she shoots a flirtatious smile in my direction.

"Thanks," I say as I sit down. The game sucked, and the fact that she thinks I played well means she's not a true fan. A real fan would point out my flaws and tell me to do better next time.

The table is small; my knees almost touch the underside. If I stretch out, I'll take up the space that Daisy is occupying, too.

"Do you think we could sit in that booth over there?" I point to one a few rows down and near the window. The hostess sighs as she picks up our menus and walks over. I let Daisy lead the way, with me following close behind.

"We'll take some coffee, please." The hostess nods and walks away.

Daisy leans forward and says, "She wanted to stay and flirt with you."

I look over my shoulder to find her returning with our coffee. She sets down two full mugs, along with a carafe and a bowl of creamer, before walking way. I push one mug toward Daisy and wrap my left hand around the other one. I'm not much of a coffee drinker, but if my hand is holding something it may not twitch that badly. With my free hand, I decide to take a gamble and pick up Daisy's hand, threading our fingers together.

"She doesn't interest me. I'd rather flirt with you."

Daisy goes rigid, and fear rushes through me. I've crossed the line. I pull my hand back and slide it under my leg.

"I'm sorry. I was out of line."

"No, it's—"

I hold my hand up. "It's cool, Daisy. We just met and I'm being pushy. We're good." I hand her the menu and hold mine in front of me. I don't want her to see the look of annoyance on my face. I'm Ethan Davenport, starting third baseman for the Boston Renegades—getting women isn't a problem for me.

We order breakfast engulfed in an awkward silence. I shouldn't have tried to force anything on her. We just met and we're both sober . . . and it's not like we're playing off residual feelings from a night between the sheets.

"Do you work?" I finally ask, breaking the tension.

Daisy sets her fork down and places her hands in her lap. "No, not exactly." Her answer is curt and to the point. No elaboration on what she does during the day or when she's not at the stadium watching the game.

My frustration level is growing by leaps and bounds. I'm tempted to pay the check and bail, but something holds me back. I lean forward and pull her chin up with my index finger.

"Okay, I'll start. I'm twenty-two years old. I graduated from Oregon State University with a degree in communications. I play third base for the Boston Renegades. My name's Ethan Davenport, what's yours?"

"Daisy Robinson."

"Hi, Daisy, it's nice to meet you. Where are you from?"

"Boston, born and bred. How about you?"

"Seattle, Washington." I can't help but smile, happy that she's playing along. "When you leave here today, what are you going to do?" I ask before she has a chance to ask me another question. She sighs and looks out the window.

"I'm a student at Boston University. I study journalism."

Now we're getting somewhere. "How old are you?" Please be legal.

"I'm twenty. My birthday is April thirtieth, and before you check, it's an off day," she says with a small smile and a roll of her eyes.

A grin creeps across my face as I pull out my phone to verify that she is, in fact, correct. "That's a shame. I would've had everyone sing to you. What time's your first class?"

"I missed it. My next one is at ten."

I lean back, flabbergasted that she'd skip class if she wasn't interested in me. "Why would you do that?"

Daisy shrugs. "I needed to return your sweatshirt."

"You could've brought it to the park tonight."

"Yes, but then people would talk, and you don't need any more rumors being spread around. You have enough."

I smirk and lean forward. "You shouldn't believe everything you read."

"I'm sure some of them are true."

"If they were true, they wouldn't be rumors," I say, shrugging. I need this conversation to go somewhere else, because I don't like the current direction. I'm not perfect. I never claim to be. I'm also no different than any other single man in the league. I like women and they like me. Some just like to blab louder. She stares at me like I'm supposed to dispel or confirm what has been written about me, and that pisses me off.

My mood changes in an instant. Here I am trying to figure this girl out, get to know her, and she's bringing up the rumors floating around about me. I finish my coffee and signal for the check. I can't change her mind, and I honestly think she's okay with that. I have a game to prepare for, a title to win.

"I'd offer you a ride, but you're going to tell me no or ignore me, so... I guess I'll see you at the game or something." I throw down some money and leave her sitting at the table. I don't look back to see if she's watching me walk away or getting up to chase after me. I already know she's not. I have the feeling she met with me out of obligation and that's it, just to appease me. And I don't need those kinds of people in my life.

It sucks, because I think she's hot and she definitely causes a reaction, but so will the next one, and the one after that. Besides, with the road trip coming up, there will be plenty of opportunities to take out my frustrations.

As I drive toward the ballpark, hours before I'm due to be there, I think about the almost-kiss last night. I'm not stupid enough to read into things. She felt something, and whatever happened after we parted last night has changed her mind. When I had her in the clubhouse, she was in her own world, getting lost in the memorabilia that we keep in there. I was able to do that for her, and that brought something out in her. I guess it just wasn't enough. It's not like I was asking for a commitment or professing my love; I was just hoping to hang out and see where things go. No pressure.

My phone starts beeping and I reach for it, even though we're in a hands-free state. If it's Daisy texting, I want to know what she has to say. Thankfully, my light turns red and I'm able to check. It's not from Daisy, but from Sarah.

> **Sarah Miller:** 25 days / dinner with my folks?
> *Is this a countdown to sex?*
> **Sarah Miller:** Yes. I miss you. Work sucks. M&D say hi!
> *Miss you too. See you in 25*

Daisy's name is right below Sarah's. It's funny; here I am trying to put the moves on Daisy, and my ex is texting about hooking up when I get to town. My relationship with Sarah is the one thing the BoRe Blogger doesn't know about, and hopefully never will. I don't know what I'd do if he found out about her and started posting shit. Besides, I'm not the only guy on the team who has women in the towns we visit.

I think about erasing Daisy's number. I don't need it and will probably never use it again. Thing is, though, I can't bring myself to swipe left and hit the red delete button. And that alone speaks volumes.

SIX

I strike out for the third time in this game, ending the inning. I slam my bat down, breaking it in two, and throw the piece left in my hand toward the bat boy. The umpire says something, but I'm walking away from him so I can't hear him. My batting gloves and helmet are next as I throw them toward the dugout and walk to third base. The only saving grace is that we're winning.

The bat boy brings my glove out without saying a word to me. Usually, he has something sarcastic about the umpire to offer up after I strike out, but not today, and it's probably for the best. My current mood is less than stellar. Not only did my morning not go as planned, but as the guys started showing up, so did the razzing. I get it. I do the same thing when one of the guys hooks up. It just sucks that it was over before it even started. Everyone had a comment about Daisy, and each one pissed me off more than the last. I know we're family, but sometimes shit goes too far.

During warm-ups, I positioned myself so I could watch for her to come down the stairs to her seat. When she finally appeared, I changed positions and kept my back to her. Part of me was hoping she'd bring someone with her to show me she's with someone and it's not just that she's not interested in me. But, as always, she showed up alone, wearing the same hat, with her long hair in a braid and her bag crossed over the shoulder of her white-and-black Renegades shirt. I didn't want to see her looking for me or catch me looking at her. I haven't looked over once since she arrived. I refuse to acknowledge her. It's petty, but my damn feelings are hurt because she thinks the rumors she's read about me are true. She didn't even try to get to know me to form her own opinion, just went straight to what she's been led to believe by people who know me about as much as she does.

"I think someone is trying to get your attention." Easton Bennett, phenomenal shortstop for my beloved Renegades, motions toward the stands. He's standing next to me as we take practice grounders while our closer, Kenjiro Tomita, warms up.

"Eh, she's just another fan," I say, shrugging it off as if she's no big deal. In the grand scheme of things, she's not. I shouldn't care about what happened this morning, but I do. I had hoped she and I could have a good time together. That's what I get for thinking.

"Hit it and quit it already?" He bends to field the ball and does some twisty shit to get it back to first basemen Kayden Cross.

"Not even close." I field a ball and send it back to first. "I think I came on too strong and scared her away."

"I'd say she probably wants a second chance." Bennett walks over to his spot on the field and pushes the dirt around where he's going to stand. I'm tempted to look over at her, but it's not worth the aggravation.

I want to get this game finished and get on the plane. Three days in Florida will be a welcome reprieve from the cold weather. I'm ready for the sun, the sand, and plenty of women. I think that's what I need, someone to get my mind off the little mind fuckery I was trying to play on it last night and this morning. Thinking that I could get to know a fan was a momentary lapse of judgment and something I'll never do again. I'm better at the no-name ladies who like to pay attention to me. It's better that way. They know what they want and how to get it—and most don't ask a lot of questions. Plus, I'm usually drunker than shit.

The top of the ninth gets underway and just like that, Tomita has two batters sitting down. I raise two fingers in the air for the outfielders, even though all they have to do is turn around and look at the scoreboard to see the outs. It's a practice from Little League through high school and college. It makes me feel better knowing I told my teammates, just in case.

There's one batter left and then we're on the road for six days. After Tampa Bay, we're heading to Baltimore to face the Orioles again. Hopefully, we fare better than the two and two we did for this home stand. A sweep would be nice.

The last pitch is sent toward home; it's a swing and miss, with another broken bat. I feel his frustration. We meet at the pitcher's mound, raise our hats, and start tapping each others' ass in a sign of solidarity after our win. Most of us wave to the crowd, as I usually do after the game, but not today, especially not toward my favorite side of the field.

I'm the first one off the field and quickly make my way to the clubhouse. As usual, the reporters call my name, but after today's performance, even if I were allowed to talk, I'd have nothing to say. I played like shit. I let a chick get in my head and distract me from my game and that can't happen. Even back when Sarah and I broke up, I was focused. I have to be focused at all times, because at any given moment my name could be on the waiver wire. I don't want to give general manager Stone any reason to trade me.

As soon as I'm in the clubhouse, my gear comes off. My hat and glove are first, followed by my dirt-filled cleats. My mother used to make me undress in the garage when I was younger, saying her house isn't a locker room. I never understood it until I got to high school and had a locker room to change in. After the first time I took off my cleats and dirt piled up in front of my door, I was thankful I didn't have to clean up the mess.

The guys come in, loud and rowdy. They're satisfied with the win. Most played well and have reason to celebrate. I exchange some high fives with them before I head to the shower. The night before a road trip, things are hectic. We leave right from the stadium and fly at night. By the time we get out of here, two buses will be waiting for us, one for the team and the other for personnel. The best part is we don't have to go through security. We have our own TSA personnel on site that check each of us before we board the bus. Then the police escort by Boston's finest gets us to Logan Airport.

Our chartered flight, on our custom plane, will be ready when we arrive. Each flight has the same flight crew, which makes it easy. They know what we want without asking. The flight attendants are strictly off-limits; at least that is what Diamond says. He doesn't want anyone screwing up the relationship we have with the crew. I don't blame him, and I think maybe the same rule should apply for fans. Although if that rule existed, none of us would ever find dates.

As soon as we land, I'm jostled awake by Kidd. I slept through the three-hour flight and feel like complete shit. My neck is stiff, my mouth is dry, and my ears are plugged. I don't even remember getting on the plane, much less deciding to take a nap.

"Now you'll be good to hit the bar," Kidd says. His words are muffled, but it's the same thing every time we land someplace. I move my jaw back and forth, trying to unplug my ears, but it's not working. He takes my head movement as a positive response and slaps me on the back. He's ready to party and get laid.

The air is stifling when we step off the plane. It's unusually warm for Tampa Bay this time of year, and an early heat wave mixed with the ocean air has laid down a thick blanket of humidity. Still, the heat is a welcome reprieve from the cold of Boston. I'm cautious and hold the handrail as I descend the stairs onto the tarmac. My head is still in a fog from my impromptu nap; mix that with the heat and I'm feeling less than stellar at the moment.

Two charter buses and a U-Haul truck idle not far from the plane. The second bus is always for the players; it's how the Renegades staff has set it up. Traveling, at least for the team, is easy. All we have to do is check our travel bag in, the same one every member uses, and get on the bus. Renegades staff does everything else for us. We're spoiled, but we appreciate it.

I follow my other teammates as we step onto the bus. A few of the guys have their usual seats and most of us know not to even think about sitting in them, but for the most part it's a free-for-all. I like to sit in the third row, on the left side, next to the window.

Kidd sits down next to me and pats my leg. "You, me, and a dozen single ladies."

Sometimes his enthusiasm goes overboard and other times it's catching. I can't help but smile. I'm game to go out and have a good time, even if that just means the hotel bar. We can usually find a few girls to party with and have a good time. The only thing that sucks is that Kidd and I share a room. We're not the only ones, but I do dream of the day when my contract says I get my own room.

The hotel is nice. A six-star resort, as my mom would call it. I don't pay attention to shit like that. I only care if the room is clean, the food is hot, and the bed is comfortable. Everything else is just a luxury and makes me wonder if it'd be cheaper for teams to start buying hotels in each town they travel to. It might save them money and make them able to offer lower ticket prices to fans. But what do I know? I'm only a baseball player.

By the time we're ready to get off the bus, our room keys are being distributed. Kidd and I take ours, exit the bus, and head straight to the bar. As soon as we walk in, the bartender tells us we have an hour. Kidd and I sit down and order.

"No way are we picking up chicks in an hour." I turn, resting my elbows on the bar, and look out over the patrons. There are four, not including the two of us. The other people are couples and looking very cozy with each other.

"I guess you're my date for the night." Kidd puts his arm around me and bats his eyelashes. I push him away and turn back toward the bar. Sports highlights are playing on the television. Right now we have basketball, base-ball, and hockey—it's fan central overload for a true sports fan. On any given night, you can flip through at least three channels to watch some type of sporting event.

I fish my phone out of my pocket and take it off airplane mode. It's only a matter of seconds before the notifications come in.

"Why do you even have notifications on?" Kidd is looking over my shoulder, watching as my phone keeps registering text messages, Twitter alerts, and Facebook posts.

"I like to see what people are saying about me," I say, shrugging. I pick up my drink and almost spit it out when I see Daisy's name come in as a text message. I angle my phone away from Kidd and contemplate whether I want to know what she has to say. I opt to read my Twitter alerts first.

> **BoRe Blogger** @BoReRenBlog—4hrs
> Renegades win despite @TheRealEthanD striking out 3xs! 2
> much hype?

My temperature starts to rise as I read the tweet that started the flurry of notifications. This blogger is a piece of work, and I can pretty much guarantee you that he's never played a professional game in his life. If he had, he would show a bit more respect in his posts. These people who hide behind screen names and do nothing but incite hate piss me off. There needs to be a law about this kind of crap.

I scroll through the responses. Some agree, while others disagree. A few women tweet that I'm hot, sexy, and they don't care if I strike out, as long as they don't. Classy. Another tweet by the blogger catches my attention.

BoRe Blogger @BoReRenBlog—3hrs
Seems @TheRealEthanD didn't bother exchanging numbers...

There's an image attached and I'm almost afraid to scroll up to see it. I can tell by the small sliver showing that there are people in the background. I down the rest of my drink, letting my thumb hover over my screen. When there isn't a drop left, I push down, dragging my thumb up.

Fuck me. It's a picture of Daisy holding a sign that says "Call Me." *This* has to be what Bennett was referring to during the game when he said she wanted a second chance. I shake my glass for a refill and look over at Kidd, who is engrossed in his phone. We're a sad, sad example of single men. Once my drink is refilled, I down it, needing the liquid courage to read Daisy's text message.

I close Twitter and press the green Messages button. My mom, dad, sister, and Sarah have all texted, along with my agent, but it's only Daisy's message that I'm interested in. The first line is visible without even opening the message.

Daisy: Sorry...

That's all I can see without opening the rest. It makes me wonder what exactly she's sorry for. The sign? Or the fact that she mentioned rumors? The guy who wanted to get to know her yesterday wants to hear what she has to say, but the asshole in me doesn't care. She's just another chick in the pool of millions. Unfortunately, I'm my own worst enemy, and I love to torture myself.

> **Daisy:** Sorry...
> I'm sorry for the stupid remarks I made, how closed off I am &
> the sign. I tried calling you but couldn't bring myself to actually
> press your name. I thought the sign would work but I guess it
> didn't. I just wanted to say thank you for breakfast and I'm sorry.

I read and reread her babbling message. She's sorry for being closed off? Doesn't she realize that most of us want to be like that, but our privacy is invaded? We're followed, spied on, and can't do a simple thing like go to the mall without being hounded. She's lucky that she *can* be closed off, especially from ridiculous media agencies. *They* tell the world everything and would probably even like to document when we take a shit if they could.

"I'm going to head out," I tell Kidd, who nods. We both throw a couple of twenties down on the bar and tell the bartender we'll see him later. He'll likely be our best friend for the next couple of nights. "I need to call home," I tell Kidd as he turns for the elevator. I walk toward the door, slipping off my sport coat as I step outside. The grounds of the hotel are expansive and illuminated by ground lighting. I walk down a path until I come to a bench and sit down.

I look at my phone and read her message again. This time I don't hesitate when I think about calling her. I press down on her name and listen to the ringing on the other end.

"It's two a.m." Her voice is hoarse, sexy. The sound of her on the other end of the line is like music to my ears and sends chills down my spine. I know in this moment that unless I cut her off completely and ignore her, I'm going to fall hard for her. There's something about her that I can't put my finger on, and it's driving me crazy. I don't know if it's the innocence in her eyes, the pinkness in her cheeks, or the fact that she's a baseball fan, but she's doing something to me and I'm not sure I'm going to survive whatever it is.

"You didn't specify what time you wanted me to call you," I tell her, trying to keep things light when I really want to ask her what she's wearing and if she's been thinking about me.

"Hmm, I guess I didn't." The way she hums sends a jolt to my system. I adjust the way I'm sitting to circumvent any building pressure.

"Do you want me to hang up and let you get some sleep?" Please say no. Please stay on the line and give me some hint that we can go on a date, or at least get coffee.

"No, I wanted you to call."

I let out a sigh but hold back the "Thank God" from escaping my lips.

"Oh yeah?" I ask.

"Yes, I need to apologize. I was wrong to assume. And I'm very closed off, but for good reason. I thought that maybe I could treat you to breakfast when you get back?"

"I'd love that," I tell her without hesitation. We talk for another hour until we're both yawning and trying to find the words to continue.

"Sweet dreams, Daisy," I say as I hang up. I hold the edge of my phone pressed against my chin for a beat longer before I tell the world how I feel.

EDavenport @TheRealEthanD
I'm falling…

BOSTON RENEGADES

The Renegades are BACK!!

The second major road trip of the season didn't go in our favor. Tampa Bay came out ahead, winning two of the three games, and the Renegades didn't fare much better against the Orioles. Sunday's game against the Os had us giving up 18 runs.

Three weeks in and we're giving up more runs than we're scoring: 108 earned / 114 given up.

Manager Cal Diamond chose not to speak to the press after Sunday's game. Could his time in Boston be coming to an end?

First baseman Kayden Cross is the only notable player from this road series. He had a hit in every game and drove in at least one run a game.

The Renegades are 12 and 10 going into this nine-game home stand, with two days off. Let's hope those days are spent on the much-needed...well... *everything*.

GOSSIP WIRE

I'm hearing more and more rumors that Steve Bainbridge is out at the end of the year. Cooper Bailey has been in a Lowery Field meeting with upper management while the Renegades were on the road. It's also being rumored that Bainbridge may have strayed from his marriage and his wife is giving him an ultimatum to get the hell out of Boston or else. Clearly, divorce is not an option for Bainbridge's wife. It's probably the ironclad prenup she had to sign before they were married, but nonetheless, a wife scorned is never fun.

Surely if Cooper Bailey comes to Beantown, Ethan Davenport will no longer be Boston's most eligible bachelor. It'd be nice to see Davenport get a run for his money in that department.

It'll be interesting to watch Twitter in the next few days to see how many "hookups" the Renegades had on their road trip.

One thing is for sure: Ethan Davenport seems to have fallen, at least according to an early-morning tweet after the team reportedly arrived in Tampa Bay. Let's hope he didn't hit his head too hard.

The BoRe Blogger

SEVEN

The first thing I do after my shower is text Daisy to see if she'd like to meet for lunch. I'm still in the dark about a lot of personal things when it comes to her, and it didn't escape my notice that each time we spoke while I was away it was about my game. She would rarely answer questions, except for the basics like favorite food and color. I get why she keeps everything to herself. I'm a wild card where she's concerned. She's read the rumors, and while some are true, others have been made up purely to get traffic to a certain website. Nonetheless, I'd be hesitant, too. Most people only dream of meeting celebrities, sports figures, and the like, but to have one calling you at odd hours just to talk has to be pretty freaking surreal.

She answers when I call at one a.m. after being in the bar with the guys. She doesn't ask what I've been doing or if I've been with anyone, even though I want her to. I want to be able to tell her that she has been on my mind since that first morning in Tampa and that I can't wait to see her again. I hold back, though, because I don't want to scare her away. It's important for me to pursue her the right way and not like the sex-crazed twenty-two-year-old that I am.

For the first time in a long time, I want this girl to like *me*, and not the one who makes a regular appearance in the sports pages in the tabloids. Rarely do I find a woman who isn't related to me who can talk shop and understand what I'm saying. Although that could come back to bite me in the ass if I keep playing like shit. I have no doubt Daisy will tell me where I fucked up and what I need to do to get better.

Daisy texts back saying she wants to meet at T. Anthony's Pizzeria. Between the pizza joint and the place we had breakfast, I can pretty much guess that we're meeting in between her classes, even though she won't tell me what her schedule is. I'm going to have to find a way to get it out of her, because I'm hoping there will be a day where I want to surprise her. I can see myself showing up on campus and leaning against my car as I wait for her to come out of her dorm or class. I'm getting ahead of myself here, having these thoughts. I don't even know if she likes me or just feels sorry for me right now.

The BoRe Blogger was quiet while we were on our road trip. The losses diminished most of our spirits and no one wanted to do anything. I didn't play as well as I had been, which is bringing my batting average down. My father doesn't like that and expressed his displeasure with my strikeouts after one of the games. Even though I'm playing at the highest level possible, you're never too old to take feedback from your first coach, especially when he's your dad.

There's a light drizzle falling as I drive over to T. Anthony's. I hate thinking Daisy is out walking in this. I shake my head, trying to clear my thoughts. My first thought about rain shouldn't be about Daisy, but about whether we're going to play tonight. We have three games until we get a day off. And that day off just happens to be Daisy's birthday. I'm hoping that I'll be able to see her, but I'm assuming her family will want to take up all of her time.

I park across the street from the restaurant and jaywalk through traffic. Definitely not the brightest decision I've made today. I half jog, half speed walk to get out of the light rain, and as soon as I reach for the door, Daisy is there, pushing it open for me.

"Hi." You would think that I'm out of breath from zigzagging my way over here, but I'm simply out of breath from looking at her. Today, there's no BoRe fan staring back at me, but a sexy coed whom I want to get to know better. Her blond hair is flowing in long curls that I want to twist around my fingers or pull on to see if they bounce back. She's wearing a light coating of makeup, nothing too heavy, but enough to make her eyes stand out even more. She's wearing a black sweater and jeans with boots, and as much as she looks like every other college girl in town, her sheer beauty makes her stand out. When she smiles, I am done for. If I weren't holding the door, I'd be on my knees in front of her.

"Hi," she says back, sending my nerves into a tizzy. One freaking word and I'm a borderline pansy boy. At least, that's what Kidd would say. I need to rein it in, because if I'm not careful, I could be making a fool out of myself where she's concerned.

"Hi," I say stupidly and end up blushing, which, in turn, causes her to laugh. I give in to temptation and pick up one of her curls and pull it between my thumb and finger before letting it go. It bounces back into place like a spring. She laughs, and all I can think about is giving her a hug. It'll have to wait until after lunch.

"I already got us a table." She motions behind her, the grin never leaving her face. Maybe we needed that hiccup to get past the awkward stage to where we are now.

I take her hand in mine and let her lead the way. As we walk down the aisle, my name is mentioned in loud whispers. I nod and smile at each person who's looking, hoping that they give Daisy and me some time alone before they start bombarding me with autograph and photo requests.

I sit down across from her and place my hands on the table. "I have questions." She blushes, but nods.

"I figured. Go ahead, but I'm warning you now that I reserve the right to not answer." Her hands are folded on the table like mine. I use this to my advantage and move my arms a bit closer toward hers. My index finger lightly strokes her knuckles and when she doesn't pull away, I take it as a good sign.

"Are you in between classes or skipping again?" I cock my eyebrow at her.

She smirks, beating me at my own game. "What if I were skipping?"

"Well, I'd feel bad. I know my schedule isn't that flexible, but I don't want you skipping to spend time with me…" I trail off, realizing that didn't come out as planned, so I try again. "What I mean is that your education is important."

"Well, thanks for that, Professor Davenport! No, I'm not skipping." Her lips curl into a small grin before she continues. "Is it okay if I ask questions, too?"

"Of course," I tell her.

"Okay, do you regret tweeting out your address?"

I hang my head in shame and nod. When I look up, she's laughing at me. I don't blame her. I'd laugh at my stupid ass too if I were her. "Worst mistake ever."

"Why'd you do it?"

"I was new in town and wanted to meet my neighbors so I thought I'd have a little get-together at my place, but no one showed up, so I sent out the tweet. I deleted it a few seconds later, but the damage was already done."

"Do you have random people showing up at your house?"

"No, not anymore, but I used to."

Daisy leans closer and whispers the next question. "What do you do in the off-season?"

"I go home and visit, but I spend most of my winter in Boston. I love the winter festival downtown, and I had my family out here for Christmas last year. With my brother-in-law being deployed, I tried to make Christmas as fun as possible for my sister and niece. What type of pizza do you like?" I spot the waitress out of the corner of my eye. I want to be able to order and send her on her way.

"Most anything, really. Sausage and mushroom is my favorite from here."

"I've never had the pie here. I'm looking forward to it."

"It's really good." The movement is subtle, but I notice it when she pushes her hand into my touch. To me, this is a sign, and I roll with it by taking her hand in mine. It's a bit awkward to hold hands on top of the table, but I'm being a gentleman. Next time I'll share a booth with her.

I quickly place our order and turn my attention back to the beauty across the table from me.

"So, Daisy, do you live in the dorms?"

She takes a drink of water and dabs her mouth with her napkin. "My freshman year I did. Since then, I moved home to save money."

"So no wild sorority parties?"

Daisy laughs, but doesn't exactly answer me. She stares at her lap, like she's thinking of something, so I tell her about my wild days.

"At Oregon State, I was in a fraternity. I wasn't going to pledge because of baseball, but my buddy thought it would be a great way to meet chicks."

"Was it?"

I nod. "Yes and no. I had a girlfriend when I went to college so I never really did the party thing, plus I was busy with baseball. But my junior year—that's when the parties were off the hook. For every party we had, though, we were also doing community service and fund-raisers. Some of them were a bit scandalous."

Her eyes pop when I mention the word *scandalous*. "Like what?" she asks, leaning forward.

"Well, this one year, the baseball team did a car wash...in our underwear...in November."

Daisy covers her mouth to stifle a laugh. "You can laugh all you want. It was the most ridiculous thing I have ever participated in, but it gave some orphans a chance at a decent Christmas."

"That was very nice of you."

I shrug and reluctantly let go of her hand when our pizza arrives. Our water glasses are refilled and we're asked if we need anything else. Daisy is the one who tells her we're fine and digs right into the pie. I like a girl with an appetite and who doesn't want to eat rabbit food all the time. Sometimes you need to indulge in some carbs to survive.

We eat the first couple of pieces in silence until I open my mouth and, in true Ethan Davenport form, ask the dumbest question yet.

"Do you have a boyfriend?" I catch her mid-chew, and she shoots me what can only be described as an "Are you kidding me right now?" look. She puts her fork down and covers her mouth with her napkin while she finishes chewing.

"If I had a boyfriend, I wouldn't be here right now."

"Fair enough," I say, knowing that's not even remotely enough to satisfy my mind. "I'm sorry. It was rude of me to ask or to make the assumption." I don't want to say that I made the assumption that she would, in fact, cheat, because I really do feel like she's different from the others out there.

"Are you going to the game tonight?" This is my roundabout way of trying to find out if I'll see her in the stands, even though I know she'll be there. More important, it gives me a chance to ask her out for later.

"I haven't missed a game in years, even when I had the flu."

"Wow, now that's dedication. I don't know if I'd get out of bed if I had the flu."

Daisy laughs and sets her hand back down on the table. Is this a sign that she wants me to touch her, or is she simply resting her hand there?

"Not to be rude, but most men think they're dying when they're sick."

I pretend to be insulted, but she's telling the truth. "Being sick hurts every single bone in my body."

"Yeah, but you can dive headfirst into a base and get up just fine."

I lean forward so the gap between us isn't so big. "But our bodies are trained for that. We aren't trained to expel the contents of our stomach. If we were, being sick would be called something else."

"Good point." I love that she concedes, but the glint in her eye tells me that even though I may have won this round, the next won't be so easy. Sadistically, I look forward to an all-out heated battle with her. I have a feeling she's a fiery little devil when she wants to be.

When the check arrives, I quickly pay and balk at her offering me her half. I give her a stern look, telling her that I don't want her money, before I crack a smile. The eye roll is epic and so worth it. I'm comfortable with Daisy and am sensing that she feels the same way.

As I leave the table, I take her hand and pull her behind me. My palm is on fire from her touch, sending my mind into overdrive. I don't give her any option but to follow me to my car across the street. Her short legs have to work double-time to keep up with my long strides. That is something I'm going to have to make an effort to change when I'm with her.

When we get to the side of my car, away from traffic, I pull her into my arms. She gasps, caught off guard, but I can't wait any longer. It sucks that I have to bend to hug her, but it's worth it to be able to have her pressed against my body. Her arms slide under my jacket and around my waist, as I take a deep inhale of her neck and hair. It's not flowers that I smell, but the sun and beach. Her hair smells like coconut, causing me to linger longer than what is deemed acceptable for a friendly hug.

Touching her in the most innocent way—a hug—is killing me. My nerve endings are on fire, like they're exposed, and I'm finding that I have to grit my teeth to keep some semblance of composure. I let my lips graze her cheek, hoping to convey my intentions.

When I pull back to see if Daisy is feeling what I am, she doesn't meet my eyes, effectively killing my mojo. I know for a fact that if she had looked at me, I would've kissed her. And I would've loved it. Instead, I'm forced to find any excuse to touch her. I push her hair behind her shoulder, tempted to pull it forward again. She looks at me, but the moment isn't right.

"What time is your class?"

"I have class at two."

"May I drive you?"

She nods, and my inner self is fist pumping like there's no tomorrow. I open the door and help her slide in before running around to the other side. At least for today, the inside of my car will smell like Daisy, and that makes me very happy.

EIGHT

After dropping Daisy off on campus and watching her walk away, I drive around town trying to stay enveloped in everything of her that's been left in my car. I need to find a subtle way to figure out what fragrance she wears so I can make sure she's always fully stocked. It's hard to describe and seems ridiculous for me to say she smells like warmth and home, but that's what it is for me. She makes me feel comfortable.

I stop at my brownstone before heading to the stadium. I plan to ask Daisy if she wants to do something for her birthday, preferably at my place, so we can have some privacy. When I open the door, I can tell that my maid service has already come and gone. It doesn't take them long to clean during the season, since I'm hardly home. The winter is a different story. There are days when I refuse to leave because it's so cold, and I dread the winter workouts.

As I look around, I wonder if Daisy will like my place. All my walls are gray, but with white woodwork and cabinets. I went with black, red, and white furniture to blend with the gray. My guest bedroom has a white comforter while mine is dark blue. My leather couch and comforter are the only things I picked out. My mom and sister did the rest.

I look at my king-size bed and imagine Daisy lying there, with her blond hair contrasting with my blue sheets. She's going to look pale, gorgeous, and sexy as fuck, and I can't wait until I'm lying next to her. I want to see her in my home, to see if these things I'm feeling are the real deal or just from the excitement of knowing someone new. What I *do* know is that my senses are heightened when I touch her and my nerves are zinging with electricity when she's near. I never felt like this with Sarah. That has to mean something, although I'm not sure what. What I *am* sure of is that my gut is telling me I can't push her, no matter how much I want to get to know every inch of her body as soon as humanly possible.

When I arrive at the stadium, there's a note in my locker to go see the GM. If it were serious, he would've called me and asked me to come in. As it is, it's still nerve-racking climbing the stairs to see the man who can change your life in the blink of an eye. What's worse is that he's only a few years older than me.

Wendy is sitting at her desk, typing away. When I walk in, she stops and smiles. "Mr. Stone is waiting for you."

"Thanks," I say. I knock on his door once before I twist the knob and enter. Ryan Stone is standing at his floor-to-ceiling windows that overlook the field. He truly has the best view, but there's nothing like being down where the action is. "Hey, boss."

Ryan turns around and motions for me to sit in one of the chairs that are situated in front of his desk. Last year, I walked in to talk to him about the BoRe Blogger only to be interrupted by none other than Hadley Carter, whom I had a massive crush on. Turns out, Hadley and our boss used to be an item, and she was here to win him back. If it weren't for her, I wouldn't believe in love. She won her man back, and they ended up getting married on the field.

"How are you feeling these days?"

I know he's asking about my nervous tic. Honestly, I haven't felt it during the past few days. Come to think of it, this afternoon at lunch I didn't have to hide my hands at all.

"I've been trying acupuncture, and I think it's helping, but not all the time. When I'm nervous, it's always worse."

Ryan opens a file and briefly picks up a sheet of paper before setting it down on top of the open folder on his desk. "I'm not seeing it affect you on the field."

I shake my head. "No, sir. I'm comfortable on the field and when I'm batting."

"The extra time with Diamond paid off, then?"

"I believe so."

Ryan makes a note and closes my file. He's been a hands-on general manager, making sure that everything is okay with his players.

"Are you ready for some media training?"

I can't help the smile that spreads across my face. I've been waiting for this moment for more than a year now. "Yes, sir. Tell me what I have to do."

Ryan slides another sheet of paper toward me. I take it and read it two or three times before my mind starts going crazy. I'm to attend media marketing at Boston University. I'll be on the same campus as Daisy for two weeks.

"Sir, here I was hoping your wife was going to teach me!"

"Nice try, Davenport," he says, rolling his eyes. "Everything good? Are you still obsessed with the BoRe Blogger?"

I grind my teeth and clench the armrests of the chair. Ryan knows how I feel about the blogger. I know some of my issues with the blogger are from my own stupidity, but everything I do, or the team does, is posted on this blog. Can't he write about baseball and call it good? The other day he implied that Bainbridge is cheating on his wife. That shit isn't cool.

"Unfortunately, I don't see my obsession going away anytime soon." It's probably best for me if I learn to ignore the blog, but I don't see that happening.

"Well, Hadley read it and she saw that you've been spending some time with someone. She wants to know if you want to bring her to dinner."

"Um..." I run my hand through my hair. Dinner with Hadley Carter is at the top of my must-do list, but having the boss there—not so much. However, it would be stupid to pass up an invite from him.

"I can tell you're uncomfortable, so I'll make sure to extend the invite to the team. We'll make it a party. Hadley will have fun with something like this."

"Okay, boss. Let me know when."

I stand and shake his hand, taking my class assignment with me and leaving his office. I pull out my phone and text Daisy as I walk back to the clubhouse.

> *Do you have Media Marketing?*
> **Daisy:** No, why? Do you need media training?
> *Sadly, yes! I'll tell you about it later. Dinner tonight?*
> **Daisy:** Only if you win ☺
> *Thanks, no pressure now! Can't wait to see you...*

I hit Send before I can erase the last sentence, and I shut off my phone so I'm not waiting for her response. I want her to know that I want to see her. I hope my message conveys that I haven't been able to stop thinking about her.

Despite the early-afternoon drizzle, the evening has shaped up to be pretty pleasant. Even at the end of April, it's still chilly at night but getting warmer each day. Tonight, when I step out of the dugout for batting practice, my eyes are right on Daisy's seat and, much to my surprise, she's sitting there with her elbows leaning on the visitor dugout, watching our second baseman, Bryce Mackenzie, take his swings. She hasn't noticed that I'm on the field yet, and as much as I want to go over and talk to her, I can't. I need to maintain some sort of professionalism right now.

Instead, I walk over to the stands and start signing autographs. The little kids, and even some big ones, flock down to the fence to get a signature on their ball, glove, or bat. A few of the other guys join me, making this a team effort.

I move along the fence, making sure everyone is getting a chance instead of having to wait in a large crowd. I really like giving kids one-on-one attention. The bigger kids tend to squeeze the little ones out, and that annoys me. I take a ball from a little guy dressed in BoRe gear. His toothless grin reminds me of myself when I was about his age. For the longest time, I missed my four front teeth. Eating food that summer was difficult, especially Popsicles.

It's still not my turn for batting practice so I move over to the third base side of the field, just steps away from Daisy. I know she can see me now, and when I look toward her, she's smiling. I've impressed her, or at least I think I have. I'm waiting to see if she'll come down to the opening. Each time I glance at her, it seems like she's thinking about it. I sign a few more items before moving to the other side of the dugout, where Daisy is sitting.

A few of the fans rush down, but my eyes are locked on hers. Before I left the clubhouse, I grabbed a brand-new baseball and wrote *Will you go to dinner with me tonight?* on it. I did this with the intention of giving it to her after the game started, but I don't want to wait. She walks down the few steps to get to get to me, saying, "Excuse me" along the way. At first the fans balk, but I think they get the drift that I want to see her, because before I know it, she's standing in front of me.

"Nice hat," I say as I tap the brim. It's the same hat she wears for every game, but my brain can't come up with anything else to say right now. She makes me fumble through my thoughts just to say the simplest things. I don't know if it's her smile, her eyes, or her sheer presence that gets me tongue-tied, but I don't want this feeling to stop. What I *do* want to stop is the twitching my hand is doing. I have a hard enough time around her as it is, and I don't need her distracted by this ailment. I pull the ball out of my back pocket and squeeze it, trying to control the shaking.

"I think you might like my jersey," she says with a hint of humor in her voice. She turns around slowly, showing me my name and number on her back. A few of the adults near us snicker, making me wish I could flip them off and tell them to get the fuck lost so I can bask in the fact that this girl, whom I really like, is going to sit in the stands with my name on her back. If I didn't have my cup in, everyone would see the fucking woody I'm sprouting right now, because this is hot…not to mention that it's also a sign that she's actually into me.

"Wow," I say, stepping closer. My hands rest on the railing that she's pressed against, and I let my right hand touch her thigh. I have to lean down to do this, but it's worth it. Even with all the cell phones out, it doesn't stop me from touching her. "You really know how to impress a guy."

"Davenport, you're up." I look over my shoulder and nod. "I gotta go," I tell her as I fight every muscle in my body from leaning forward to kiss her. We are going to have our first kiss soon. I just don't know when. I do know that I'm going crazy with the need to feel her lips pressed against mine. "I have this for you." I hand her the ball, and her fingertips brush mine, sending a jolt to my system.

Daisy reads the words and looks up, her green eyes piercing mine. "Yes," she says loud enough for me to hear, giving me the sweetest smile in the process.

"Fuck me," I say as I turn away and adjust myself. I don't know where the BoRe Blogger is now, but I hope he isn't counting how many times I'm adjusting myself, because I have a feeling I'll be fixing my cup all night.

Branch Singleton, our designated hitter, is finishing up when I get there. I use the extra minutes to put my batting gloves on and take a couple of practice swings.

"Hold the bat, Davenport." Cal Diamond is walking toward me, and all I can think is that I'm not starting because of what I just did with Daisy, even though it's nothing different than what any of the other guys have done. "Bainbridge had something come up and I need you to take his place at the Rotary dinner Thursday night."

Thursday is Daisy's birthday.

"I have plans," I blurt out.

Diamond stands firm with his hands on his hips, glaring at me. He glares at everyone. He's the manager; it's allowed. "Yes, you do...at the Rotary dinner. You were requested after Bainbridge, so get your tux out, get it pressed, and show up for dinner with a speech."

I look over at Daisy; she's too far away for me to truly see what she's doing, but I feel her eyes on me. "Can I bring a date?"

"As long as she's not a hooker." He slaps me on the arm and laughs as he walks toward the dugout.

Well, shit, this is great. I had plans to do something with Daisy and can only hope she'll agree to go with me. If not, I'll have to meet her after, if she'll even feel like going out later. My good mood is now soured by a baseball commitment. I shouldn't be surprised. It's how things go around here. Even our off days are baseball days. And organizations plan events around our calendar so we can attend. They use our names and the fact that we're appearing as a way to sell tickets. We could essentially send one of the guys lower on the totem pole of the forty-man roster, but people aren't paying to meet him. They pay to meet players like me.

I step up to the plate and wait. Each swing is powerful, and balls are flying out of the park, much to the fans' pleasure. I usually hit like shit when I'm angry. Maybe this is a sign that I'm not pissed off, but looking forward to a night with Daisy—who, mind you, would have to be dressed up. The thought of Daisy in a dress sends me into overdrive.

If I can continue to think about her in a dress, and maybe with that dress hiked up over her hips as she lies on my bed after the party, I may bat for the cycle tonight...or hit three home runs. That would be something, considering I've yet to do that in my Major League career.

NINE

Despite my stellar batting performance, we only win by one run. That win puts us at thirteen and ten—not anywhere near where I thought we'd be this early in the season. Athletes go into their new season with expectations. GM Stone made some solid off-season trades and drafted well. On paper, we should be number one. However, the standings do not show that. I can't let the rankings get to me, though. I have a job to do.

Tonight, Daisy is meeting me in front of the fan store across the street from the stadium. It's a good thing she texted that suggestion to me, because I forgot to send an usher to get her. That's probably why she's across the street—all because I forgot. This time when I go to meet her, my hair is dry and I'm dressed for the weather, although it's fairly calm out. My jeans hang off my waist and my crisp black button-down sits perfectly. I left my jacket in my car, not that I need it right now. I'm hoping for a walk along the harbor, where she'll need me to keep her warm.

As I step out of the stadium, a few fans approach me and ask for my autograph. I sign their memorabilia and pose for a quick picture before I excuse myself. The store is busy and mostly everyone is dressed the same. Being tall has its advantages, and this is one of them...I'm able to scan the crowd for the one person I want to see. I weave through the crowd, waving when my name is called and smiling when I'm patted on the back and told "Good job." I'm starting to panic when I don't find her, and I head back to the entrance so I can go outside and call her.

That's when I see her. Right inside the entrance, off to the left, is one of our old seats. It's there for display and clearly says *No Sitting*, but Daisy seems to be hell-bent on breaking that rule. As soon as we make eye contact everything around me freezes. The boisterous laughter that follows a win is silenced. It's just the two of us in this store. No one else exists as I walk toward her. I have a feeling she's been watching me since I stepped into the store. "Hey," I say, as she stands to meet me. My hand is instantly on her hip, sliding underneath her jersey, which bears my name. The feel of her bare skin against mine stirs a plethora of feelings inside me. It's intense. If she doesn't feel the connection like I do, then I'm screwed. I thought I was in love with Sarah, but what I'm feeling for Daisy right now is so much more. I never felt like this with Sarah.

With Daisy, my heart races from being near her, or with the knowledge that I'm going to see her. My palms sweat, and the anticipation of knowing I'll be gazing into her eyes has me on edge. It's a good edge, one that I want to be on.

"I'm sorry I forgot to send an usher for you. Tomorrow, you won't have to worry. I'll make sure you have a pass to get into the wives' lounge." The fact that I just said "wives' lounge" doesn't even faze me. I want her there when I come up. I want to see her waiting for me.

"It's okay," she says, as her hand finds mine. I want nothing more than to kiss her right now, but this isn't the place. Us being here, touching like this, isn't good for her. Fans can be relentless with the taunting, and I'm only setting her up by acting like a fool in lust…love…in public with her.

"Let's go." There's more to talk about, but not here. In the privacy of my car, or her place, or mine—any other location is better as long as we don't have an audience.

I pull her behind me through the parking lot. Her smaller strides make it seem like she's running. I *really* need to slow down for her. When we reach my SUV, I'm pulling us both in between my car and the one next to mine. There's slightly more privacy here, but not much. Video cameras overhead capture everything. With her back pressed against my car, my arms lock her in.

"I like you, Daisy."

"I can tell."

Not the response I was hoping for, but I'll go with it.

"I want to kiss you. Would that be okay?"

Her eyes travel to my lips and back to my eyes. Her tongue darts out, wetting her lips. These simple gestures have me getting hard just thinking about what I want to do to her.

"Yes," she whispers huskily. She wants this as bad as I do, but not here. Not when people are watching.

"Later," I say with a satisfied smirk, kissing her forehead. It actually physically pains me to have to put this off, but she's going to have to trust that I'm doing this for her and not because I'm a giant piece of shit. I open the car door and help her get in before running around to the other side. Once I'm in, I reach for her hand, and as much as I want to put her hand in my lap, the space in my car is too great, leaving our hands in the middle on the console.

"That was mean," she says as we pull out onto the streets.

"What was?"

"That almost-kiss you gave me. Teasing isn't nice."

Teasing isn't nice? Is she serious? Doesn't she realize that each day I see her she's teasing the shit out of me with the way she walks, smells, and bats her damn eyes? When she smiles, the sight of her dimple hits me right in the groin.

When we get to a stoplight, I turn and look at her. "I thought you'd much prefer our first kiss to be a bit more private. I know I would, because I don't plan to just kiss you, Daisy." I bring her hand to my mouth and press my lips to her skin, never taking my eyes off her.

"Oh," she says, as her breathing catches. Unfortunately for me, the light turns green and I'm forced to drive. I take us to a little restaurant on the outskirts of the city. I have a table reserved in the back, which will allow us some privacy from the rest of the restaurant. Tonight, I plan to get to know Daisy more, and if a good-night kiss is in order, it shall be had.

With my hand on her back, I guide her into the restaurant. The hostess greets us with a smile and says she has our table ready after I give her my name. The ambience is subdued, with low lighting. Even though the restaurant is busy, the noise level is kept low. It's almost like one of the Italian places in a mobster movie where everyone is just waiting to get blown up.

Our booth is in the back corner, and although I said I would sit next to her given the opportunity, it's not wise. I won't be able to keep my hands off her, and I'm not looking to embarrass her.

"I don't think I should be here," Daisy leans across the table and whispers to me. I look around, confused.

"Why do you say that?"

"Look at how I'm dressed." She speaks through gritted teeth, clearly angry with me.

"This is a casual place. The lady behind you looks like she's wearing slippers." Daisy looks over her shoulder and stifles a laugh. "Seriously, I would never do anything to make you uncomfortable or embarrass you."

She looks at me questioningly.

I shrug. "Unless you're at a game. Then all bets are off."

"What's good here?" she asks as she picks up the menu. I rattle off a few of my favorites, which ends up being half the menu. When the waiter appears, I order a rib eye and she orders a small salad with a French dip.

"I have something important to ask you."

"What is it?" she asks.

My hand starts to twitch at just the thought of saying the words that are about to come out of my mouth. Right now, I'd like to cut the stupid thing off, but I'm sure my right hand would take up the slack from missing the left. I place my left hand under my leg and prepare for her answer.

"What are you doing on your birthday?"

She tries to mask a pained look before she forces a smile. "Nothing. I don't have any plans," she says, shocking me. How can she not have any plans for her twenty-first birthday? She should be out celebrating and having dinner and cake with her family and friends.

"Your family doesn't expect you anywhere?"

"My family is dead, Ethan." I sit back, shocked by what she just said and wishing she could take it back.

"I'm sorry," I tell her earnestly.

Daisy looks away, unable to maintain eye contact with me. I get up and move to her side, sliding in next to her. Something tells me I need to give her a hug, so I do. She only lets me hold her for a few seconds before she pulls away.

"You don't need to be sorry. This week is a rough one for me, and I didn't expect you to ask about my birthday. I'm usually at a game. It's just dumb luck that it's an off day this year."

"It's fate or kismet, or some of that other Shakespearean bullshit we learned about in school, because I wanted to ask if you'd go to a charity event with me." I push her hair off her shoulder and leave my hand on her neck, letting my fingers play in her hair.

"I'll go, but I'll have to meet you there."

"Why can't I pick you up?"

Daisy shakes her head, and I'm starting to put the pieces together.

"Hey," I say, pulling her chin up. "I don't care where you live. Material things don't matter to me at all. I want to pick you up. Hell, I want to drive you home tonight and have been thinking about ways to find out where you live since we met."

She doesn't say anything, but she rests her head on my shoulder. It's an avoidance tactic, but she's touching me so I'm happy.

"My parents died when I was three," she mumbles. "It was a freak accident. The ice shanty they were in collapsed, and as they were trying to get out, my mom slipped into the fishing hole. My dad thought he could save her. They both drowned. I've lived with my grandparents ever since, but my grandma died two years ago and my grandfather and I moved into a low-income apartment."

"Excuse me for being stupid, but how do you have season tickets to the Renegades?"

Daisy sits up and pushes her hair out of her face. "My grandfather gave up a luxury to have those."

"A luxury?"

She nods, taking a sip of water. "Uh..." She shakes her head. "He's in a wheelchair and we live on the third floor of an apartment building with an elevator that only works occasionally. After my grandma died, he sold his van to pay for the tickets. Said he refused to give up the seats his father worked so hard for."

"He's never at the games, though."

Daisy shakes her head. "We don't have a car, and I'm not strong enough to help him walk down the stairs. The visiting nurses come to the apartment to check on him, and they'll take him out occasionally, but it's not like I can ask them to drive us to the game. They'll take the cost of the tickets and count it as income. We won't be able to afford them."

Her words hit home. I've never been in a situation in which my parents couldn't afford anything. My sister and I always had everything we asked for. Call us spoiled, but my parents worked hard to provide us a good life. And here sits the girl I'm interested in, spilling her guts about how she doesn't have any money, because I asked about her birthday. If I didn't know any better, and she was the one pursuing me, I'd say she was a gold digger. I know once people find out about her and dig into who she is, they're going to say shit like that, and it's going to piss me off.

When our meal arrives, I stay where I'm seated. It feels wrong to move back to where I was. Besides, I rather like feeling the body heat radiate off her. After a few bites, I'm putting my fork down to talk to her.

"About your birthday, do you *want* to go with me? I understand if you want to stay home with your grandfather." In my head, I'm silently begging her to say she wants to go.

"Do I have to wear a dress?"

I nod as fear sets in that she's a strict tomboy. She doesn't seem like the type, but you never know.

"Is it a date?"

Her question catches me off guard. Have I not given her enough indication that I want to be with her? I lean in and graze her cheek with my lips until I'm at her ear. "Every time we're together, you should consider it a date. In fact, you should consider us dating." She leans her head into my lips, trying to hold me there. Another time, another place, and I wouldn't move, but right now, my body temperature is rising and I know I need to pull away from her and try to adjust myself as discreetly as possible.

"You know," she says, abruptly changing the subject, "that blog is going to mention how many times you adjusted yourself during the game today."

I roll my eyes and stab at my food. "Well, if someone hadn't worn my shirt to the game, I probably wouldn't have had the urgent need to adjust my cup so many times during the game."

"Is that so?" she asks with a wicked gleam in her eye.

"Yes, it is," I say quietly as I lean in. "You see, I have fantasies of you in my clothes, in my bed, and under me . . . Any bad press I get for that kind of stuff is because of you."

I leave her with those thoughts as I try to finish my dinner. I watch her out of the corner of my eye and try not to laugh. She's stunned and I love it.

TEN

I can't get Daisy off my mind. She's in my dreams at night. When I wake, she's there in the images I've stored in my mind. I see her in every woman I encounter. It's getting to the point where every smell, every color, even every freaking pizza topping reminds me of her. It doesn't matter what I'm doing or where I am because I see her *everywhere*. It's a curse. That's what I've determined, because with each thought comes another one that takes me down a path I have yet to travel with her.

The other night after our dinner date, I tried to drive her home. She wouldn't let me, and I didn't force the issue. I like her too much to be that guy—the one who is demanding and overbearing. She's been riding the trains and walking the streets a lot longer than I have; I can't come swooping in to save her like some kind of superhero if she's not asking to be saved. Sadly, not being able to drive her home also meant no good-night kiss. I don't want to settle for some cheapened peck on the cheek while standing on some street or on the subway platform. I want to hold her in my arms. I want to caress her face and let my lips linger over hers until neither of us can wait any longer. I want it to be something for her—for us both—to remember.

I also want to stop sounding like a girl. This is the shit I used to make fun

of my sister about when she'd ask me to take those stupid tests from her mag-
azines. As much as I try not to, I can't help but think of Daisy as this delicate
flower. I don't know if it's because of her name or the fact that I'm so damn
attracted to her that this mushy shit is flowing from me and I can't turn it off.

Tonight, the kiss is happening. It's her birthday and I can't think of a better way to cap off the night than a good-night kiss. Actually, I can think of
about ten other ways to end the night, and if I can get her to come back to my
place for a small birthday party, I may try to make them happen.

I grab my phone from my bedside table and scroll through my contacts
until I find my mom's picture. It's of her holding Shea while my mom beams
with pride. I press her name, and she picks up on the second ring.

"Hello, Ethan."

"Hi, Mom." I've never been one to open up about my feelings, but there's
a first time for everything. I don't know how to tell if what I'm feeling is lust
or genuine feelings, and I'm hoping my mom can help me figure it out. I can't
compare Daisy to Sarah—I've tried, and it's not working. They're completely
different.

"You had a good game last night."

"Thanks. We're still not doing that well. We're already behind and it's
only April."

My mom sighs and I can hear her moving around the room. The sound of
a door closing makes me wonder if I've woken her up.

"Dad says the team is young, and you guys have a lot of rebuilding to do.
You'll be fine. It may just take a bit longer than you expect."

"Yeah, but I'm impatient and used to winning."

"Well, everyone has to grow up eventually. You can't win everything,
Ethan."

I want to ask her why not. I'm Boston's most eligible bachelor. Surely I
should have whatever I want whenever I want it. Isn't that part of having this

title? I want Daisy, yet I have a feeling that if I don't act fast enough I'm going to be friend-zoned. The problem is, if she's giving me a sign, I'm obviously missing it and finding excuses as to why I shouldn't kiss her whenever I have the chance. Something is holding me back. It's as if I'm stuck behind bars and unable to reach her, even though she's right there.

"I need to ask you something, but I also need you to keep it between us."

"I'm all ears," she says, but there's a hint of worry in her voice. I'd be worried, too, I suppose, if my son said this to me.

I take in a deep breath and exhale slowly as I close my eyes and prepare for her reaction. It doesn't matter that my mom is three thousand miles away; she'll be giddy and want to know everything about Daisy.

"How did you know you were in love with Dad?"

The slight intake of air on the other end tells me she's smiling. Knowing my mom the way I do, she has her fist clenched and is doing her own impression of Arsenio Hall. My only fear is that, given our history, she'll think that it's Sarah, and I don't want to disappoint her.

"Is it the girl the BoRe Blogger has written about?"

I go silent and wish I could hang up on my mother. However, I'm sure that action would have her on the next plane out. I'm never too old for a spanking, according to her.

"Ugh, Mom, why do you read that garbage?" It's not all garbage. The BoRe Blogger is fairly accurate with his baseball knowledge, but the gossip part is what kills me. Why can't the blog be about baseball and only baseball? Why must our personal lives be subject matter?

"I can't help it. *You* aren't forthcoming with a lot of information, and the BoRe blog is. Besides, why are you only now telling me about this?"

"There was nothing to tell."

"Then why do you think you're in love?"

I stand and walk over to my bedroom window. The line of cars parked along Marlborough Street in the Back Bay makes it hard for people to drive down the road. Horns honk and people yell, most of them in their Boston accent, making me laugh and cringe at the same time. I love where I live. I love my neighbors, and they like me, even after my Twitter incident. My place is relatively small, but it's perfect for me. I *do* long for a house, though, with a yard…for a dog…

"Because…" I pause and try to gather my thoughts. I take a deep breath and spill. "This is going to make me sound like a girl, but here it goes. When I look at her, Mom, I see sunshine and happiness. I see someone who is the light at the end of what used to be a dark tunnel. And I know that sounds cliché, but there's no other way I can describe it. It's the way she smiles, and the way she watches the game and can carry on a conversation. And her sports knowledge is second to none. It literally scares the living daylights out of me that she may know more about baseball than I do, so I've steered clear of any sports talk. I think about her every day. Everything I see reminds me of her. It's like…I want to call her at random times in the day just to hear her voice. It's driving me crazy, but in the best possible way. I want to touch her, and by that I mean even just hold her hand…I just…Ugh."

"Ethan, it's okay. I'm not asking about what you've done with her."

"That's just it, Mom. We haven't even kissed. I've held her hand, and that's it. I'm trying to be a gentleman here."

"And I'm sure she appreciates your efforts."

Well, I'm glad someone does, because my freaking Johnson doesn't appreciate anything I'm trying to do. He's constantly carrying a semi each time she's around—but this is all shit I can't say to my mom.

"Oh, Ethan, it sounds like you've really fallen for this girl, and I can guess from what you're telling me that this is different from your relationship with

Sarah. To answer your question, I just knew. Everything will just feel right, from the tips of your fingers to the ends of your toes, every bone in your body will gravitate toward her. Your father was my every thought. He still is, even today."

"Right now, Daisy is my every thought."

"Daisy." My mom sighs when she says her name. "I like that name."

Me too, and I've been trying to come up with a nickname for her, but nothing seems to fit. I thought about calling her D, but then my jackass teammates would be saying shit like "She wants the D." It's funny but crude. I don't think she'll appreciate it too much.

Before my mom and I hang up, I tell her about my plans for tonight and promise to send her a photo of us all dressed up. She asks me to tell Daisy hi for her, and even though I agree, it's not gonna happen. It's far too early to bring parental units into our relationship.

The team has sent a car and driver for tonight. I couldn't be happier, because that means I can focus my attention on Daisy when she gets in the car. I thought about driving to her neighborhood after she gave me her address, but I figured she'd catch me and it'd piss her off. She's embarrassed by where she lives, and I don't know how to convey to her that shit like that doesn't bother me.

As we drive, I'm constantly looking at my watch. I want to see how far she lives from me. I don't know why it's important, except that I have a great amount of hope that she's going to be spending a lot of time at my house, and I want to know how long it'll take me to drive her home every night.

Seven minutes. That is how long it took us to get from my house to hers.

"Is this it?" I ask, slightly confused.

"Yes, sir," he says as he looks at the GPS mounted on his dashboard. I look around and nothing screams low income. I don't know what she was going on about the other night, but this looks like a place I'd live in.

"All right," I say, as I get out of the car. I contemplated buying her a corsage, but felt like that would be overkill and more like prom. I did, however, buy her a birthday cake in the hope that she and I can have a little celebration tonight after the dinner.

As I approach the door I notice a keypad. I drag my finger down the names, looking for Robinson, but don't see it. I step back and look at the address before pulling out my phone to match it with the address she sent to me. As I unlock the screen, I notice a message from her. Shit, she wants me to call her so she'll come down, instead of me going up to her door. I don't like that it isn't as personal as meeting her at her door, but I'm left with no choice.

I start to dial when I see an elderly woman with almost blue hair and a cane walk out.

"Hi, excuse me. My name's Ethan Davenport and I'm here to escort Miss Daisy Robinson to the Boston Rotary dinner tonight. Do you happen to know which apartment is hers?"

She eyes me up and down before lifting her cane. I think for a moment that she's about to beat the shit out of me until the driver of my car steps out.

"Are you going to hurt her?"

"No, ma'am," I say, shaking my head. I still have a feeling she's going to hurt me. I keep that thought to myself, though. It's a fear I have. Daisy's been closed off. She's held back even though I've pushed. She's going into this relationship with an advantage over me. I'm a public figure, but she's an enigma.

"You'll find Daisy in three-C, but if you hurt her..." She trails off, pointing her cane at me and huffing before walking down the street. I nod to the driver that I'm okay as I step inside the building. The hall smells like urine and there are kids screaming at the end. A wooden staircase is off to the right, with built-in mailboxes on the left. I walk down the hall, hoping the elevator is in service, but as my luck would have it, it's not today.

"Three flights of stairs in a tux, no problem." I take the steps two at time. The second floor gives me a long hallway to walk down before I have to climb the next set of steps. This floor smells better, but is messy. There are toys in the hallway and one resident has the door decorated for the holidays, which are still eight months away.

When I reach the third floor I stand straighter and fix my bow tie. I hate that I'm empty-handed. I should've asked my mom what to bring that wouldn't be considered stupid and over the top. My stroll to her door is casual, with my hands in my pockets to help control the twitching.

The black C is mocking me as I stand in front of it, poised to knock. My knuckles rap on the door twice before I lean against the doorjamb, trying to play it cool. A flash of black catches my eye as the door swings open. I swallow hard when Daisy stands before me, as the fingers in my pocket pinch the shit out of my leg, trying to make my mouth work.

I stand up straight and take her in. Her blond hair is pulled up, and I'm not talking piled on top of her head. It's in big curls like my grandma used to wear in her heyday. Daisy's cheeks are rosy, with her lips painted red. Her black dress sits somewhat off her shoulder and just below her knees and she's finished off her ensemble with red high heels.

"You look . . ."

"Like a pinup model?"

I catch her eyes and immediately look at her lips again. I feel myself getting hard just picturing her red lips wrapped around my cock.

"Fuck me," I say as I try discreetly to adjust myself. She catches the action, but doesn't have to say anything because the smirk is enough. She knows she turns me on.

"Daisy, you look fucking stunning." This time she knows I'm serious as her cheeks darken. "You're a classic beauty, and I'm so honored to have you on my arm tonight."

"This old thing?" she says as she brushes her hands down the front of her dress.

"I don't care if it's brand new, vintage, or what—the fact is, you're gorgeous, and I'm going to have to fight every man as they try to get your attention."

"Are you up for the challenge?"

I step into her apartment and place my hand on her waist. I bend only slightly, her heels making our height difference less of a challenge, and whisper into her ear, "If it means I get you all to myself, I'm up for anything." I brush against her dress so she knows what I'm talking about. I don't miss the sharp intake of air she takes, either.

"Who's at the door, Daisy?"

Daisy steps out of my hold and looks at me quickly before answering. "My friend, Papa. Remember, I told you I was going to dinner."

"I need to meet him and make sure he's a respectable young man."

"Shit," I mutter as I look down at my semi. I start filtering images through my head of the nastiest things I can while Daisy takes my hand in hers and pulls me into the other room.

Her living room is decorated like everyone else's, with artwork and pictures on the wall. There's a television in the corner, with a love seat and recliner along the wall. Her grandfather sits in the recliner with his wheelchair next to him. Just by looking at it, I can tell it's old and probably doesn't function properly.

"Papa, this is my friend, Ethan. Ethan, this is my grandfather, John."

I step forward and shake his hand. I have no doubt that, in his prime, he had a firm handshake, and I make sure to show him that I do, too. It's a sign of a confident man, according to my father, and I want her grandfather to know that that's what I am.

"It's great to meet you, sir."

"I know you," he says in a thick Boston accent. "You're behind in home runs if you think you're going to be voted in for the derby. Don't they have you practicing?"

I step back, not entirely shocked that he knows me, but more that he's hounding me about my percentage. "I'll work on those at bats, sir."

"Be good to my Daisy. She's fragile and the only woman who loves me enough to put up with my cranky ass."

"I plan to take very good care of her." When I say the words, I'm looking directly at her so she knows I'm serious. She looks away, and for the life of me I can't figure out why. It's not that I want her to fall at my feet and profess her undying love, but I want her to trust me. It makes me wonder who has hurt her in the past to make her like this.

"Sir, we have to go, but it was very nice meeting you." I shake his hand again, and this time I feel him put a little more strength into it.

"Someday I'll see you play live."

"I'd like that," I tell him as Daisy motions for me to go to the door.

Daisy says her goodbyes and meets me out front, shutting the door behind her. Right now would be the perfect time to kiss her, but I want to do it after she blows out the candles on her cake tonight.

ELEVEN

I may be biased, but if that's the case, I'm okay with having that title. Everywhere I look, men are staring in my direction. I'm a confident man; I know I'm good looking, but they're not looking at me. No, these fuckers that I have to play nice with tonight have their eyes focused on Daisy. I don't blame them. She's fucking hot. She's the hottest woman in the room and everyone knows it.

From the minute we walked in, men have drooled from a distance while the women have flocked to her. You would think that she's famous or the honoree tonight, but that's not the case. In fact, the honoree, who will be sitting at our table tonight, has barely even been spoken to. To me, that proves one thing: these women are motivated by their jealousy and only befriending Daisy to keep her away from their husbands, which shouldn't be a problem since she came with me.

Every lady in here looks the same, except for Daisy, with their long gowns and hair piled on top of their heads. She stands out among the drab and tired old looks, and has something that these women could only dream of pulling off. I know this because the lady next to me won't stop yammering away about how she wishes she could pull off the fifties look.

For the first time in a long time, I'm not the one talking. I'm not the focus of attention. I'm not sure how I feel about that, but I am happy to play the supportive role for Daisy, although the constant fashion talk is boring as fuck.

I've also yet to wish her a happy birthday. That fact alone makes me feel like a complete ass. I had a plan when we walked in. I was going to lead her to the bar and buy her first legal drink. I was going to give a toast and then wish her happy birthday.

When dinner is about to be served, I place my hand on her waist and nudge her in my direction. She understands my hint and excuses herself from the conversation. I lead us over to the bar, and while we wait, I look down to find a smiling, radiant Daisy.

"Are you having fun?"

"Yes and no," she says, causing confusion. She stands closer to me, pulling me down slightly to speak into my ear. "I'm having fun because I'm with you, but those women are talking about things I don't have any clue about, and it's hard to play along."

"High-society women are like that," I tell her. "They all have an agenda, and you're a fresh face in their pond of groupies."

Daisy looks at me with bemusement, and I shrug. It's something I've come to learn about people who have too much money to throw around. We step up to the bar when it's our turn. My hand is on her back, refusing to move.

"What would you like to drink?"

"Um…a whiskey and Coke?" By the face she makes, I know for certain she hasn't had a drink like this before. I find that odd, since she's in college, but it also makes sense, since she's been taking care of her grandfather. The last thing I want is for her to be puking on her birthday, especially tonight. Maybe on my next off day we can tie one on.

"The lady will have a sea breeze and I'll have a Sam Adams," I tell the bartender, who looks at Daisy for a brief moment. I'm guessing he's trying to figure if she's legal or not, or he could be eyeing her like every other dude in this place.

"What's a sea breeze?" she asks, leaning into me. I find this naïve part of her cute. My sister likes this drink, so I figure it's a safe bet.

"It's vodka, cranberry, and grapefruit juice. I'm hoping you like those juices?" She shrugs in a sort of noncommittal way.

The bartender places her drink and my bottle of beer on the bar. We thank him and take our drinks. With my hand on her back, I guide her in the direction of our table, only stopping twice for people to talk to her. I like that they're interested in her and not me. When we finally get to our table, I set my beer down so I can pull her chair out.

When she sits, her dress poofs out around her, and I try not to laugh as she attempts to tuck it under her legs. I help her pull her chair in before sitting down. Once I'm seated, I'm holding her hand.

"In case I haven't told you, you look stunning."

Her cheeks darken as she bows her head, turning ever so slightly to look at me. "I do believe I remember the words you said when I opened the door."

I lean in, taking a deep whiff of her perfume. "Care to repeat them?"

Daisy shakes her head but can't hold back the grin forming on her lips.

"Happy birthday, beautiful," I say as I kiss her just below her ear. "We can celebrate later." I'm unable to gauge her reaction because my name is being called from the podium. I have to give a speech tonight, and it's on the top of the list of things I didn't want to be doing this evening. I leave Daisy seated at our table as I make my way to the front of the room. Once in place, I take a deep breath to calm my nerves and control the inevitable twitch that starts in my hand.

"Good evening." The applause is loud and continues on for a moment.

Once it dies down, I look down at the typed words on the cards in front of me and clear my throat. I should've read this before I arrived, but I was too preoccupied with thoughts of seeing Daisy. For someone who hasn't had any media training, they definitely sent the wrong guy. As I read over the speech, I realize I can't say any of this stuff.

"I want to say thank you for having Daisy and me tonight as your guests. I think this is the first time I've been in a room where no one wants to talk about baseball. I know she's beautiful, but she's going home with me."

Everyone laughs and I half expect Daisy to turn away, but she's focused on me.

"Steve wanted me to let everyone know that he's sorry he couldn't be here, and he was kind enough to write my speech. Thing is, I didn't read it before-hand and I'm not sure it works for tonight.

"We've all come together for one reason—to raise money for the community. I'm not going to ask you to open your checkbooks and start scribbling your name. Instead, I'm going to ask that you think about what it means to give back, because sometimes it's not always about the money. When I'm not playing, I'm walking the children's wing of the hospital or I'm down at the community center helping to repair a swing set or painting over the graffitied walls. I could just give them money, but without volunteers to actually do the work, that money is being spent on contractors when it could be spent directly on the children. My mom always used to say, 'Give a man a fish and you feed him for a day. Teach a man to fish and you'll feed him for life.' Even though I know we're not teaching these kids to make their own meals, I'd like to think that the same applies here.

"So tonight, when you're asked to open your checkbooks, please consider volunteering your time as well. One is good but without the other, neither one will go nearly as far."

Daisy is the first one to stand and start clapping. Others quickly follow her, as the applause grows louder. I've had standing ovations before, but this one is by far the best.

"That was amazing," she says as she molds herself into my arms. Holding her has to be the best thing on earth, especially right now. I have no doubt that after tonight, other things are going to start ranking up on the best list right along with her.

I'm nervous about taking her to my place. All night I've thought about how I would ask her to come to my place, only for our night to end before the words could be said. Call me a chicken or a coward, but it's just hard to grasp whether she likes me or not. Sure, tonight she was on par with the likability, but there are times when I can't read her at all.

The driver stops, and suddenly my hands are twitching and my palms are sweating. My mouth is dry and my tongue feels like it's three feet thick in my mouth. My fear is that when I finally have the guts to speak, I'll be too hard to understand and she'll make fun of me.

"Is this your place?" she asks, breaking the ice. God, she's amazing and perfect. I don't know if she senses my unease or what, but she has a way of making me feel comfortable.

"Yes. I thought we could go in for a bit and celebrate your birthday."

"I'd like that." Even in the dark of the backseat I can see her smile. As soon as I pull the handle to open my door, the driver is out of the car and opening the door for Daisy. I stay seated, watching as she takes his hand to get out and her dress falls perfectly into place. I groan, thinking about what's underneath, wondering if I'm going to get a visual or have to rely strictly on my imagination.

"Will you be needing my services?" the driver asks when I come around the back to meet Daisy.

"No, thank you," I tell him. Daisy will have to go home eventually, but I'll be driving her there and walking her to her door like a proper gentleman.

I hold Daisy's hand and walk slowly up the steps to my brownstone. I have a feeling she already knew where I lived but was playing along to save my dignity. Once inside, she lets go of my hand and walks straight into my living room. I have the lights on timers to ward off burglars. Plus, it's nice coming home to a few lights on after a game. Makes me feel like someone is waiting up for me.

"Feel free to look around." I set my keys on the table and slip off my tuxedo jacket as I follow her around. She moves from the living room into the kitchen, touching various things. I stand in the doorway when she walks into my room, watching her take everything in.

When she turns, I'm already undoing my bow tie. The air between us is crackling with a combination of what I can only hope is sexual tension and nervous excitement. We each take one or maybe two steps and then our mouths are crashing into each other. I hiss at the contact. My skin burns when we touch, and my ache grows. My desire for her is fueled when her tongue seeks permission to enter my mouth. There's nothing slow about this kiss. It's nothing like I ever imagined it would be. Her fingers are in my hair and my right hand is cupping her face while my left arm is holding her to me. Her hands start roaming up and down my chest, and with the slightest tug of my buttons, I'm walking her backward toward my bed.

I hate tearing my mouth away from hers, but I only do so to enable me to take off my shirt. With each button that comes undone she eyes me, watching me work. I capture her mouth again, our tongues meeting and working to increase the passion between us. She tugs at my undershirt, causing me to stand back up. I pull my hands through my sleeves, popping off my cuff links. They clank somewhere in the room, no doubt to be found by my housekeeper later. Daisy kicks off her shoes as I pull off my undershirt. She scoots to the middle of my bed. The vision of her lying there is sending all the blood in my body to my increasing bulge.

My pants stay on, but I shed my socks and shoes before climbing onto the bed to join her. I don't know whether to lie on top of her or beside her. Everything I know about women is all for naught, because this girl is different. Her eyes are rapturous, and I want to ravage her. I want to feast on what she's bringing to the table and never let her go. I trail my finger down her chest and run it along the top of her dress. Daisy takes my hand, kissing my palm, before sitting up and turning around. Her head turns slightly over her shoulder and she looks at me with nothing but pure desire.

Her zipper moves painstakingly slowly. My fingers glide along the back of her shoulders, pushing her straps down. It's only then that I take in what's she's wearing under her dress: a black lace bra with the sexiest pair of black panties. Secretly, I'm happy she's not wearing a thong, because now I have more to imagine.

I pull her dress up over her head and lay it behind me, near the edge of the bed. It's as delicate as she is, especially since I heard her tell one of the ladies tonight that it was her grandmother's. I pull her to me and press my lips to her neck, then her collarbone. Her breathing is rapid, causing me to pause.

"What's wrong?"

"Not..." She clears her throat. "Nothing." She tries to smile, but it doesn't reach her eyes. I turn her around so she's facing me. Her eyes are downcast, avoiding me.

"Daisy," I say as I lift her chin to look at me. "Please don't shut me out."

She closes her eyes and tries to relax. "I've never done this before." Her words are matter-of-fact and have me both rejoicing and freaking the fuck out. I can't let her see that I'm panicking, though.

"We can go slow, or we can put our clothes back on. Nothing has to happen." I'm such a liar. I want her legs wrapped around my waist in the worst way.

"I want to try. Maybe not everything, but I want to try with you."

"Are you sure?" My voice breaks like a puberty-stricken teenager.

She nods and lets her fingers dance over my skin. With each touch, she leaves a path of intense feeling behind. I don't know what it is about her touch, or about her, but my body enjoys the ache she brings. It welcomes her with open arms, begging for her to be near.

This time our kiss is slow as I cradle her face in my hands. I nip at her lower lip, teasing her and myself until I can't take anymore. My tongue glides along her lips, asking for entrance into her delectable little mouth. She moans when our tongues meet and her hand tugs at my hair. I pull her closer to me until I'm leaning over her and we're falling back onto my bed.

"Is this okay?" I ask, trailing kisses down her neck, chest, and over the valley of her breasts. I tug slightly on the cup of her bra, freeing them.

"Tell me when to stop," I say, giving her all the control right now. When she arches her back, I continue, bringing her peaked nipple into my mouth. I bite down gently before lapping at her sensitive bud. My hand kneads her other breast, letting my finger tweak and pull until I'm ready to show it the same attention.

Her legs fall open, welcoming me to her center. I'm so hard I can feel my head pressing against the zipper of my pants as I deftly remove my belt. I grind into her core, rocking back and forth. The friction is welcome, but it's not enough. I haven't dry humped since high school, but this is as good as it's going to get tonight.

Her flesh is on fire, her mewling is encouraging, if not frustrating. I want to be buried to the hilt inside of her. I need to know what she feels like wrapped around my dick. For weeks I've been waiting for this moment.

Daisy pulls me back to her mouth and drives her tongue deep inside. Her hands push down on my ass, encouraging me to move faster. Each moan is swallowed. Each thrust is welcomed. I rub my hand over her panty-covered core and just about lose my shit. She's so fucking wet that it's taking every ounce of willpower not to rip her panties off and plunge deep inside her. That bitch of a devil is snickering in my ear to do it while the angel is reminding me that Daisy is fragile and this is new to her. She may be a virgin, but I'm getting the impression she's at least made it to second base.

I lean back, pulling myself away from her. My palm rubs up and down my bulge while Daisy lies in front of me, her chest moving up and down in a lust-filled rhythmic motion.

"Can I touch you?" I hook my fingers into the sides of her panties and give a slight tug until her hands clamp down on me. I ease up, waiting for a signal to either stop or continue taking her clothes off.

I kiss the insides of her thighs, leaving my hands gripped at her sides. With each kiss, I'm watching her, waiting until I'm at her center. I inhale deeply, taking in her scent. She's going to destroy me if I'm not careful.

My lips press down on her lace-covered pussy, much to her delight. Her thighs quiver and her breathing picks up. I slide my finger into her panties, my knuckle grazing her sensitive bud. Her breath hitches, and my cock throbs for attention. I don't have the heart to tell him he's going to stay behind his cotton barrier tonight.

I maneuver my body so I can take off her panties one leg at a time. The woman whom I have been watching, the one I've been trying to get to know, the one who has pushed me to put myself out there, lies bare before me.

"You're so beautiful," I say as I kiss my way up her body. A lesser man would have gone to town and not made her feel comfortable, but that's not me.

"I don't know what to do," she says as she runs her fingers through my hair.

"About what?" I ask stupidly. I roll off of her, settling in by her side.

"Sex. I don't know what to do. Like right now, should I be touching you?"

I can't help but rub my hard-on against her leg. "Do you feel that?"

She nods, pulling her lower lip in between her teeth.

"I want you, but I'll wait until you're ready."

Daisy turns onto her side, and I use this as an opportunity to hitch her leg over my hip. I'm so fucking happy that I can only see her eyes and breasts right now because any visual of what's going on any lower and I'll be ripping my trousers off.

"What if I'm ready now?"

Fuck me sideways. I groan and kiss her hard.

"You're not," I say, pulling away. "But I can get you ready if you want."

She nods, and I swear my fingers fucking dance for joy. I bring her to me, pressing my lips against hers. My hand massages her leg as I work my way to her core. The slightest brush of my finger against her center has her squirming. I deepen the kiss when my finger is at her entrance. I give a small push, earning a gasp.

She's so fucking wet, it takes nothing for my finger to glide in and out. I hold back from kissing her so I can watch her eyes. They focus on me as her hand tugs at my hair. My room is starting to fill with the smell of sex, accompanied by the fucking sounds coming out of her mouth. Each gasp makes it harder for me to remain in control. My dick is going to fucking explode if I don't relieve the pressure soon.

Daisy hitches her leg higher. I love that she's so into this. Her hips rock with the movement of my hand. She pulls me to her, taking my mouth with hers and sucking on my tongue. I'm about to fucking die, right here, right now.

"Oh no," she says as she moves faster. My thumb presses against her bud while I slide another finger into her pussy.

"Oh yes," I say, encouraging her to accept what's happening to her body. "Go with it, baby. Let your body take over."

"Oh shit. Oh my. Oh shit." She strings together words in between gasping. "I'm…it's…Oh shit, I'm coming…" Her walls flex as her juices coat my fingers. I slow down and let her ride out her orgasm before pulling out completely. Her leg falls tiredly back down onto the bed and Daisy looks like she's about to fall asleep.

"Did I bore you?" I ask, unable to keep the laughter away.

She shakes her head. "God, no. That was intense."

"Was it your first one?" I'm asking for my own stupidity. I want to be the only one who has done this for her.

She shakes her head. "Self-induced, but nothing like that." She doesn't meet my eyes when she says that. Maybe out of embarrassment? She shouldn't be. I jack off all the time. In fact, I need to right now.

"I'd like to watch you do that sometime," I tell her, kissing her softly on the lips before extracting myself from her. "I'll be right back." I climb off my bed and take the painful steps to the bathroom. My cock is out of my pants before I'm even five feet away from her and about to blow its load by the time I get to the bathroom door. Even if he got to touch her pussy, he would've pumped and dumped before I had a chance to have any fun.

TWELVE

When I walk out of the bathroom, Daisy's back is to me. The streetlights shine through my sheer curtains, casting a soft glow around her. Dressed in black lace, she looks like an angel with a little hint of the devil. I step toward her and ghost my fingertips along the back of her shoulders. Goose bumps pebble her skin, causing her to shiver. I hold back the urge to rub against the swell of her ass. Doing so would only end with us in bed. Not that I don't want to be there.

"Are you cold?" My lips follow the path of my fingers as I kiss along her collarbone. I'm torn in two right now, struggling between wanting to take her back to bed and celebrating her birthday. I *did* buy her a cake and want her to make a wish—a wish I hope I can make come true—before her birthday is over. I glance quickly at the clock on my bedside table and see that my time is running out.

"A little," she says so quietly that I can barely hear. I kiss her neck and tug on her ear before moving toward my dresser. I pull out a T-shirt and look at her as she stands in the same spot. Her shyness makes her more desirable than I could have ever imagined. I want to pull her into my arms and hold her, cradle her, and keep her out of harm's way, even though I know that I can't. Daisy is far from meek or needing to be saved and I need to stop thinking like that.

I hand her a BoRe T-shirt. It's white and almost touches her knees because it's too long for her. The fabric is slightly see-through, showing just enough of her bra to give me a semi. She's so fucking hot right now with my shirt on and her hair falling out of her updo.

"In ten minutes, your birthday will be over."

She glances at the clock and nods. "I had an amazing birthday."

I brush some imaginary lint off her shoulder. It's really just an excuse to touch her. "Did you get anything for your birthday?"

"I got a lovely dinner and a fancy ride in a black car where a very nice man opened my door. I got to dress up in my grandmother's prom dress, something I've wanted to do for years, and received the biggest smile from my grandfather. Then I got to be with a man that I really like, in a way that we'll always remember." She stretches up on her tiptoes and brushes her lips to mine. My hand rests on her hip, intent on keeping her close, but she pulls away.

"I have something for you." I take her hand in mine and lead her out of the bedroom and into the kitchen. She props herself up on the white marble countertop, and for some reason I find that extremely sexy. She's now my height, and it's something I'm going to take advantage of. I step in between her legs and slide my hands under her shirt and into the waistband of her panties. Daisy wraps her legs around me, caging me in. There are quick flashes of us like this in the morning, and something deep inside tells me that I could get used this. But even I know it's too soon to think about a future together. We're just starting out. Everything is new and fresh with us, exploratory. In a week, she could hate me.

We share an intense kiss that has me on edge. The thought of spreading her out on my counter and feasting on her runs through my mind. Except I really want to finish celebrating her birthday. Reluctantly, I pull away and let my fingers drag along her body until I'm no longer touching her. I keep my back to her as I pull out the cake I ordered. I set it on the counter nearest my refrigerator and lift the lid. This has to be my hardest purchase to date, ordering a cake for someone that I'm trying to get to know. Thankfully, the baker gave me some insight and collectively we decided that a white cake with chocolate mousse filling, topped off with buttercream frosting, would do the trick. *Happy Birthday, Daisy* is written in elegant script and is surrounded by white flowers with black and red accents. I went with black and red because of our BoRe connection. For all I know she hates these colors, but it's the thought that counts.

I set a single candle deep into the frosting and light it. It crackles like a sparkler. As soon as I turn around with the cake in my hand, I'm singing to her. I can't carry a tune, but the expression on her face right now tells me that it doesn't matter. Her hand is covering her mouth and tears form in her eyes as I hold her cake out in front of her.

"Happy birthday, Daisy."

Daisy drops her hand from her mouth and clutches the edge of the countertop, leaning forward.

"Make a wish," I suggest, even though I'm sure she knows to do that. She breathes out, and the flame disappears into thin air. "What'd you wish for?" I ask, putting the cake down next to her.

"I can't tell you. If I do, it won't come true."

"Is that so?" I ask over my shoulder. I pull out two plates and grab two forks from the drawer, along with a knife.

"It's what my grandma used to say."

"Do you miss her?" Let me stick my foot in my mouth with that question. "I'm sorry. I know you miss her." I slice a piece of cake and set it on the plate, handing it to Daisy along with a fork. She scoots back onto the counter and crosses her legs.

"I miss her, but she was sick, so I'm happy she's not suffering anymore. I know my grandpa misses her a lot. I catch him, every now and again, talking to her as if she's in the kitchen."

I don't know what it'd be like to lose my grandma or my parents. We have such a strong family bond that I think we'd fall apart. I know for certain that I wouldn't be who I am today without them. And here Daisy is, with only one grandparent left.

"You don't have to feel sorry for me," she says, before taking a bite of her cake. Her lips wrap around her fork and her eyes close as she savors the taste. "Oh gosh, this is freaking heavenly," she says as she looks at me.

"Um…" I'm thankful that I'm partly hidden by the counter right now because my growing dick is begging for a small bit of action. "I'm glad you like it." Fuck, I love it and want to stand here all night and watch her lick her fork.

"Can I ask you something personal?"

She nods. "I think after what you did for me, I should answer everything you ask."

I place my hands on her thighs and massage them. "I did that for us. I enjoyed it, too. Everything that we've done tonight, it's all for the both of us," I tell her. "But I was going to ask if you remember your parents."

Daisy puts her fork down and slides herself toward me. My hands slide up her legs as she moves. I don't hesitate to make sure my fingers go under her panties and use my hands as leverage to bring her closer.

"I have pictures, but no real memories. I have some things that I made up from the photos and stories I've heard, but I don't remember them."

"I'm sorry," I say for lack of a better response. I lean forward and kiss the tip of her nose. Daisy rests her forehead against mine while her fingers play in my hair. My hands move from her ass to her waist, and I hold her against me with my arms wrapped around her. As much as I want to think otherwise, I know I've already fallen for this girl in front of me.

She kisses me quickly, and as much as I want to hold her mouth to mine and not let go, I do. This isn't the time or place to start making out, especially since I just asked about her parents. Daisy puts her head in the crook of my neck and sighs.

"I should be getting home," she mumbles, effectively ruining any chance of her waking up in my arms. It's for the best, though. If I had her in bed, I'd be on my knees begging her to let me take her. It would be a selfish move on my part, but I've been walking around with a raging hard-on since I met her, so I can't help it.

"For the record, I want you to stay." She looks up and smiles.

"Someday, I'd like that, but not tonight. I didn't make arrangements with the nurse and can't leave my grandpa alone at night."

"It's okay. I understand." I try to fix her hair, but learn quickly that I don't know what the hell I'm doing. I help her down and hold her hand as we walk back into the bedroom. My bed mocks me, reminding me that I'll be sleeping in it alone tonight. That fact shouldn't bother me, except I had my hopes up that Daisy would spend the night.

Daisy excuses herself to get dressed in the bathroom, and I use the opportunity to change out of my tuxedo pants and into some sweats. I plan to put on the shirt that she's wearing so I can feel like she's near me after she leaves. When she comes out, she looks almost as good as she did earlier, but I see the difference. Her hair isn't as perfect and her lips are slightly redder. She comes to me, and I brush my thumb over her bottom lip, wondering if my whiskers hurt her.

"It's worth it," she says, holding my hand to her face. She moves my thumb slightly, kissing the pad before linking her fingers with mine. "You should probably put a shirt on. It's cold out."

"I was planning on wearing the one you had on."

"Why? It probably smells like me."

"Exactly!" I wink and take my shirt out of her hand, putting it on. I go back to holding her hand because it feels good and I want to.

We walk outside and the early-spring air is frigid. I shiver, forgetting to grab a sweatshirt, and run us down the stairs and to my car. I help her in before sprinting to the driver's side. I start the engine and crank up the heat, flipping the switch for the heated seats to come on while both of us shake from the cold.

"I'm an idiot. I should've grabbed you a jacket."

"It's okay. The car will warm up in a minute."

I reach over the console and pull her into my arms. Science class taught me that body-to-body friction is the best way to combat the cold. Also nakedness, but I don't see her letting me take her dress off. It's only a matter of seconds before my butt starts getting warm from the seat and warm air is blowing in from the vents. I hate to let her go, but getting her home to her grandfather is her priority, and I'm not about to put her in a position to choose. I can wait.

The drive to her apartment takes only seven minutes due to the lack of traffic this late at night, or early in the morning, depending on how you look at it. I park along the street in the no-parking zone closest to her door and jump out, racing to the other side so I can open the door for her. It's evident that any guy she dated before me never opened her doors. She needs to get used to me doing this for her. It's the way I was raised.

I'm sure her neighborhood is safe, considering Boston's finest take pride in every neighborhood they work, but I'm still leery and hold her hand until we're at the front door of her building. I stand behind her while she unlocks the door and I step in with her.

"Do you think the elevator is working?"

"You don't have to come up," she says, standing on the first step. Even now, with her heels on, I still have the height advantage.

"It's not that I don't want to walk you to your door. I just thought we could make out in the elevator."

Daisy laughs and pulls me up the stairs. It's nice to see the tenants are quieter now than they were when I came to pick her up earlier.

"Our luck, we'd get stuck and the fire department would have to come. If they showed up, we'd be all over the news and the BoRe Blogger would have a field day with you."

"Ugh, don't get me started on that site."

"That bad, huh?" she asks as we reach her floor.

I shrug and lean my arm against the wall as she unlocks her door. "Like I said before, some of the shit that gets posted isn't accurate, and it's hard to have a life when he's always lurking. I'd like to meet him and give him a piece of my mind."

"He? What makes you so certain it's a guy?"

"Because all the women love me," I tease, pressing my lips to hers. The kiss is chaste, but lingering. I cup her face with my hand and hold her as long as possible. When she pulls away, she covers her lips briefly.

"I need to go," she says as we hear rustling behind the door.

"I'll see you tomorrow. Sweet dreams and happy birthday, Daisy." I brush my lips against her cheek and turn away. Each step is more difficult than the last, and while part of me wants to turn around and go back to her, another part wants to nurture whatever this is between us and see where it goes.

BOSTON RENEGADES

Boston's beloved Renegades are falling!

What the hell happened?

We're five games into a nine-game home stand and things are not looking good, people. It's time to put your rally caps on and start yelling at these guys. Come on, we pay good money for our tickets. At least they can show up for us!

Of course, with the Yankees in town, the Renegades cower in the corner. Listen guys, the "curse" is dead. It's long gone! Stop letting them win. Maybe Curt Schilling needs to remind us what the bloody sock looks like... that is, if he weren't suspended from broadcasting right now.

Down in the minors, center fielder Cooper Bailey is looking fantastic and batting .393. The prediction is that he'll be called up soon, rather than waiting for Bainbridge to retire or ask for a trade.

We in the Renegade community are thankful that our runs batted in are still (somewhat) higher than the runs we're giving up—154/139.

Silver lining, folks, we gotta find it!

GOSSIP WIRE

It took much digging, but I've been able to unearth the identity of Mr. Ethan Davenport's girlfriend. Yes, even though he has yet to confirm that they're dating, taking her to the Rotary dinner was HUGE and didn't go unnoticed by anyone. The young woman occupying Boston's Most Eligible Bachelor's time is none other than Boston University's Daisy Robinson. We wish her luck!

Travis Kidd was spotted at the Chevy dealership the other day. Why is this news? Well, because his father owns a Ford dealership. I think Thanksgiving may be a bit awkward in the Kidd house this year.

Manager Cal Diamond has been seen going in and out of the cancer clinic recently. A call to the front office yielded nothing. We hope that whatever's going on, Mr. Diamond and his family are in good health.

The BoRe Blogger

THIRTEEN

I hate the Yankees.

Of course, I grew up a Seattle Mariners fan, so it's what we do. We hate teams that continually beat us and win every possible title that comes their way. When the Renegades drafted me, it basically became law that I not be a fan of the Yankees. Honestly, you don't find many people in Boston who are. And if they are, it's because they're not from here. Although, if you go to any other city, chances are you'll find Yankees or Braves fans everywhere. We can thank cable TV for that. Another thing you never do once you've been a Renegade: leave and become a Yankee. It's a guaranteed way to lose the respect of your fans.

As a Major League player, I have goals: win a batting title, a Home Run Derby title, a World Series title, and bat for the cycle... just to name a few. I like to remain optimistic and think that I can achieve each goal with the Renegades, but in order to do so, I need to be consistent, and right now I feel like I'm not. It's still early in the season, but that's no excuse. My off-season training prepares me for these moments. I shouldn't be failing my team or myself.

It's the bottom of the fifth and I'm on deck. Preston Meyers is up to bat, ahead in the count with no outs. Steve Bainbridge is on third.

One look at the scoreboard tells me that if we want to win this game, we need to get some hits and base runners, otherwise we're going down...again. And frankly, I'm sick of losing to the Yankees.

Meyers drills one out to center field, scoring Bainbridge easily, and makes it to second, standing up. Bainbridge and I exchange a high five after he crosses the plate, and he tips his hat to the fans, thanking them. I've wanted to talk to him about the rumors that the BoRe Blogger keeps posting, but the time is never right. Personally, I don't want him to leave. He's my mentor, someone I look up to on the team.

The closer I get to home plate, the more my eyes are trained on Daisy. The BoRe Blogger asked me to comment on whether or not she's my girlfriend, and I gave the same standard "no comment" tweet back. She's a girl, and definitely a friend, so the title makes sense. However, it means something when you put those words together and label them. In this day and age it's hard to tell if women want a label or if they're too independent for something like that. It's also an awkward conversation to have, and something I'm not good at doing. Hell, just thinking about bringing it up with her makes my hand twitch with nerves.

Daisy cracks a smile, but shies away by pulling her hat down. The BoRe Blogger published her name, effectively ruining any privacy I thought we'd have and making her a target of sorts at the game. If I don't do well, people are saying shit to her, and that pisses me off. My game performance has nothing to do with her...Okay, maybe it does a little bit, but not much. If anything, she makes me want to work harder to impress her more. It's stupid, I know. I should want to work hard to better myself, not for some chick. But I can't help it. One look at Daisy and I'm weak in the knees and willing to follow her around like a lost puppy dog.

After adjusting everything humanly possible, I step up to the plate and show my bat. With it cocked back and ready, I wait for the first pitch. This pitcher is taking his sweet-ass time, and it's pissing me off. He looks from me to Meyers—who is just off second, waiting to see what I'm going to do—and back to me before delivering the pitch. I know I'm swinging for the fences on this one. He sends me a meatball right down the center. I step forward, rotating my hips and shoulders as my bat comes around. The sweet sound of wood and hard rubber colliding has the stadium of fans up and out of their seats. Someday I want to be so respected that I can wait and see who catches my home run, but this is not the time. I drop the bat, watching the ball fly into the stands before I start jogging to first to start my trip around the bases. Fireworks go off in center field, music plays, and my teammates are at home plate to greet me as soon as I cross.

I glance quickly at the scoreboard and see that now we're only down by three runs. We have a few innings left to score and hold the Yankees to no more runs. More high fives are given when I enter the dugout. The adrenaline is pumping and I find myself clapping loudly as our designated hitter, Branch Singleton, walks toward home plate. Everyone's on their feet with their rally rags flying through the air, cheering as loud as they can over Branch's music.

"Why don't you move her to the correct side?" Travis Kidd stands on the stairs beside me, cocking his head in the general direction of Daisy and smirking.

Shaking my head, I spit out a few of the sunflowers seeds I've been sucking on and continue to lean on the railing with my arms dangling over. "She has season tickets and likes it over there."

"But if she's behind you, or with the other wives, she can ogle your ass a bit more."

"You're such a dumbass."

"Just sayin'," he says, as he spits out whatever's in his mouth.

"I don't want her hassled by the wives. You-know-who's wife is out for blood right now, and Daisy doesn't need to be subjected to that shit. Plus we just started seeing each other. I don't want to scare her away."

Bainbridge's wife is on a rampage and hell-bent to find out who Steve has been screwing behind her back. She's texted all of us, asking questions, but the truth is, if he *is* doing something like that, none of us know about it. Not that we'd tell her, either. There's solidarity in our brotherhood, and that pisses her off, so she's been going after the wives.

We all stand tall when Singleton smacks the ball into the outfield. We raise our arms, thinking it's gone, and groan when the center fielder jumps up and snags the ball out of the air before it clears the wall.

"Shit," a few of us mumble as Singleton returns to the dugout. He's pissed and throwing his helmet at the wall with a string of slurs coming out of his mouth. To make matters worse, he was traded from the Yankees to Boston a few seasons back and has held a grudge ever since. The trade didn't make sense—Branch is one of the most consistent designated hitters in the league—and once his name hit the trade wire, teams started a bidding war. Even if they didn't need him, they *wanted* him. Boston wasn't even the highest bidder, but they are the archrival of the Yankees, and Branch wanted to stick it to them. Most of the time he does.

There are those moments when you're in the lead and the outfielder makes an amazing catch and you give props to your teammate for hitting it deep enough that the outfielder has to work to stop the run. But then there are times when you don't speak about the almost home run that would've put your team within two runs rather than three down. This is the time when you just ignore the "what could have been" and let your teammate stew.

Jasper Jacobson, our catcher, is up next. He takes the first swing and hits a grounder right to the shortstop. Jacobson is fast and has the ability to beat out the throw to first, but not today. Next, second baseman Bryce Mackenzie steps up to the plate. The crowd is still somewhat loud, but it has died down considerably after the last two outs. Mackenzie takes the first two pitches without even flinching. The third pitch is also a ball, giving me hope that the pitcher is tiring and maybe we can wear him down in the next inning, as long as his relief doesn't come in.

Mackenzie swings at the next pitch, and I'm thinking it must've been a damn meatball because he was ahead in the count, and now the right fielder is taking a few steps in to catch his pop-up. The inning is over and we're still down by three runs. We take our sweet time coming out of the dugout as the music starts to play and the Jumbotron lights up with the kiss cam. I'd love to take Daisy to a game and get on the kiss cam. It'll never happen, though, unless we go to a Celtics game, because there is no way in hell I'll stand out in the freezing cold in Foxborough to watch the Patriots. Checking out the Bruins, on the other hand, would be on my list of things to do in Boston.

After we've taken our warm-up grounders, the heart of the Yankees lineup steps up to the plate. I take a step back and get into position. My eyes are steady on his bat, watching every wiggle that it takes. He starts the rotation and the wooden weapon comes around, smacking the white leather ball toward me. I move into position, ready to use my body as a shield to stop the ball. It bounces nicely into my glove, and in one swift rotation, the ball is in and out of my mitt, into my hand, and being thrown accurately to first base.

It's a three-up, three-down inning; in fact, the rest of game is played out like that, with us losing 8–5 and dropping yet another home game to the Yankees. This loss puts us even, at fourteen and fourteen—a shitty way to start the month.

Our cleats clank as we walk down the corridor to the clubhouse. The press is already there, waiting for interviews. The mood is subdued. It's not just the fact that we lost, but that we have put ourselves in an early hole, and holes in the majors are hard to climb out of.

"Ethan, care to give us a few words?" Yes! I'd love to talk about my home run or the outs that I made, but I'm not allowed, not yet, at least. I want to talk about how well we play together as a team and how I support our pitching staff. I know I can answer simple questions with canned answers.

I smile my normal half grin, half grimace and wave. Media training starts tomorrow at Boston University, with a ten a.m. class. I thought about complaining, but it means I can see Daisy earlier and maybe even eat lunch with her while I'm there. That thought, alone, makes me turn in my man card. It should be the other way around. She should be asking me for time, and yet here I am mapping out when I can see her, eat with her, and just be near her. I'm turning into such a girl.

When we are traveling, I'll take the class via live feed. It's not ideal, but I want to be able to give interviews, and this is what the GM thinks is best. I only have to take the course for two weeks and let the class interview me before I'm cleared for press interviews.

The vibe in the clubhouse is subdued. No one is talking; the only noise being made is by us when we undress. I suppose there isn't much to say. We lost, yet again, and have to face the Tampa Bay Rays tomorrow and the following two days before we have an off day and fly to Toronto.

"Do you have plans tonight?" Kidd asks, as he stands next to me, nothing but a towel around his waist, which he is holding together with his thumb and forefinger.

I shake my head and pull off my shirt, tossing it into the laundry bucket. "Sleep."

"With your girl?" He waggles his eyebrows and steps away before I can punch him in the shoulder.

"No. I have class tomorrow. I thought it'd be best if I showed up without any bags under my eyes."

"Man, I can't believe Stone is making you take media classes."

"Yeah, well, when you tweet out your address like a fool, management starts to wonder how fucking smart you are. Clearly, I'm an idiot."

"You said it, not me," he says as he slaps my back. "What are you going to do about your girl back home?" he asks as he waits for me to head to the showers.

"What do you mean?" Truth is, I haven't even thought about Sarah for a few days, especially after my epic date with Daisy. She's been the only one on my mind, and between the phone calls, texts, and seeing her for a few minutes after the game, she's all I've had time to think about.

"Don't you have, like, a standing hookup deal?"

His words cause me to freeze. My mother knows about Daisy, but I'm sure Sarah hasn't read up on it or seen us online because she's busy training to become a doctor. Sarah will be expecting to hang out. I'm now in a situation where I don't know what to do. Any other time, it didn't matter because I haven't had a girlfriend since Sarah. Do I call Daisy my girlfriend? Do I give her that label?

If it were anyone but Kidd asking me the question, I'd dodge it, but he's my best friend. "I don't know," I say as I head toward the showers, hoping that the hot water will provide the answer to my upcoming conundrum.

BOSTON RENEGADES

Even after valiant efforts by Preston Meyers and Ethan Davenport, the Renegades came up short against the Yankees, dropping all three of their home games to them with a cumulative nine to 15 in the runs category. It wasn't until Sunday's game that the Renegades were able to get their bats swinging and break out of the two-run hold the Yankees had them in by putting five up on the board.

Branch Singleton tried to make the Yankees pay, going deep each time at bat, but the acrobatic skills of the Yankees' outfielders proved to be too much for Singleton's longball game. Better luck next time.

The Tampa Bay Rays are in town for three games, followed by an off day.

Thursday, the Renegades will be doing arts and crafts with their littlest fans at Beth Israel Hospital. Sorry, adult fans, you must be under 18 and kicking cancer's ass to be a part of this.

On the minor league front, Cooper Bailey hit for the cycle yesterday, paving his way to move up. Even if Bainbridge stays, the front office can't afford to keep Bailey in the minors. He'll be demanding a trade before too long. GM Stone needs to make a move...and soon.

GOSSIP WIRE

Ethan Davenport is heading to media training. I guess we now know why he hasn't given any interviews before or after games. Apparently, a pretty face can only get you so far and Mr. Davenport will be learning how to speak, act, and socialize on television when he takes a two-section—not course—at Boston University, the same school his current flavor of the month attends. I wonder if they'll carpool.

There's still no word on why Cal Diamond has been spotted at the cancer clinic. Once we find out, we'll update you.

Bryce Mackenzie is making it official with his girlfriend, model turned designer Gabby Nolan. He popped the question two weeks ago when she came into town, and tonight she was spotted with a four-carat princess-cut diamond ring on her finger. I guess the rumors about her and pro tennis player Ralph Amato are just that—rumors!

The Bainbridges were seen heading into marriage counseling. By all accounts, Steve looked like he didn't want to be there when caught by a photographer as he was being pulled into the building by his wife. She's gotta hang on to the money!

The BoRe Blogger

FOURTEEN

Freshman year I was that eager student who signed up for eight a.m. classes because I thought it would be best to get my day over sooner, even after my six a.m. workouts. That lasted exactly one week until I was groggily dragging my ass out of bed and barely making it to class. "Naps" became my favorite four-letter word, and a shower turned into something I had to schedule. Second semester I planned a little better, but by the time I was a sophomore, I refused to take any class that started before eleven. The six a.m.'s never went away, but that nap right after my workout was the best part of my day.

For the past few weeks, I've been getting up uncharacteristically early so I can spend time with Daisy. The minute my alarm would sound, I'd hop out of bed, shower, shave, get dressed, and leave with a damn smile on my face. Today is different. Now, as my alarm is buzzing, my pillow is once again being held to my face by my forearm as I pray that the noise will stop and I can fall back to sleep. Even knowing that I'm about to see Daisy doesn't rouse my sleeping body. The fact that I have to go to school—a place I've already graduated from—is keeping me in bed. The mere mention of class and my body is tired and exhausted, even though I got plenty of sleep last night.

I roll over with a groan and slam my hand down on the clock, silencing it before it makes my ears bleed. I let out a cough and quickly convince myself that I have a cold, and there is no possible way I can make it to class. It would be unfair of me to infect the student body with any illness.

Reaching for my phone, I rise up on my elbows and type out a text to Daisy.

I have a cold. Can't go to class.

The conversation bubble pops up immediately, making me smile. I know she wasn't waiting for my text, but the fact that she stopped what she was doing to reply means the world to me.

Daisy Robinson: Well, that sucks. I thought we could make out behind one of the dorms today.

My eyes bug out at her text message, and sure enough, my happy stick likes the idea of making out with her, although not in public.

I'm feeling better.

I type back and hit Send before it dawns on me that she just played me. I'm slow to get out of bed, and I contemplate going to class looking like the quintessential college kid. No one would really care. Chicks dig the messy "I just rolled out of bed" look on guys just as much as dudes like the "I just got fucked" look on a chick.

Each step I take on my way to the bathroom has me thinking of another excuse to stay home. I don't know why I'm being such a baby about taking this class—it's only for two weeks, two hours a day…and half the time I'll be on the road. But I'll be on campus with Daisy, and I think that's what's scaring me. I don't want her to get sick of me because I'm around too much, or worse, act like we aren't seeing each other to avoid scrutiny in the press, even though everyone knows we've been hanging out. The BoRe Blogger made that public for us.

My hair is an unruly mess and standing on end. I run my hands under the water and through my hair but nothing changes. It's definitely a hat day for me. I finish up the rest of my necessary morning crap in the bathroom before slipping on a pair of sweats with a Nike T-shirt and shoes. The ladies in the front office of the Renegades were gracious enough to buy me a few school supplies, which I gather up before heading out the door. The thought hadn't even crossed my mind that I would need a pen and paper.

The drive over to the university takes longer than I had planned, and once I find a parking spot that seems far enough away to be in another country, I'm running to class with a map in my hands like a lost freshman. "Official Nerd Alert" should be flashing across my chest right now. I enter what I hope is my class, out of breath and with a hundred or so eyes staring at me. There's clear recognition of who I am as eyes go wide, mouths drop, and the eager whispers and texting starts.

"Mr. Davenport, it's so nice of you to join us," the professor so nicely announces, pointing out that I'm late. I nod in his direction and take the first available seat, which happens to be between two girls, both brunette and both watching my every move.

They lean toward me in unison as I get comfortable. The one on my right hands me the paperwork that I need.

"Thanks," I mumble, keeping my eyes focused on the professor.

"You're welcome, Ethan," she says dreamily, which really makes me uncomfortable. I'm used to this kind of attention, but something about her and her friend on my left seems odd. I can't put my finger on it. Tomorrow,

I'm going to have to be early so I can pick another seat and maybe pay some dudes to sit next to me.

"Social media is a powerful tool," the professor starts. "It can be used for just about everything. Many people announce their engagements, the birth of a child, or when they're in a relationship. It can also be used for bad news, like when you change a relationship status from 'In a relationship' to 'It's complicated.' Most of you don't realize that it wasn't *that* complicated until you made it such on social media."

He has a good point. When Sarah and I decided to part ways, she changed her relationship status from "In a relationship" to "Single" and her friends posted that I was a jerk, an asshole, and that she could do better. She spent hours defending me, saying that our breakup had been mutual, and that we were still very good friends, just going in different directions in life. We collectively had decided it'd be best to part while we were happy with each other instead of fighting. We didn't want to end up hating each other.

"Social media is also an avenue for awareness, such as an accident on the route you usually drive, or for a fund-raiser. What a lot of people don't realize is that media and social media are the same thing, with the only difference being live footage. For example: I can go on live television and give an interview. Someone sitting at home with nothing to do can take bits and pieces from said interview and mash them together, creating something new and the exact opposite of what I actually said during my live interview, and post it on social media. My interview has now gone from media to social media. Sadly, this cannot be prevented, but what can happen to prevent this type of thing from happening is for people to utilize their social media pages for the positive. Direct them to the correct interview, even if it's not yours."

As I look around, everyone is either typing on their computers or writing notes by hand. I'm doing neither because I thought this class was going to prepare me for what I need to say to the media and what not to post on social media. I don't care about interviews gone bad—that shit happens all the time—which is why I'm here. The Renegades want to prevent me from putting my foot in my mouth or being labeled stupid due to nerves.

After the first few minutes, I'm zoning out, not focused on class as the professor continues on about the differences and similarities of all forms of socializing. I can feel my phone vibrating against my leg, tempting me to take it out and see what's going on, but getting scolded again isn't high on my priority list. Now that I'm sitting here, staying in bed with that fake cough is becoming more and more appealing. I thought this guy was going to teach me how to give an interview, something my college should have taught me. I suppose I could tell Stone that I don't want to attend and just accept the fact that I'll never have any television time.

I must've zoned out because the girl next to me is tapping me on the shoulder, telling me to pack up. She says something about following her and her friend to the library for an assignment, and I figure I better do it since I haven't a clue what just happened. I keep pace behind them as we walk through the busy campus. Instead of looking around at the scenery, I'm looking for a familiar pair of green eyes.

I really wish I had paid attention to what the professor was saying, because I don't want to do homework club or whatever it is that has me following these two girls up the stairs and into the library. I need to be better than this first showing. Right now, I'm showing everyone in that class I'm nothing but a dumb jock.

It's been a couple of years since I've been inside a college library, or any library, for that matter. I've forgotten how quiet everyone is. That is unless you're Ethan Davenport and you just walked in and everyone stops, stares, and pulls out their phone to take your picture. I wave and break off from these classmates of mine in search of a corner I can hide in. My plan is to text

Daisy and ask her to come and save me…only I don't have to, because I spot her sitting at one of the computer terminals. I walk up behind her, thinking I should scare her, but think better of it. Making her scream from shock in the library, where you're required to be quiet, might not be the best thing for her. The last thing I want is for her to get into trouble.

"Hey, babe," I say, letting the term of endearment fall easily from my lips. My arrival has clearly caught her off guard, as I happen to see what's on her screen before she fumbles to close the window, and my heart sinks. I know declarations haven't been made, but I had hoped she'd respect me where certain things are considered…the BoRe Blog being one of those things. By the look on her face—eyes down and no smile—she knows I'm not happy. I pull out the chair next to her and pull hers so she's facing me.

Her hair is down, the ends curled, and I find myself playing with a tendril. It's soft and curves around my finger like it belongs there. Against my better judgment I lean forward and press my lips to hers.

"Please don't read that shit," I beg as my lips ghost over hers. The last thing I want is for her to read the BoRe Blogger and assume that anything on there is legit.

Even though her birthday was just the other day, I've seen her every night since. After the games she waits for me, we get dinner, and then I drive her home. I park illegally in front of her building and we make out like horny teenagers, steaming up the windows of my SUV. It had been years since I'd reached first or second base in a car, but damn if it doesn't feel good. Everything is so much more exciting and dangerous when you're trying to get your girl off with your hand down her jeans, hoping no one will walk by and see what you're doing. And when she moves to straddle you in your seat, pressing against your erection…Yeah, your next off day can't come soon enough because all you want to do is take her back to your place and be deep inside her.

We have three more games until we leave on a ten-game road trip, a road trip that is going to include a trip back home, where Kidd so kindly reminded me that my ex is waiting and expecting sex. I haven't found the nerve to tell her that I've started to see someone. I don't know what's stopping me. Maybe it's because I'm waiting for Daisy to introduce me as her boyfriend.

"I'm sorry," she says, as she pushes her fingers under my hat so she can play with my hair. She deepens the kiss with a sweep of her tongue against my lips, and just like that I'm getting hard in a place where none of this shit should be happening.

"Wanna get out of here?" I ask, pulling her up with me as I stand. She nods and reaches over to shut down the computer she was working on. She takes my hand as I lead us out of the building and back through the students, to the parking lot, which feels a million miles away.

"Where'd you park?"

"New York," I say sarcastically, making her laugh.

When we finally reach my car, at least ten minutes have passed. I help her into the passenger seat and move to my side, tossing my notepad, sans any notes, onto the backseat. Before I have a chance to start the car, she's in my lap, attacking me. She grinds against me, bringing me back to life once again. This isn't the time or place, as it's daylight and people can see through my front window. I can't imagine what pictures will be all over the web when I get home. This probably goes against all the social media training I sat through today.

"Daisy," I say, trying to gain her attention as I lightly push her away. "Do you want to go back to my place? I have a couple of hours until I need to be at the field."

I don't care if it's only been a few weeks since we've officially met; the cat-and-mouse game of staring at each other for a year has been like foreplay without touching... It's been mental foreplay.

She pulls her lower lip in between her teeth and nods. My next movement is a blur. I do believe I may have thrown her into her seat out of sheer excitement to finally have my way with her. I can't be sure because I'm a dude, and she's fucking sexy and horny, which is a really dangerous combination, but who cares? I have a few hours to kill with my smoking-hot girl and I'm going to use them to my advantage. The only problem is—it's lunchtime in Boston, so traffic is going to be a bitch.

FIFTEEN

Fucking Boston traffic.

We would've been better off taking the T from the campus to my place instead of driving. I wasn't thinking with the right head and now we're sitting in bumper-to-bumper congestion due to what I'm assuming is an accident. Any other city and I could take the side roads, but the narrow streets coupled with on-street parking make maneuvering my SUV a bit difficult. So we sit here and wait.

Reaching across the console, I pick up her hand and interlock her fingers with mine. Gazing at her, I let my thoughts run rampant. Her smile is soft, rewarding, and I ask myself if I'm doing everything I can in this short amount of time to show her how much I like her and want to spend all my free time with her. Or does she just see this as a casual hookup? Because the thought of sleeping with her, while at the forefront of my mind, isn't a be-all that ends all. I hate that we're rushing back to my place for our first time. I'm not even that guy who has to do the whole song and dance, either, but I don't want her to get the wrong impression. She's too important to me.

There's something else bothering me: finding her looking at the BoRe Blogger page at the library. She knows that I was ready to give up on even being her friend when she brought up rumors. Stupid on my part, yes, but I don't need that shit hanging over my head or her questioning my motives because of what some dumbass who doesn't even know me decides to write about me.

I bring her hand to my lips and place a chaste kiss on the back of her hand. She smiles and leans over to kiss my cheek. Acting like this with each other makes us seem legit, but I can't be sure that's how she feels and I don't want to be lame and ask her if she wants to be my girlfriend. Do men even ask that question anymore?

The longer we wait in traffic, the more frustrated I become. I can't get the image out of my mind of her looking at that website and quickly closing the window when I walked up behind her. Why would she do that when she knows how much that site bothers me?

I decide to take the next exit and risk the narrow streets just to get to my place faster.

"Where are we going?" she asks, her head darting from side to side as we cruise by buildings and brownstones.

"I thought you wanted to go back to my place."

She cracks a smile and asks, "Are you in a hurry?"

Her question catches me off guard because, if my memory serves me correctly, she jumped me as soon as we got into the car. *She* was the one who started grinding on me. I know I asked her in the library if she wanted to get out of there, but I did so because I didn't want either of us to get into trouble. The last thing I need is some report being circulated that I was busted for making out in the library while taking media classes.

"Um...why were you looking at that website?" The question is out of my mouth before I even know what I'm saying.

Daisy runs her fingers along the nape of my neck, taking time to answer. I don't know if that's a good or bad thing, but either way, I don't like it.

"It's part of an assignment for my class."

"What class?" I know I sound defensive but I can't help it. The BoRe Blogger has been anything but kind to my teammates and me. It's one thing to post about the game, but to post gossip and rumors is a completely different thing.

"Sports media. It's for a research paper," she says and I want to believe her, but surely her professors would require a reputable site and not some random blog that isn't reporting the facts.

"What's wrong with ESPN or CBS Sports?"

In a rare occurrence in the city of Boston, I come upon a parking spot that doesn't require me to parallel park, and I take it. Putting my SUV in park, I turn in my seat to face her. I can't read her expression because I'm not very good with this girl shit.

"I don't understand why you don't like the BoRe Blog. It's funny and informative."

Is she serious right now? "It's anything but, Daisy. He posts rumors, falsifies information, and publicly outed you. Nothing about that blog is okay."

"Are you just angry because you think the blogger picks on you?"

"No, Daisy, I'm not," I say sharply. "I'm pissed because I asked you not to look at that shit and when I come to surprise you, you act like I caught you doing something wrong. It's not a lot to request."

I don't know what's happening here, but now I'm fucking pissed. Daisy turns and looks out the window, ignoring me. I know it's stupid to fight over a blog, but the shit that particular blog publishes is a sore subject with me, and she knew that. I thought it was a fairly simple request that she not read it, but apparently I was wrong.

When she takes out her cell phone and starts doing whatever the fuck she's doing, I know the conversation is over. I put my car back into drive, heading back onto the road, and instead of going to my house I take her home.

"I can't believe you're pissed off," she says as we turn onto her street. Truth is, neither can I, but I am.

"If that blog didn't post about my friend's failing marriage, or how many times I adjusted my cup, I might take it seriously...but shit, Daisy, it's *not* fucking news."

"Yeah, well, my friends and I like it. So what if they post how many times you pick your nose or the fact that Bainbridge is cheating on his wife? It's newsworthy to the fans. It makes us feel like we know you."

"Are you shitting me right now?" I stop abruptly in front of her apartment, failing to put my car in park. "Whatever is going on in Steve's life isn't news, and if they're getting a divorce, they certainly don't need some half-assed blogger posting inaccurate shit that's none of anyone's business. God, why can't you see it's wrong?"

"Because journalists support freedom of speech." She's out of my car, slamming the door before I can even say anything. My only comeback is the squealing tires of my car, which I hope she hears as I pull away from the curb.

———————◆———————

The only place I can go to try and get my mind off what just happened is the stadium. Once I'm there, I hit the gym. I want to lift weights and punch the shit out of the bag that hangs in the corner, but I'm too pissed and that's a bad idea. I can't afford to tear a muscle right now. My game is the most important part of me. That and my integrity, which is something Daisy doesn't seem to understand.

The whole "journalists support freedom of speech" thing is bullshit. I'd support it too if it were the truth and not some made-up gossip to stir the pot. And where does the BoRe Blogger get his information? There must be someone on the inside who leaks it, because we didn't even know about

Bainbridge, his wife, and a potential mistress until we read about it in the damn blog. Guys talk in the clubhouse—there's a code that it doesn't leave—and nothing has been said. But again, if I were cheating on my wife, I probably wouldn't tell anyone. No one can keep a fucking secret anyway.

I step onto the treadmill, put my earbuds in, and push the speed button until I'm in a steady run. My heavy metal playlist blasts into my ears, blocking out my thoughts of Daisy and the fucked-up conversation we just had. Our weight room looks out over the field, reminding us why we're busting our asses in here—so we can bust our asses out there for the fans, the town, and our team.

The grounds crew is out, mowing and fixing minute holes in the dirt infield. When I was in college, I followed the grounds crew around to see how they did everything. It fascinated me. I thought if I couldn't make it in baseball I'd get a degree doing that instead. This way I'd still be with a team, in a stadium, and part of the atmosphere. My advisor thought I was stupid for thinking about it and talked me out of it. I ended up with the standard communications degree, guaranteeing me a telecasting job when I retire or become washed up.

Still, watching these guys out there, lying on the ground making sure each blade of grass is the same length, making sure the Renegades pattern is perfect and brushing the dirt in the proper direction, amazes me. Everyone who works for a baseball club takes their job seriously, from concession stands to souvenirs to laundry. It's a high-end operation here, and if there's ever any trouble, we never hear about it.

The treadmill next to me starts up. I glance over to find Bainbridge starting a slow jog. I push the button to slow down and pull out my earbuds but leave the music playing. As far as I'm concerned, he's my mentor, and I feel like a shit for bothering him with the bullshit weighing on my mind, but I need help.

"Can I ask you a question?"

"Sure, what's up?"

"So you know how I have an issue with that blog?" He nods, so I keep going. "Well, I've been seeing this girl and I've asked her not to look at it."

"Why?" he asks, without breaking stride.

"Our second date, or meeting, she brought up something about rumors she'd heard and I told her that not everything she reads online is legit and that if she had questions, she should ask. Then, somehow, the blog came up in a conversation and I asked her not to look at that shit. Today, when I surprised her at school, she was looking at the website and when I asked her about it, she flipped out on me."

Bainbridge sighs, and I have a feeling I hit a sore subject. "I don't blame you, but that shit is addictive to them. Lisa has e-mailed that blogger before about crap in our marriage even though I've asked her not to. Whatever happens in our house needs to stay there; she knows that, but she loves the attention."

"Daisy says all journalists support freedom of speech."

"The first part of the blog is great. I enjoy his critique of the game. He's a real fan. The gossip part, though—that shit has no place in baseball and takes away from the point of the blog. At least that's how I feel."

We continue to jog for a few minutes without talking. A few of the other guys come in and out of the gym, but they lift weights or hit the massage room, leaving us alone.

"I think that whatever was going on with Daisy is effectively over." Saying that out loud actually hurts. I really like her, but I need to have her respect in regard to something as simple as not indulging in a blog she knows pisses me off. It all seems so petty now that I think about it, but I can't help how I feel.

"You're too young to be tied down, Davenport."

Bainbridge steps off the treadmill and presses stop. He looks at me, pain masking his features. I stop running so I can give him my undivided attention.

"Lisa was a fan. I hit her with a foul ball in college. I felt bad and took her out to dinner and we hit it off. But she's insecure and freaks out if I don't answer when she calls or I don't call her right back. Anything longer than five minutes and I'm screwing the secretary, the cashier, or the waitress. God forbid I get up in the middle of dinner and take a shit because she accuses me of texting my girlfriend or looking at porn. If I try to make love to her, she's accusing me of trying to appease her because I'm having an affair. Frankly, I can't handle my wife, let alone a girlfriend.

"She wants to move home, back to Indiana—I don't blame her. She's alienated herself from the other wives and girlfriends, but I'm not ready to give up on my time here in Boston. I love it here. I love the team. I hear the rumors about Cooper Bailey and they scare the shit out of me. He's young, has fresh legs and a killer arm. But I'm not ready to quit."

He wraps his towel around his neck and shuts off his machine. "If I were you, I'd forget the girl. You're young and chicks are eager to get to know you. If I could do it all over again, I wouldn't have had a girlfriend when I started playing in the majors. The only things I don't regret are my kids—the rest I could honestly live without."

Bainbridge walks off, leaving me stunned. He doesn't open up much, but when he does he pours it all out. I've always asked him for advice, but to hear him say that he wished he never married his wife is a bit of a shock. Now I know why he's never introduced us, and why he either shows up to events solo or cancels.

BOSTON RENEGADES

I feel like my pleas have fallen on deaf ears!

After dropping three to the Yankees, the Renegades could only pull out one win with the Rays. One would think that playing in Boston, the Renegades would have the advantage over a team that plays in the tropics. Apparently, one shouldn't assume.

The Renegades are starting a 10-day road trip that begins in Toronto and ends in Seattle (home of Ethan Davenport) with a stop in Oakland on the way.

Seattle is historically bad, although new management is trying to rebuild the team. Let's hope Robinson Cano isn't bringing his A game while we're in town, even though we love him for ditching the Yankees in favor of the Mariners.

The Renegades are 15 and 16 going into the road trip. If they plan to make it to the postseason, they need to start winning. Yes, it's only May. However, the clock is ticking.

Our run count is now 160/149. For those keeping count—we scored six runs in the last three games, giving up 10. That's backward, boys!

GOSSIP WIRE

It seems the romance is over for Davenport and his super fan! Sources say he's been leaving the stadium by himself these past few games instead of having his number one on his arm. It makes me wonder why it's over so fast. Maybe she has a thing for Cooper Bailey...

The Renegades put on quite a show for the Children's Cancer Ward at Beth Israel. Sources close to the team said the guys had their makeup done, their fingernails painted, and many selfies were taken.

Hadley Carter, the wife of general manager Ryan Stone, recently accepted an MTV Music Award for best video. Congratulations, Ms. Carter, even if you *are* a Yankee fan. Ick!

The BoRe Blogger

SIXTEEN

I love baseball. I love women. What I don't love is women and baseball together. Since Daisy and I argued, my game has sucked. My batting average has dropped, my on-base percentage is almost nonexistent, and when I *am* hitting the ball, they're foul or I'm dropping my shoulder and they're pop-ups. Six out of our ten away games are done with a record of three and three. In those games I didn't drive in one single run. Not even a sacrifice. At least my defensive game is still intact. I can't imagine how I'd be feeling if I were committing errors and letting my team down by not being present on the field.

My head is all jacked up with thoughts of Daisy. I've been trained to block this type of shit out, but apparently it's not working. The game should be the only thing on my mind. Even now, as I walk along the hot tarmac to our plane at the Oakland International Airport, I wonder what the hell she's doing. And as I board the plane and see the same flight attendants I have known since I joined the team, my thoughts should be about tomorrow's game, but they're not. I'm stupidly wondering why Daisy hasn't called or texted and I need to stop. This was too fast, too soon for me.

Never again will I allow a female to consume my thoughts while I'm working. My focus from here on out will be solely on baseball and the pitchers I'm about to face and about the teams we need to beat to at least be a wild card team this fall. I'm going to close my eyes and visualize myself at the plate, swinging my bat to kill the ball. From here on out there will be no worrying about how someone feels, or whether someone is looking at me...and no more going the extra mile. I don't need to.

And this pent-up frustration, well, that's what Sarah's for. She has hers, I have mine, and that is why our arrangement works. I should've known better than to fuck with a good thing.

The flight from Oakland to Seattle is under two hours, barely enough time to get any shuteye. Instead, Kidd and I take advantage of the free booze and we keep the flight attendants busy. We're not the only ones drinking, just two of the youngest, but legal is legal.

When we land I'll be heading to my parents'. It's a luxury that we're entitled to when we visit our hometowns. My parents live close enough to Safeco Field that it's only a ten-minute drive. Sarah's apartment is fifteen, and if I have my way, I'll be spending as much time with her as possible. She's exactly what I need to get over this sour taste in my mouth.

"Are you sure I can't convince you to stay at the hotel?"

"Nah, my bed at home is waiting for me."

When you're single and on the road you can have a lot of fun. The cleat-chasers know what hotels we stay at and most know our arrival schedules. We'll be in town long before the bar closes and they'll be looking for action.

"Shit, don't you mean Sarah's bed?" Kidd shakes his head as he downs his drink. If I hadn't been so hung up on that certain baseball fan back in Boston, I would've had Sarah pick me up tonight, but when my mom called, it was an automatic request. If I really wanted to, I could go to Sarah's after visiting, or she could come over to my parents' house. My mom may not understand, but she wouldn't question Sarah's presence at our house.

When the flight attendant comes back, she has new drinks for us, plus an assortment of snacks. I'm starving, but the short flight makes meal preparation a bit difficult. I'm hoping my mom has the refrigerator well stocked or that she at least cooked a big meal today.

"Does she have a sister?"

"Who?" I ask, tearing my eyes away from the window. Even though it's dark out, I know the vast mountains of the Cascades loom beneath us.

"Your girlfriend?"

I frown at the term "girlfriend." For a brief moment I was stupid enough to think that I'd have a girlfriend, but that thought is long gone. A fuck buddy is better suited for me.

"She's not my girlfriend," I say, shaking my head. I quickly finish my drink and hand my empty cup to the attendant as she passes by.

"What do you call her?"

I shrug. "I don't know. My ex? Sarah doesn't have a label."

"You know most guys label that 'for a good time, call...' and put her name and number on the bathroom wall." Kidd is laughing so hard at his joke that he wakes Bainbridge up, who is frowning at us. I grimace, letting him know that I'm sorry, but he looks pissed and will likely yell at us tomorrow in the clubhouse.

"Sarah is completing her residency at the hospital. She doesn't have time to meet guys, so this is convenient for her."

"So she uses you for your pecker jammer?" He cocks his eyebrow at me, trying to stifle a laugh, only he can't and ends up snorting and blowing booze out of his nose. I keel over, laughing, as Kidd scrambles to clean up his mess while putting together a string of curse words that would embarrass Urban Dictionary.

We get stares from the other guys, but one look at Kidd and they know he's done something stupid. It's typical behavior, especially when we travel.

He's the life of the party. As soon as he's done and the redness from his face has dissipated, I can finally answer his question.

"No. It's mutually beneficial. I get what I need without someone demanding a diamond ring, and she gets what she needs without wondering if her hookup is going to call the next day. She knows I won't call, and I know she has no desire to get married."

I do fear the day that changes. I've often thought about why she hasn't tried to meet someone new or even someone in her field. She's always waiting for me to come to town or flying out to see me when she gets a vacation. Even though she knows I've been with other women since her, it doesn't seem to bother her at all. The first time she asked, I thought she would break down and start crying, but she didn't. Now that I'm thinking about it, I actually kind of find it odd.

◆

The moment we land, I'm scrambling to deplane. I'm eager to see my parents, my sister, and my niece, Shea. I don't know who will be here to pick me up, and it honestly doesn't matter, because knowing that I'm home is a big stress reliever.

As soon as my feet hit the steps, I see my dad waving. It looks like he's chatting with the bus drivers who will take the rest of my teammates and all our gear to the hotel the team is staying at. Every bag that was checked when we boarded will be taken to the hotel. I packed extra in a carry-on so I can stay with my parents.

My dad's arms wrap around my shoulders tightly as we embrace. "So happy you're home," he says, patting my back. He has no idea how much I need this hug. I don't care how old you are, hugs from your parents are a necessity.

"Me too," I tell him, returning the sentiment. This is the only time they'll see me play unless they come to Boston or pick up an away game along the way. If I had been drafted by a West Coast team, they'd see me more. I know they miss watching me play, and college spoiled that for them. Being close meant they were at most of my games.

"Is Mom still up?" I ask, knowing it's late, and she takes care of Shea during the day so my sister can work and not have to worry about day care.

"She sure is. You know she'd stay up waiting for her baby boy to come home." My dad ruffles my hair and smiles. It doesn't matter how old I am, or what my profession is, I'll always be my mom's baby boy.

The guys all come over and say hi to my dad, shaking his hand or giving him a hug. Last year, my parents came to Boston, and my dad hung out on the field with me. The guys treated him so well.

My dad moves his hands to my shoulders, shakes his head, and pulls me into another hug. "I'm so proud of you."

"Thanks, Dad."

He takes my bag and I follow him to the car. It's the same car we had when I was in high school. I tried to buy them a new one when I signed my contract with the Renegades, but they took the money and started a college fund for Shea, something I was planning to do anyway. My parents won't take anything from me, and it's sort of nice, but also a pain in the ass because they've done so much for me that I want to help them out and make sure they're comfortable. They refuse to let me help them, though.

The drive to my parents' house takes about a half hour. Seattle and Boston aren't all that different when you compare the two. Both are harbor cities, although in Boston it's pronounced "the hah-bah." Both have these amazing waterfronts, along with excellent places to eat and shop. Faneuil Hall and Quincy Market remind me of Pike Place Market, minus the fish throwing.

And the weather is similar. I think that is why I love Boston so much; it feels like home and has since the day I arrived.

I don't realize I've fallen asleep until the car shuts off. "Sorry for dozing," I say to my dad as I come to and reach for the handle. No sooner do I step out of the car and shut the door than I hear my mother squealing. Her arms are flung around me before I have a chance to gather myself, and we fall back against the car.

"You're home," she says sweetly into my shoulder.

"I am. I wish it were for longer, though." I set my mom down, and she cups my cheeks.

"Promise me you'll come home this winter."

"I promise," I tell her, meaning it. There really isn't a reason for me to stay in Boston through the winter. The housekeeping service I use can check on my house, or I can sublet it to someone. Coming home will do me some good.

"Let's go inside. Shea is sleeping on the couch. She's been waiting for you. Shana is heating up your plate."

"The only one missing is Mike." My mother frowns, turning away to go into the house. She worries about my brother-in-law and knows how much stress my sister is under while he's gone. Each time he leaves, Shana and Shea move in with my parents because my mom doesn't want Shana to be alone. Mike's a great guy, and I'm proud of him. I only wish he were home to watch my niece grow up; although I don't have much room to talk since I'm not home, either.

As soon as I step into the kitchen, the smell of home washes over me. My sister is behind the counter, looking as beautiful as ever, with her dark hair piled high on her head. She wears a "Proud Army Wife" T-shirt. Once we make eye contact, she's sprinting toward me. I pick her up and hold her, telling her how much I've missed her. I don't care if it was last week or six months ago when I saw them last—we're a close family, and being apart from them really sucks.

"Shea is going to be so excited that her unc is home."

"I can't wait to take her to the field tomorrow." I set my sister down and look her over. She's seemed to age since the last time I saw her, not that I'm going to tell her that. Mike's tours must be getting to her. "How are you, Shana?"

"I'm good. I stay busy with work and Mike calls a lot."

"When's he coming home?"

"Soon," she says, nodding. "It'll be soon." Shana doesn't say anything more on the subject and walks away when the microwave beeps.

"Your bag is in your room," my dad says, returning from down the hall. I was so wrapped up in seeing my sister that I didn't even know he had come into the house. As I look around the kitchen, I see nothing has changed, and yet everything seems so much smaller than the last time I was here. I'm so used to my open floor plan and how everything is bright in my house. My parents' kitchen is dated and dark. The cabinets have to be from the seventies, and even though the appliances were replaced while I was in high school, they're outdated now.

From where I'm standing, I can see into the family room. The cream-colored carpet needs to replaced, the walls could use a fresh coat of paint, and the curtains should be updated. I know my parents won't let me buy them a new house, but they never said anything about remodeling.

"You should let me remodel your house," I say as I sit down. My sister puts a hot plate of food down in front of me, and I instantly dig in, having missed the taste of a home-cooked meal. She sits to my left with my mom on my right and my dad across from me. I know they hate it when I try to spend money on them, but it's something I can afford to do, and I want to do this for them.

"We don't need your money, Ethan," my mom says, putting her hand on my forearm. "You're going to need it someday."

"Mom, if I spend that much money in my lifetime, something is seriously wrong with me."

"Maybe you should take him up on the offer," Shana says. I smile at her, silently thanking her for taking my side.

"I tried to buy you a car, but you gave the money to Shea."

"She needed a college fund," my mom retorts.

"That I would've set up for her!" I counter, putting my fork down. I look at my parents, hoping to convey that I'm serious. "You guys worked your tails off for Shana and me. We had the best of everything. Let me do this for you." I turn to my mom and pick up her hand. "I know you have a Pinterest board full of ideas for the house. Let me make that happen."

"How do you know about my Pinterest?" I don't know if she's surprised I know what Pinterest is or that I know about her board.

"Shana told me." I wink at her, earning an eye roll. They may balk and try to change my mind, but deep down they know I can do this for them and I will. I look at my sister, who is beaming. "You can start making some calls."

Mom lets out a big screech before covering her mouth, hoping to have not awakened Shea.

SEVENTEEN

I let out a loud snore after Shea pats me on the cheeks. She laughs, and I can no longer pretend to be sleeping. Rolling over, I grab hold of her and start tickling her sides. Her laughter is the best medicine and worth being woken up for. My niece is wearing a Boston Renegades shirt, and even without rolling her over, I know it says Davenport on the back along with my number.

Last night, even as we carried on with kitchen planning, the excitement from my mom and Shana's voices didn't wake Shea. I know it was for the best, but I miss her and want to spend as much time as possible with her. My saving grace is that I'll be flying back by myself, since we have an off day after we finish this series with the Mariners. When we do this, we run the risk of flights being delayed, but it's worth it. I need time with my family.

"Hi, Unc," she says, as she sits back on her knees. Shea's tooth-filled smile is beaming and her baby-blue eyes sparkle. I pull to her me and kiss her cheek, pretending to eat her ear. "Nooooo, monser," she screams while laughing and tries to push me away.

My door opens and Shea scrambles under my blankets to hide from my mom. "Have you seen Shea?" she asks as she sits on the edge of my bed.

I shake my head. "Nope, last time I saw her she was sleeping on the couch."

My mom sighs dramatically and Shea snuggles into my side. "Well, I just don't know what I'm going to do, Ethan. I wanted to take Shea to the park today and thought we could stop and get some ice cream, but if she's lost—"

"Here I is!" she yells as she throws the covers up and away from her. My mom jumps in surprise and covers her mouth, causing Shea to laugh. Her blond hair is a mess, and she has to use two hands to push it out of her face.

"Oh my goodness, Grammie thought she lost you." My mom pretends to pout, and that clearly upsets Shea. Without hesitation, she's crawling into my mom's arms, patting her face, and saying, "No, no, no, Grammie." I think Shea is one of the best things that has happened to us, which is saying a lot, because we have a great family.

"What time do you have to be at the field?"

I don't know why, but I look at the clock that has always sat on my night-stand. Even today, my room is the same, with my dark-blue walls, an oak desk, and shelves that hold all of my trophies. The last time I was home I offered to clean it out, box up my stuff, and put it in the garage, but my parents said no. They said this would always be my room. Shana's was the same, too, until she had Shea, and then it quickly became a nursery.

"No later than three," I say as I sit up, my comforter falling away and exposing my chest.

Shea laughs and says to my mom loudly, "Unc nakie."

"Yes, he is. Maybe we should leave so Unc can get dressed." My mom picks up Shea, much to Shea's displeasure. She screams, piercing our eardrums, and reaches for me. My mom's a pro, though, and doesn't let Shea's little tantrum bother her.

"I'll be out in a minute," I tell them both. As soon as my mom closes my door, I'm reaching for my phone. I know I shouldn't care if *she's* texted, but I do. When I press the home screen, it's only Sarah's name that displays. She'll be at the game tonight, sitting behind home plate with my parents, Shana, and Shea. And after the game I'll be going to her place for an adult-style sleepover where neither of us has to get up and go home in the middle of the night or worry about a three-year-old barging in once the sun is up.

I shower quickly before dressing and heading downstairs for breakfast. Shea is sitting at the table, in her booster seat, picking at her pancakes. Her hair, while still messy, is now sticking to the side of her face with syrup. I sit down next to her, but far enough away that her hands can't touch me, and dish up a plate of food. Aside from the pancakes, there are eggs, bacon, and hash browns, which on the West Coast are shoestring potatoes cooked together. This is how I prefer my hash browns. Not like how they're cooked in New England.

My mom doesn't always cook like this, either, and right now I'm very grateful. There's nothing better than starting your day off right with a home-cooked breakfast.

"How's your friend?" my mom asks, as she sits down at the table with a cup of coffee. She sips it cautiously before setting her mug down on the table. I set my fork down and swallow what I have in my mouth.

"I don't know," I say honestly. "Things are difficult, I guess."

"What do you mean, you guess?"

I pour myself some orange juice and down my glass before refilling it. "I got mad at her last week for reading one of the blogs that's always posting gossip and rumors. Early on, when she and I started talking, she mentioned some of the rumors and I was defensive."

"Rightly so," my mom throws in for good measure.

"Stone has me taking a media class, which is more like a chapter in their textbook because I only have to do it for two weeks, but it's on the same campus where she attends school. I thought I'd surprise her on the first day, and when I got to her computer station, she was reading the blog. When I asked her about it later, she became defensive, saying journalists stick together, and started going on about freedom of speech."

"Is that what she's studying?"

"Yeah."

"So she chose to follow the path that many journalists have carved out. They're all about protecting their sources, their voice, and their rights to freedom of speech."

I lean back in the chair and fiddle with my fork. "I'm all for freedom of speech, but when it's lies to sell your product, in this case a high-traffic blog that reports crap, I can't support that. I've told her as much, too."

My mom rests her hands together on the table, but doesn't say anything. Even as I tell the story, I'm not sure it makes any sense. Everything that went down didn't need to. I think about calling her, but I'm not sure I have anything to say right now. Once this road trip is over, I'll see her, and I can honestly say I don't know if I'll talk to her. Those thoughts actually hurt. It also hurts that she hasn't reached out to me to apologize. Hell, maybe I'm the one who needs to grovel.

"I think it was a fair request."

"I thought so."

"You like her, though?"

I nod and pick my fork up. I hate to admit that I like Daisy, but the truth is I do. I could see myself with her in the future. None of that matters now, though.

"Maybe she'll come around," Mom says.

"Maybe I'll hit for the cycle."

My mom laughs, but I don't find that funny. "Stranger things have happened, Ethan. Sometimes you just have to put all your eggs in the basket and pray you don't drop it."

"Well, if I do that, I may not have any eggs left. Doesn't that defeat the purpose?" I look at her questioningly, willing her to hit me with a witty comeback.

"When you stand at the plate, what are you doing?"

I scratch my head, pondering her question. "Batting?" I say with hesitation.

"Taking a risk," she says. "You don't know if you're going to walk, get a hit, foul out, or get hit by a pitch, but you stand there, repeatedly, over and over again. Sometimes the risks are worth it."

Mom stands and starts cleaning off the table. When she reaches for my plate I put my hand down on her wrist and shake my head no. I'm not done eating. I refuse to let her risk her life by stealing my food.

"Incoming," I yell, giving the guys ample time to cover up before I bring Shea into the clubhouse. This isn't a surprise visit, by any means, but I do need to warn them to make sure their potty mouths are zipped up tight, because she's three and repeats everything.

Shea is on my shoulders when I walk in, having to duck under the doorway so she doesn't hit her head. All the guys love her and reach up to give her a high five once we're inside. She is, of course, decked out in full BoRe fashion, even though she's being raised as a Mariners fan. Her legs move back and forth the more attention she gets, and as soon as I put her down, she's running in a full sprint around the room. Clubhouses are big-kid playgrounds for the most part, but even the littlest of kids can have fun in here.

When Shea runs by Branch Singleton, he scoops her up in his arms and spins her around while making airplane noises. Singleton has a son, but he never gets to see him. I don't know all the specifics, but the baby-mama drama was too much, and he doesn't like to talk about it. I do know he pays a shit-ton in child support and that his son lives in Phoenix, where the mother moved after the baby was born.

I let the guys entertain Shea, although it's likely the other way around with the way she has them all wrapped around her finger, while I get ready. For being three, she's outgoing and loves attention. Shana and my parents ensure that she experiences a lot of different social situations in order to teach her about stranger danger.

Once I'm dressed and ready, I hold Shea's hand as we walk down the corridor leading to the field. She wears cleats, like me, only hers have plastic spikes, and her tiny baseball glove is tucked under her arm. Mine is already in the dugout, waiting for me.

My dad is waiting for us at the top of the dugout, since he'll be keeping a close eye on Shea during warm-ups. He and Cal Diamond, our manager, are deep in conversation, but he makes eye contact with me briefly as Shea and I climb the steps and step out onto the field.

"I'll take her with me, if you want to hit," Kidd says, as he stands near us.

"Me too," Bainbridge says. With both of them being in the outfield, she has less of a chance to get hurt.

"Do you want to go with Steve and Travis to the outfield?" I ask her, pointing toward the outfield. She clutches my hand a bit tighter and tries to mold herself to my leg. I imagine being three and looking around the baseball field. This place is enormous for an adult, so the size must be overwhelming to a toddler. It takes under a minute until she decides that yes, she does in fact want to be out there.

In a picture-perfect moment, my niece is walking hand in hand with my best friend and my mentor, and the people who are here early are eating up every minute of it.

"Hey, stud."

The sound of Sarah's voice comes from behind me. The nickname she gave me in high school, sticking even today. When I turn to see her, my world shifts on its axis. I don't know what I was expecting, maybe a white coat with her dark brown hair in a bun for starters. Instead, I'm graced with the woman I was once madly in love with, wearing a version of a BoRe T-shirt that I've never seen before, showing off her curves and ample cleavage. She beckons me with her finger and, as if it had me on a string, I'm walking toward her.

"Hey, Doc," I say, taking her all in. "Although, I have to say, you don't look much like a doctor to me right about now."

When Sarah smiles, her light-brown eyes light up. She's beautiful, always has been. And I'd be a fool to ever tell her no.

"We can play doctor later," she whispers into my ear, sending a jolt right to my cock.

"I look forward to it." I back away slowly, trying to undress her with my eyes. I know what's waiting for me. Hell, I watched her transform from a girl to a woman while I caressed every inch of her body. That's a definite benefit of being her boyfriend for so long.

I wink before turning away and adjusting myself. As soon as my hand touches my cup, I count one in my head. I'll be sure to tweet the BoRe Blogger how many times an adjustment was made tonight so his statistical count isn't skewed.

EIGHTEEN

Nothing makes me happier than a win. Actually, that may not be completely true, because the idea of getting laid has me pretty damn ecstatic right now. The win makes our manager happy, and the fact that it was a close victory, with a late two-run shot by Branch, puts a shit-eating grin on his face. With back-to-back road wins, it's a boost in the standings.

My routine is different this time around. I'm not going to linger in the clubhouse, nor am I going to shower. The sooner I arrive at Sarah's, the sooner this pent-up frustration will be released. She made the game almost unbearable today with her shy finger waves, blowing kisses, and yelling crude comments about my ass when I was in the on-deck circle. Even though she was sitting next to my parents, she didn't hold back. My sister encourages Sarah's behavior, and even though Shana is happily married, she has no qualms about catcalling my teammates who, in turn, give her what she calls the "sexy eyes."

It's no secret that we all have slump-busters or cleat-chasers in the towns we visit. I've hooked up with random women in different cities, but Sarah is my only consistent one. My parents know about our arrangement, and while they may not approve, they at least know her and consider her part of our family.

As soon as Diamond is done congratulating us on the win, I'm taking off my uniform and throwing it into the laundry hamper. My cleats, glove, and everything else I need stays in my assigned locker until I need it again tomorrow. I put my game-day attire on—dress shirt and slacks—and tell the guys I'll see them later. Kidd shows me how much fun I'm about to have when he puts his fist to his mouth and juts his tongue into his cheek.

"Be jealous," I say as I grab my dick and give it a good shake.

"Be sure to wrap your junk so your pecker juices don't sneak out."

I flip him off as I walk out of the clubhouse, laughing. At the end of the corridor the parade of women starts. Most of them filter around, but a few are brazen enough to flat-out ask you to come hang with them. At first, it's an ego boost when they choose you…until you remember they just want to say they fucked a Major League baseball player and take a selfie as proof. I won't have to worry about that tonight. Sarah doesn't care about what I do for a profession. She wants my dick, and I'm going to give it to her.

The car I had in high school and college waits for me in the parking garage, along with my overnight bag. The smell of home surrounds me as I navigate my way to Sarah's apartment. It's close to the hospital so she can walk to work, and it's not far from Safeco Field. There were many times that Sarah and I opted for the cramped quarters of the car even when we had a bed at our disposal. It wasn't just the thrill of possibly getting caught, but also how close we had to be, and how creative we had to get in order to make things work.

I pull onto Sarah's street and maneuver my Toyota Camry into a tight parking spot. Sarah's building used to be an office building until a big-time developer came along and converted the space into apartments for students.

Mostly medical students live here, but you'll find a few engineers and teachers as well.

I'm all but jogging to the main door, eager to get upstairs. As soon as my foot hits the first step, the buzzing of the door sounds and there's the telltale sound of it being unlocked, signaling I can go in. Despite everything that's happened between Sarah and me, we still have this weird sixth-sense shit going on. I guess that's what makes our situation work so well. Neither of us has any expectations, but we both know when we need that certain itch to be scratched. Sex, in general, is great, but when you're with someone who knows how to make you let go of everything, it's ten times better.

Her door is open when I round the corner on her floor. Some could take this as a sign that she doesn't care and is going through the motions, while others could take it as a sign that she's eager and ready to get shit done. It's neither for me. Sarah is very matter-of-fact about everything and simply making things easier for me. As soon as she sees me, her eyes widen. I'm dirty, probably stink, and look like shit.

"Need a shower?" she asks with one eyebrow raised. I give her a smirk and wink in return before heading toward her bedroom, where her only bathroom is, and drop my bag on her bed. Her apartment is small but cozy. After I graduated, I stayed here for about a week until we all but killed each other—it was a little too close for comfort back then. Now, I welcome it. I unbutton my shirt, tossing it on her bed as I pass by her, and undo my pants, letting them fall to my ankles before kicking them off, along with my shoes, on my way into the bathroom. She had to have known I was going to head right here, as towels sit on the counter waiting for me.

After starting the shower, I finish undressing before stepping in and letting the hot water pound down on my muscles. I rotate my shoulders and flex under the spray, hoping to get them to loosen up. I jump slightly at the feel of her hands on my sides, but quickly relax into her touch. She slowly runs her hands down my hips until she's stroking my dick. My head falls back while my hand steadies myself against the wall. I reach back with my other hand and grab her ass, pulling her to me as she nips at my back.

It's been far too long since I've had the attention of a woman like this. I find myself turning, moving her hand away. She looks confused, but I displace any errant thoughts she has when I pull her to me, kissing her hard and fast. We're all teeth until we find our familiar rhythm, our tongues gliding against each other and our hands roaming paths that had been forged long ago from years of being together.

Sarah breaks our kiss, letting her lips travel from my neck, over my chest, and stopping at my erect nipple. She bites hard, pulling on it until I'm groaning. My cock jumps, pushing against her, ready to be inside of her. Sarah looks at me with a devilish smile before dropping to her knees.

"Oh, fuck," I say, grabbing hold of the shower door to steady myself. She looks up with her brown come-hither eyes, watching me as she takes me into her mouth. I'm taken deep into her warm mouth as I slowly start to rock, and her fingers dig into my ass.

"God damn, your…" I trail off as she pulls back and slowly takes me in again, sucking and using her hand to create much-needed friction. She switches her method and starts licking me from base to tip and back down while her hand works to get me off. I want her mouth on me, though. I want to feel the suction against my shaft. Tangling my fingers in her hair, I guide her mouth back to my dick, and she greedily accepts what I'm offering. I pump my hips, fucking her pretty mouth as my orgasm builds.

"Fucking hell, Daisy, your mouth."

I freeze, as does Sarah. The water turns to ice as I stand there in silence and there's a pounding in my head. She avoids eye contact as she stands and steps out of the shower, leaving me with my demon. The one thing we've always agreed on is that if we were to start seeing someone, we'd tell each other so we wouldn't have awkward situations like the one that just occurred.

I shut the water off and step out. The apartment is silent; not even the sound of the television can be heard. Wrapping myself in a towel, I walk into her bedroom and find her standing at the window with her bathrobe on.

"I can explain." It's my lame attempt at a half-assed apology. I should be over there, behind her, telling her how sorry I am for using another woman's name while she was doing exactly what I wanted her to do.

"Who is she?" Sarah doesn't turn around, leaving me unable to gauge exactly how she's feeling. I run my hand through my hair and sigh. Dropping the towel, I reach into my bag and pull out my sweats and a T-shirt, forgoing underwear. Right now, I just want to be in clothes so when she kicks my ass out I'm not stark naked in the middle of downtown Seattle.

"She's hard to explain," I say as I try to think about how to describe Daisy to her. "We met last month, but I guess you can say I've been looking at her since last year. She's a season ticket holder, and we sort of stare at each other during games."

"That doesn't sound creepy at all." Sarah turns and when I look at her, her eyebrows are scrunched.

"It's totally fucking creepy, but you didn't need to point it out." I sit down and rest my elbows on my knees, my wet hair dripping onto my white T-shirt. Sarah walks over, taking a seat beside me.

"There are support groups for people like you," she says, but I can't figure out if she's making fun of me or being serious. I have a feeling the doctor part of her thinks I need mental help. Maybe I do.

"Do you have a number for me to call?"

She shakes her head and looks down. I've ruined everything and don't know how to fix it. Taking her hand in mine, I turn my body to face her and pull her chin up so I can look her in the eyes.

"Sarah, I'm sorry for what just happened. I can't explain it and will understand if you never want to speak to me again. Calling you by another woman's name is beyond unacceptable and I never meant to disrespect you like this."

Her face softens, and she leans into me. "I know why you did it."

I laugh. "You're in sports medicine, not psychotherapy," I remind her.

"You're in love."

Her words cause the room to spin and my heart to stop. I've only loved one woman, aside from my mother, sister, and grandmothers...and that woman was Sarah. Even in high school I knew I was in love with Sarah, and still, to this day, I would do anything for her.

"Am not," I childishly respond.

"Ethan, right now I want to punch you in the gut and maybe kick you in the junk, but I know how much you value your manhood so I won't do that. But come on, we were together for years and even after we broke up and you were sleeping with other people, you never once called me by another woman's name. I'm not exactly happy about it, but I'm willing to concede my reign over your dick and let another woman have at it, as long as you admit to yourself that you're in love."

The words "am not" repeat in my head, but I hold them back for fear she might make good on her word and pummel me. I'd deserve it if she chose to, so I'm going to sit here and play dumb.

"Doesn't matter, because I'm stupid and girls are too hard to read."

"What'd you do?" Sarah asks as she stands to face me with her arms crossed. I think her foot is jutted out, but I'm too afraid to break eye contact to look right now.

"Freaked out because she was reading a blog that I asked her not to," I mumble and lean back, making the gap between us even larger. Sarah is of average height so I'm calculating that the distance between her arm and me is in my favor.

She rolls her eyes and places her hands on her hips. "You're right. You are stupid."

I throw my hands up and sigh.

"So what if she wants to read a blog? I read gossip columns all the time. It's an easy way to relax and remind yourself that your favorite actor or musician is still human and can't actually walk on water or get away with murder."

"I find them dumb."

Sarah scoffs. "It's because people write about you. Grow a set, Ethan. Who gives a shit? You're Boston's most eligible bachelor, so regardless of what you do, they're going to write about you. Whether you help an old lady cross the street or kick your neighbor's cat—you're news! Suck it up, buttercup. This is what you wanted."

"Ugh," I say, throwing my hands up in the air again before flopping back onto her bed. She laughs from somewhere behind me while I bury my face in her comforter. We should be having sex right now. Sarah's a fine piece of ass and her beautiful tits should be bouncing in my face while she rides me, but no, we're having girl talk, and I'm about to cash in my fucking man card.

"Sarah," I whine, feeling the bed dip next to me. I turn my head and see nothing but a creamy thigh mocking me for being such a pussy. "What am I going to do?"

"Well, for starters, you're not getting laid unless you hit the corner bar and find someone who doesn't care what you call her, and second, start thinking of a grand gesture, because I have a feeling this girl is worth it."

She's right. She is, but how does she know that? How do women have all the answers?

"How?"

"I've never seen you like this, Ethan. She must be something else if she has you tied into knots." Sarah runs her fingers through my hair, calming me. "Come on, let's get some sleep."

I crawl into my spot and push the covers down with my feet. "Where are you going?" I ask as she gets up.

"Bob and I have a date."

"Who the fuck is Bob?" I ask, seeing red. How the fuck could she have a date knowing I was coming over?

"Bob is my dildo. He's my go-to cock, always hard, always ready. He never lets me down. You didn't get me off, so someone...or some*thing*...has to." With that she closes her bathroom door, leaving me in her bedroom to listen to her fucking moaning and telling him yes, yes, yes repeatedly while my sorry excuse for a dick laughs at me.

NINETEEN

In true Sarah fashion, she threw some hard facts at me the other night, reminding me of just how stupid I can be. Even though I spent the night with her, in her bed, we never touched and honestly, it broke my heart. It hit me like a ton of bricks that we were finally over, that our relationship had met its end. I hate that my last encounter with her was a quick blowjob in the shower where I referred to her by another woman's name. She deserved better from me.

Sarah told me that I need to come clean with Daisy when I see her and not hide what went down in Seattle. It's really not a conversation that I want to have with Daisy, if she were ever to speak to me again, because in my mind that just solidifies the rumors from the blog.

First things first, I have to get Daisy to speak to me, and right now that's not happening. As much as it pained me to leave Seattle a day early, I chose to fly back with the team after our last game. I wanted to use the off day to see Daisy and apologize.

The downside of returning with the team means I'm required to attend class, even though this is my last week. The professor is going on and on about the importance of clean enunciation when speaking publicly. He's right. Far too many athletes don't enunciate when they speak, oftentimes leaving people scratching their heads at what they're saying. I shouldn't complain about it, though, since they're allowed to be on television and I'm not. Clearly it's working for them.

Maybe that's the key to life—never speak clearly. It'll leave people wondering what you're saying and often agreeing with you because they don't want to be rude and ask you to repeat yourself. It's something I may need to try when I meet with Stone and we go over what I learned. Somehow I don't think he'll be impressed.

As soon as class is dismissed, I'm running across campus to the library. That is where I found her last time, and I'm hoping she's a creature of habit. What I'm going to say, I have no idea, but I am hoping that the words will flow once I see her. Except I don't, because she's not in the cubicle I was hoping to find her in. It's now being occupied by the Jolly Green Giant, whom I don't want to tap on the shoulder to ask if he's seen Daisy.

Feeling defeated, I start the long trek back to my car, pulling out my phone to text her. It's one of two or three dozen texts I've sent since I fucked up with Sarah, and none of them have been answered. A normal person would start to think that maybe the object of their affections had fallen ill or was in the hospital, but since I stalked the shit out of her and have seen her leave her apartment, I know that's not the case. I curse the parking in Boston, because when I saw her I was looking for a place to park and couldn't just jump out of my car and chase her down.

I was hoping we could grab some lunch today . . .

It's a desperate attempt to get her attention, and I've failed to tell her exactly how sorry I am because Sarah beat it into me that those words need to be said to her in person and not through text message. I hate it when Sarah's right, which is more often than not. I wait to see if she's going to respond before I pocket my phone and get into my car. I could go home and practice my public speaking in front of a mirror or go to the stadium.

The stadium always wins out for me. It's my home away from home. My serenity.

After splitting with the Mariners two games to two, we're hosting the Texas Rangers for three games before the Los Angeles Angels come to town, bringing their power hitter, Albert Pujols, with them. That man scares me when he's up to bat; he makes my hand twitch like there's no tomorrow. I've caught a few of his line drives and have had to hide the fact that my palm was burning from snagging the ball wrong. I could tell he knew, though, as he stared me down on his walk back to the dugout.

As soon as I step into the clubhouse, I'm called to Stone's office. The walk can be daunting, but I have a lot of respect for him, and the fact that we're somewhat close in age helps. His secretary isn't at her desk when I arrive, so I walk in, knocking on his doorjamb.

"Ethan, come on in. Take a seat," he says as he looks up from his paperwork.

I do as I'm told, burying my hand under my leg to keep it still.

"Hand bothering you today?" I both hate and like that he notices. I don't want him to think it'll ever affect my job on the field, but it worries me that he does.

"Sometimes you make me nervous, sir." I finish off by calling him "sir," hoping to ease the building tension.

"Just worried about you is all," he says, folding his hands on his desk. "How's the media stuff been working out?"

"It's okay," I say, honestly. "I've learned the dos and don'ts of what to post on social media, how words can be misconstrued, and to always enunciate my words when giving an interview."

"That's good. I've spoken to your professor, and he's assured me that he's taught you everything from the course, so tonight after the game you can speak to the media if they ask for you."

I can't hide the grin that I know is plastered all over my face. I stand and shake his hand, elated that he has enough faith in me to not screw up. I hope that I don't make a fool out of myself when given the opportunity and that I do something tonight that will be newsworthy.

"I heard about your secret project," Stone says, causing me to sit back down.

I run my free hand through my hair, trying to decipher if I'm in trouble or not.

"It's a nice thing to do—to help out like that."

I nod and say thank you, hoping that what I've done doesn't cause upset or fall on deaf ears. Frankly, I'm out of options. Stone dismisses me, but not before telling me that his wife's parents are in attendance tonight. Why he felt the need to say this is beyond me, but he loves taking every jab he can to remind me of who he's married to and where they sit.

I opt not to work out, but to start changing for the game. The routine is the same: socks, cup, jockstrap, Under Armour shirt, and finally my pants, but not my jersey. I'll change into that later. I leave my cleats untied and sit on my stool, waiting. My thoughts return to what Stone said, about how it's nice to help out. I don't know if what I've done is a good thing or not, but it's the only thing I can think of to get Daisy's attention. If it's successful, I owe the ladies in the main office lunch, roses, and a day of pampering.

The clubhouse opens for the media and I find myself sitting tall and proud. As soon as the reporter from NESN comes over to me, I know I'm ready.

"Ethan, care to chat today?" That has been their standard question every day since I joined the team. I nod eagerly like a damn buffoon.

"Great. Your batting average is one of the highest in the league and there's chatter that you'll be a shoo-in for the batting title. This is only your second season. Are you surpassing your personal expectations?"

What the fuck is this noise? Why didn't media training train me on how to answer these types of questions instead of worrying about my relationship status on Facebook?

I pretend that there's something fascinating on the floor and bend sideways to pick it up before answering. This sly move gives me only seconds of a reprieve before the microphone is being thrust into my face.

"Each day that I go out there, it's to win for Boston and my teammates." The reporter smiles and thanks me for my time. I close my eyes and mentally kick my ass for being so fucking dumb when it comes to this shit. It makes me want to call my college coach and tell him to mandate that a class on answering these questions be taken.

As soon as it's time, I'm out of the clubhouse and onto the field. I find myself looking for Daisy every chance I get, only to find her seat empty. When we start stretching out in center field, I angle myself so I can spot her when she starts descending the stairs. My stalking levels know no bounds right now, and I'm ashamed of myself.

By the time batting practice is over, she's still not here, which is late for her. We head back into the clubhouse to change and meet with Diamond and the other coaches to go over the game. It's hard to predict how a game is going to go. If pitching is tight, but batting isn't, the game could be a battle. End up with a shitty night of pitching and swift bats—we could be putting up matching runs. Ideally, you want your strong pitcher to outduel theirs and let the bats do all the talking. The guy we're facing tonight gave me my first grand slam last year. I thanked him by having him sign a game ball, since the one I hit over the wall was taken by a fan. It probably wasn't very nice of me, but I needed the memento.

We come back out to do some more game prep and to start the pomp and circumstance that goes into every game. As I step out, the music is a bit louder, and the fans are filling their seats. Looking around, I see people stuffing their faces with hot dogs, nachos, and popcorn, with beer as a chaser. It's been so long since I've been a spectator at a game. I miss those days.

My eyes finally land on Daisy's seat and, much to my surprise, it's empty. I try not to let this bother me, but it does. Meyers slaps me on the back as he passes, reminding me that standing here looking like an idiot isn't doing anyone any good.

I take my spot on the track and take off my hat. Everyone is instructed to rise for the national anthem. I keep my eyes focused on the flag while I sing the words in my head. The moment the singer has finished, fireworks go off, signaling the start of the game. I turn away from where Daisy usually sits, unwilling to see her seat still empty, and head to the dugout to grab my glove.

We tell each other good luck and then we all pat Hawk Sinclair on the ass as we go by him. He's in the zone and doesn't pay us any attention. Once he gets the first batter under his belt, he'll loosen up.

The moment my cleats touch the warning track, I'm looking left. My feet halt in their tracks and my heart stops. Sitting in the seat next to Daisy is her grandfather, and it's my grand gesture, as Sarah calls it, that put him there. After my calls and texts to her went unanswered, I had to come up with something to let her know that she's important to me, so I made arrangements to have the Renegades staff do what they could to bring her grandfather to the game, and it looks like they've succeeded.

I should walk over to her and say hi, but I don't. I need to let everything settle and see if she comes to me. I've extended the olive branch—hell, it's a fucking tree—and if she wants to be with me, the ball is in her court now.

BOSTON RENEGADES

After a tough week and a half on the road, the BoRes started a five-game home stand with a win over the Texas Rangers, besting them by one run.

Tonight's game was a nail-biter, down to the ninth inning when with two outs, shortstop Easton Bennett hit a solo shot deep into center, putting it out of reach of Delino DeShields.

The bats were decent for the Rangers, who were leading the game from the first inning. However, solid batting from Branch Singleton and Ethan Davenport kept the BoRes on the cusp most of the night.

Welcome home, boys! Boston missed you.

GOSSIP WIRE

Congratulations to Easton Bennett. Not only did he have the game winner but his on-and-off-again girlfriend gave birth today to a son. No word from the Bennett camp on who the father is, and considering Easton was busy playing... Well, you can fill in the blanks.

The BoRe Blogger

TWENTY

The hot water warms my sore shoulder muscles, allowing me to rotate my arm with ease and prevent injury. There was a slight chill in the air that I didn't prepare for during tonight's game and I'm afraid I may end up paying for it tomorrow when I wake up.

All night I watched Daisy's grandfather observe the game. You could tell by the way he participated between innings that he was in his element. If given the opportunity, I'd like to sit him down and ask if he played when he was younger. Some people enjoy the game, but those who grew up playing ball in the streets until the streetlights came on, they *love* the game. It's a different kind of love than the kind one has for a family member or friend— it's hard to explain. For me, the game means everything. As for Daisy's grandfather—well, I'm not sure I'll ever know.

Bringing Daisy's grandfather to the game was Sarah's idea. We stayed up most of the night talking about Daisy and how I feel. I thought it would be weird to discuss the girl I want to be my girlfriend with the girl who used to be my girlfriend, but it actually wasn't. Sarah said a grand gesture was needed. I thought sending roses to school would do the trick. That thought earned me a slap on my bare shoulder as Sarah and I lay side-by-side in her bed, fully clothed and not touching, after she had been satisfied by Bob. It was Sarah who suggested that Daisy's grandfather come to the field, and if it weren't for her, tonight wouldn't have happened.

During the game, the bat boy for the Rangers gave him a ball and the BoRe squad made sure he "caught" one of the shirts they hand out. The shirts are cheesy and often filled with sponsor promos, but it's the excitement of having one land in your hands that makes it worth it. Each time I checked, I purposely avoided eye contact with Daisy. I didn't know what to expect, so I thought it best that we not look at each other. I could've pissed her off with this stunt. I'm hoping that I haven't, but at least I was able to help her grand-father see a game—one that she probably wouldn't otherwise be able to get him to. I'm tempted to call her, but I'd really like her to make the first move. I want to hear her voice. I'm not looking for a thank-you. I am only looking for the door to open again.

Shutting the water off, I step out of the shower and reach for my towel. The doorbell rings as I run the towel over my hair, trying to dry it off as much as possible. I curse myself for not drying fully as I leave a trail of water behind me, but I'm more worried about who is at the door than ruining my floors. A quick glance at the clock tells me it is half past eleven, and I know I didn't order any food. Kidd was threatening to have a "nurse" stop by and visit me later tonight, and if he actually called for an escort I'm going to string him up by his balls.

Everything moves in slow motion as I pull open the door and stand naked, except for the towel that is cinched around my waist, staring at Daisy. The soft glow from my porch light makes her look angelic and peaceful. She looks at me, opening and closing her mouth as if she's unsure about what to say. I know what it's like to be unable to find the words that you need to say to someone. It took me far too long to reach out to her, and once I started, she ignored me. My hand absentmindedly rubs over my chest, causing her mouth to drop open. I can't help the smirk that forms as she watches me.

It's as if time stands still as her gaze slowly meets mine. I don't know if it's desire or hatred that I see. Her fists clench at her sides, her shoulders are square, and her luscious lips are in a thin line, making me want to throw her over my shoulder and put her down on my bed so I can have my way with her. My thoughts drift back to the night of the Rotary dinner, of her naked and on my bed. Her body responds to my touch so easily, giving into the temptation that both of us were feeling.

"I'm wicked pissed at you," she blurts out, interrupting my recollection of the other night.

"Huh?" is the most intelligible response I can come up with, because right now I'm very distracted by picturing her in very compromising positions far from my front porch.

"You," she says angrily as she points toward my bare chest. My hand covers the imaginary spot that she stabbed as I step back, away from her dagger. "What you did…"

Daisy looks away and sighs, her shoulders slumped. My hand reaches for her, but I pull it back quickly. She's not mine to touch right now. When she meets my eyes again, there are unshed tears dancing along her green orbs.

"Daisy…" My voice cracks as if my heart is breaking. It's not, but I *am* trying to show her that I care, that I'm really the good guy here regardless of what people post about me. Yes, I like women and sex, but I'm human and single. I'm not hurting anyone by having one-night stands. The women I pick up aren't looking for a long-term commitment, nor do they care if I call.

I *called* Daisy. I *pursued* her. I *want* to be with her.

She shakes her head, bringing her fingers to her lips as if she's trying to keep her words trapped inside. I look out over her shoulder to see a lady walking her dogs. She gives me a slight wave, looking unsure of herself, likely because of the way I'm dressed. I wave back, careful to keep my hand on my hip where I'm holding my towel.

"Today, for the first time since my grandma died, my grandpa laughed. He smiled, ate a hot dog at the ballpark, and heckled the opposing team. He was able to do all of this because of you, and I want to know why."

Shit, what do I say? Is it because I want to make her smile or get into her pants? Is it because all I do is think about her? I'm not sure I can tell her that the reason I did it was so that she'd talk to me, because that's purely selfish, and the intent of the gift wasn't meant to be that way.

"I did it because going to a game seemed important to him."

Before I can register what's going on, Daisy has her arms wrapped around my neck and her tongue deep in my mouth. She moans when I start to return her kiss. My towel falls away, leaving me bare-ass naked for all my neighbors to see. I fumble with the door and try to move us away at the same time without rubbing my junk all over her leg. I kick the door shut and blindly fumble with the lock. The last thing I want is for someone like Kidd to come over, even though it's too late for visitors.

Cupping her ass in my hands, I pull her legs around my waist and walk us toward my bedroom, leaving my towel on the floor. I'm being presumptuous, I know that, but I can't help it, because she's working my mouth like a pro while her hands grip my hair. I set her down and pull away, using my thumb under her chin to bring her eyes up to look at me.

"Do you want this?"

The subtle nod she gives me has my dick hardening.

"We can't take it back once we do this. You have to be sure."

"I am," she says softly.

"Is this because I brought your grandpa to the game?" This is my fear. I don't want her thinking she has to sleep with me to return the favor. That's not why I did it. I just wanted the opportunity to talk to her.

Daisy stands so she's pressed against my chest. I'm trying not to think about how fucking hot it would be to put my dick in between her perfect mounds and titty-fuck her. I know it's too much to ask for, but a guy can fantasize.

"No, it's because I want this with you. You're always in my thoughts, in my dreams, and I think about having you inside me. At night, when I'm in bed, I touch myself, imagining it's your fingers moving over my body."

Her fingers trace the outlines of my muscles, causing my skin to pebble. I'm trying not to let her words get to me, but it's no use. My heart is beating faster and my muscles constrict as she touches me. My skin is on fire, just like every other time her skin comes in contact with mine. My throat aches, even though it's not sore, but the excitement is so much that there's a pang there keeping my voice on lockdown while my cock has a mind of its own and is ready, straining to have some action.

"When I let my fingers push into me, I picture you doing it. I think about you being the one to cause that warmth to spread through my body."

My head falls back when her mouth latches onto my nipple. She bites and I groan, grabbing her shoulders in reflex.

"I'm here because I want to be, and tonight showed me that I've been wrong about you and us. I'm here if you want me."

"I so fucking want you," I tell her as I pull her shirt up and over her head. With a flick of my thumb and index finger her bra is off. Her breasts brush against my abs and my dick thinks the attention is all for him. He jerks against her skin, asking her to touch him.

And when she does, I have to think about baseball stats so I don't come before I have the opportunity to get inside her. Her small hand wraps around the base of my dick and starts pumping slowly.

"Tell me if I'm doing this wrong."

"No such thing as wrong when you're the one who's touching me," I tell her, reassuring her that I'm fucking putty when it comes to her hands and lips.

"I want to make you feel good." She has no fucking idea that the images she has put in my mind will make me feel good for days to come. Knowing she touches herself and wants it to be me strokes my fucking ego like there's no tomorrow. When her fingers make her come, she's wishing it was me doing that to her.

Tonight, I'll make her fantasies come true.

"Fuck, Daisy, just your being here makes me feel good."

Placing my lips on hers, I give her a long-overdue kiss. One that I hope curls her toes and makes her weak in the knees. My tongue dips into her mouth, slow and languid, setting a sweet and steady pace. My hand cups her cheek while the other massages her breast. Our lips move against each other while our tongues meet in unison. The heat inside me starts to build as I pull her flush to my body.

Daisy's hands roam over my body, from my hair to my cheeks to my chest, finally resting one on my dick, returning the attention she was giving him moments ago. As much as I want her to keep going, I want her naked and laid out on my bed. Dropping to my knees, I kiss along the waistband of her shorts before unbuttoning them and sliding them down her legs. She steps out of them, placing her hands on my shoulders to keep steady. I pull off each of her flip-flops and toss them into a pile near where I threw her shorts.

I nip at her skin near her panties before hooking my fingers into the sides to bring them down her legs. When she lifts her leg to step out, I hook her leg over my shoulder.

"Can I kiss you here?" I ask as I run my finger over her clit and into the chasm that will certainly be my death. Her head falls back as I pump in and out of her. She doesn't answer, and maybe that should be a sign that she does want my mouth on her. If the moaning that's coming from her or the rocking of her hips as she rubs herself against my hand is any indication, I don't think she'll care.

I pick her up, putting her other leg on my shoulder so her pussy is right where I need it. I don't wait as I dive right in. Lapping between her lips and up to her clit, I suck gently before doing it again. Daisy grips my hair, pulling handfuls that hurt like a motherfucker, but I love it. I welcome it. The moment my tongue plunges into her pussy, I'm gone.

Carrying her over to my bed, I set her down roughly. She bounces, and all that does is give me more of her sweet taste. I palm my cock to ease some of the tension and silently tell him to calm down because he'll get his time soon.

"I could do this every day," I say against her skin as I insert two fingers into her. She's tight and I'm afraid I'm going to hurt her.

"This...this..." Her hips start rocking and her hands dig into the blanket. Keeping my fingers pumping, I suck on her clit, watching her body get worked into a frenzy by me this time and not from her own doing.

As much as it pains me, I move away from her and head to my nightstand, pulling open the drawer and grabbing a condom. One look from her and I'm on top, mouth-to-mouth, chest-to-chest, with my cock nestled between us. My hand ghosts down her chest, over her breast, until my mouth can follow. Her nipples are peaked and I bite gently, pulling one into my mouth. Her back arches, pushing her breasts into my face.

"Ethan..."

"Yeah, baby?"

I sit back and push her knees wide, spreading her before me. Even my wide frame is going to stretch her and hurt. Running my finger down her slit, I know she's flush and eager when she pushes her hips toward me. Ripping open the condom packet, I pull out the rubber that's going to keep us both safe, even though I look forward to the day when I can feel her bare.

The moment I grip my dick, I hiss. I'm sensitive and throbbing. I never take my eyes off Daisy's as I roll the condom on. I want to see her eyes. I want the acknowledgment in her face of what we're about to do. My hand trails up her hip, gripping her lightly.

"I'll go slow."

"I'm not afraid," she tells me with confidence.

Centering myself, I nudge her core, pulling away quickly.

"You okay?"

She nods and bucks her hips, asking for more.

"Fuck, you're going to kill me tonight."

And probably the next night as well; I have a feeling Daisy is going to destroy me.

"Ethan, please," she begs. The desire is there in her voice. She wants this as much as I do, and I'm going to give it to her.

Inching forward, I ready my cock and slowly push into her. Her legs start to close and her eyes widen.

"I'm sorry," I say, leaning forward and kissing her tears away. "Do you want me to stop?"

"No, I want this," she says, closing her eyes.

"Look at me, Daisy." Her green eyes glisten, her eyelids almost shut as I move farther into her. For every quarter of an inch, I pull out and start over, helping her body adjust. By the time I'm fully sheathed, I'm about to lose my shit. She's so fucking tight that she's squeezing the hell out of my dick. Pulling fully out, I enter her again, this time a little faster.

Hovering over her, I kiss her deeply, swallowing her sweet mewls as her fingernails dig into my back. It only takes a few thrusts until she's into it, bringing her hips to meet mine. I'm fucking drunk off her and feel delirious. I know this one time won't be enough. I brush my lips against hers as we find a rhythm that works for us.

"Watch us," I tell her as I sit back on my haunches and pull her hips to meet my thrusts. "I've had dreams about this." My thumb brushes against her clit, hoping to give her an orgasm even though I know it's unlikely because it's her first time, but that doesn't stop her walls from squeezing me even tighter.

I moan and move faster, falling on top of her. My hips buck as I capture her mouth and empty into the condom. I jerk a few times, riding out the aftershocks of finally getting the release I've been waiting for.

Rolling over, I pull out and bring her into my arms. I know what just took place and try not to freak her out by removing the condom and tossing it on my bedroom floor. I kiss her sweat-laden forehead and run my fingers gently over her arm.

"I think you're going to be sore." I'm only guessing. I don't make it a habit of popping cherries so I'm not entirely sure.

"It'll be worth it."

Moving to my side, I adjust the way we're lying. I push a few strands of hair behind her ear and kiss her.

"Can we do that again?" she asks when I pull away. A shit-eating grin takes over my face as I nod like the eager, horny guy that I am.

"I have a feeling I'll never say no to you, Daisy." Grabbing her hips, I pull her on top of me, setting her right on my semi. The little minx rubs herself on my dick, waking him up. I have a feeling that tonight is going to be a long one, a fact that I welcome wholeheartedly.

TWENTY-ONE

It's after one in the afternoon when I finally roll out of bed and flex my aching muscles. As soon as my feet touch the floor, memories of last night and this morning come rushing back. Daisy's clothes are strewn all over my room. I thought I had put most of them in the same place. Apparently not. The bed shifts behind me and small hands wrap around my waist.

"I think you missed school," I tell her as I weave my fingers with hers.

"I have finals this week, so my schedule is sporadic."

I turn and face her. Her beautiful breasts, marked with small bruises from where my fingers dug into them, are on full display. Even though this is all new to her, I encouraged her to ride me, and she did, coming all over my cock for the first time. It was a glorious sight watching her breasts as they bounced up and down while she took my dick deep inside her. Of course, seeing her let go of her inhibitions was the sexiest thing I've ever witnessed. Sex is by far the most natural experience our body goes through. No one needs lessons if you listen to what your body wants and set your mind free.

Lying back down, I use her hip as my pillow and rub my fingertips along her bare stomach. She threads her fingers through my mop top, which is in need of a haircut. No words are spoken, just simple touches. I should be the girl I've become and ask her what all of this means. Surely, for her, considering what she just gave me, it means we're together. I don't want to assume, though, or come off as too eager. Again with the labels and the branding that society requires you to conform to. For all I know, Daisy wants to just *be* and not have to answer whether or not she's my girlfriend. As far as I'm concerned, she is.

"I have to get ready." It's game day, and for the first time in my life I wish I didn't have to play today. I'd love to crawl back into bed next to her and make love to her all day long, breaking only for sustenance, which would mean she's walking around my place naked. Sounds like a good day to me.

"Thank you," she says sweetly, causing me some confusion.

"Why are you thanking me?"

"Because you didn't slam the door in my face when you had every right to, and for what you did for my grandfather. He was so happy yesterday." Her eyes mist up and she tries to hide her face, but I stop her. I don't want her to cry.

"I like you, Daisy. A lot, actually, and when you wouldn't return my phone calls or text messages I had to do something to get your attention. It's a win-win all the way around. We're together and your grandfather is happy. I'll do it for every game if you want."

She nods. "He'd like that."

"Consider it done," I say, moving closer to kiss her. Once our lips meet, there's no turning back. Her hands are everywhere—in my hair, down my back, gripping my ass, and finally grabbing my erect cock. The moment she starts stroking, I'm a goner. Daisy knows I'm not leaving this bed until we've both found our release. She already knows how to press my buttons and make me submit to her.

"Aren't you sore?" I ask as she continues to drive me toward the edge.

"Yes," she says breathlessly. As much as it pains me, I move out of her grip and lay beside her.

"Don't think you have to do this. If you're sore, you should rest."

She turns on her side to face me. "What do you do when *you're* sore after a game? Do you stop and rest? Do you wait for the ache to go away or do you continue to play?"

"Play," I say, winking my eye.

"Let's play, Ethan. Come hit a home run," she whispers against my lips.

Her baseball analogy has me scrambling to my bedside table and yanking the drawer open, dropping it to the ground. The contents start to spill out, but not before I can grab the string of condoms. Yanking one off and ripping it open, I quickly sheath myself. Daisy's focus is on me: her eyes are full of lust and her bottom lip is pulled between her teeth. My dick jumps with excitement, knowing that it's about to be buried deep between her tight walls.

When Daisy sees me moving toward her, she kicks off the sheet that was barely covering her and she spreads her legs for me. I love how it's automatic, how she knows what she wants. She's not shy or hesitant about having sex again and I really like that, especially considering last night was her first time.

I tease her briefly before dipping my head in and pulling back out, letting my thumb tickle her clit. We're short on time or I'd be working her body over, bringing her to the brink before pounding into her.

"This is what we call a quick-hitter." I thrust quickly, pushing our rhythm faster than I want to.

"You're already scoring," she says, biting into my shoulder.

I love that she's a sports fan, but I never knew that would turn me on so much. My fairly new bed is creaking with each thrust. Daisy is moaning as her fingers dig into my back. Each grunt I give brings me closer to the edge, and when her eyes look into mine and her back arches, I start praying that she's close because I'm about to fucking explode.

Adding slightly more pressure to her clit, she starts to buckle and move her hips faster. The squeezing of her walls around my throbbing dick is all that I need to let go.

———————◆———————

"You're late," Kidd says as I stagger into the clubhouse. The other guys are talking among themselves and aren't paying attention to me. To say I'm hungover would be an understatement, even though I didn't drink an ounce of booze yesterday. I'm tired, my muscles ache in both good and bad ways, and the euphoric high I'm feeling right now makes it seem like I'm floating.

I quickly glance at the clock and see I have about thirty minutes before we're supposed to take the field, and by all accounts, I really am late. I'm usually one of the first to arrive, often getting in some cardio before it's time to change, or teasing the reporters in here because it's fun and easy to get the women to swoon with a simple wink.

"Had stuff to get done today," I say, slipping my watch off my wrist and placing it in my locker, followed by my phone.

"Oh yeah? What's her name?"

I shake my head and reach for my uniform, which is nicely folded and waiting for me. It's too bad that the in-house laundry can't wash the rest of my clothes, because I hate doing laundry.

"Was she a hooker?"

I choke and start coughing. Kidd pats my back while laughing his ass off. Fucking jerk.

"I think I'm capable of picking up women of the non-charging kind."

"Stripper?"

I shake my head no as I take off my shirt and hang it up. I instantly regret getting undressed in front of him.

"Son of a bitch, you fucked a vampire." He's seen the bite marks Daisy left on my shoulder and chest. I didn't mind them then and I don't now. I honestly don't give a shit what Kidd or anyone else has to say about them, either. Last night...I don't want to be cheesy and say it was magical, but damn if she wasn't made for me. We fit together perfectly, even if the elephant in the room sat there mocking me while I got my rocks off. We need to clear the air about the whole blogger bullshit before it escalates. Sarah says she should be allowed to read it because it's fun and can give you a different perspective of what's going on. We're famous and need to accept that people want to know *everything* about us. I hate to think Sarah is right, but I know she is.

Everyone in the clubhouse stops talking. I don't need to turn around to know that everyone is staring at me. I can feel their eyes boring into my back.

"You're an ass."

"Yes, but you knew that. Spill. Let's be girls and gossip."

"No thanks," I say as I focus on getting dressed. Kidd finally drops the inquisition. I know it's not over and he'll be up my ass again, but for right now he's quiet.

As soon as my cleats hit the concrete walkway out to the dugout, my heart starts racing. I'm eager to see her, and even though I see her almost every day, everything is different. Sex changes everything. The only time it doesn't is when it's a hookup and you never intend to see that person again. I intend to see Daisy every fucking day until she tells me to stop.

The moment I climb the steps I'm looking left. She's there with her grandfather. I'm not close enough to see his expression, but that's about to change. I can't help the movement of my feet as I walk over to her. Kids come rushing down for autographs, and I oblige each and every request, looking at her briefly in between each signing.

When the usher stands by the gate blocking people from being near her, even though that's not really what he's doing, I know it's my opportunity to talk to her.

She stands when she sees me walking toward her. I wave to the usher, who nods and moves up a few steps so she can come over to the gate.

"I really want to kiss you right now," I say, clasping my hands together in front of me. My cup prevents anyone from seeing the semi forming in my pants.

"I think the staff would frown on such behavior."

I nod in full agreement. "So would your grandfather. I think his idea of how baseball players act would not coincide with me sticking my tongue down his granddaughter's throat."

Daisy laughs and covers her mouth. She looks over her shoulder, beaming at her grandpa, and I'm instantly jealous that she's getting moments like this with him. I miss mine, and now I'm going to call my mom and arrange for everyone to come out here for a week.

I do something that isn't against the rules, but frowned upon nonetheless. I open the gate and take the few steps to talk to John. Fans see this and start rushing my way, but the usher calls for them to back up, and now we're being blocked from people bum rushing us, giving us minimal privacy.

"How are you doing?" I ask, shaking his hand.

"Oh, young man, I'm a very happy man right now, and I have you to thank for this." He spreads his arms out and looks over the stadium. I don't miss the slight watering in his eyes, but that doesn't need to be brought to his attention.

"I like hearing that. I hope we can make it worthwhile for you. I know you're missing *Jeopardy*."

He laughs and squeezes my hand. I pat him on the back and walk back toward the gate, subtly touching Daisy's hip when I pass.

"I'll be over tonight," she says, winking and sending the nerve endings in my body to heightened alert.

"Fuck me," I mumble when I pass through the gate. I look over my shoulder and smile. "I'll be there."

I jog out to the outfield to see Kidd and the other guys. If I don't do it now, it'll happen in the clubhouse, and I'm not sure if I'm ready to answer any of the media's questions about Daisy. My teammates are a different story.

Bainbridge wraps his arm around my neck and rubs his knuckles over my hat. "Fucking wrap that shit tight, Davenport. The last thing you need right now is a pregnancy."

"It's okay, Bainbridge. His pussy packer is weak in that department," Kidd yells as he catches one of Meyer's pop flies.

"Fuck you, Kidd. I don't see you with anyone."

He looks at me after tossing the ball back toward the infield and says, "Why do you think I keep having parties that you never attend? I'm testing out the finer qualities of the Massachusetts women."

"You're going to get into trouble if you're not careful," Bainbridge adds.

"Nah. I know what no means."

When I look at Kidd, I'm not so sure he does, but I hope that when a woman says it, it registers.

BOSTON RENEGADES

No one considers May to be a midseason slump, unless you're a Renegades fan. We're racking up more losses than wins right now, and heading into June, we're well under .500 with a 24-and-30 record. This isn't how our season is meant to go and it's probably time for general manager Ryan Stone to take a look at the coaching staff.

Why staff, you ask?

Right now the Renegades are the youngest team in the league and it doesn't make sense to break them up. With the exception of Bainbridge, the team age is an average of 24. They're young men in their prime and not so far removed from their college days that they still understand the concept of hard work.

Is our coaching/management staff bad?

No, not necessarily, but they're not showing stellar improvement either. Clearly the lineup isn't working and could use some fine-tuning. And management needs to make a move on Cooper Bailey before it's too late. Rumors are milling around that he's seeking a trade because he's ready to play in the big leagues. And honestly, we can't really blame him. His batting average is through the roof, as is his on-base percentage. Those are numbers the Renegades need right now.

No one is consistent right now for the Renegades. When one is hot, the rest are fizzling. The guys need to find their happy medium as a team and deliver the wins they're being paid to deliver.

GOSSIP WIRE

Even though they're going to counseling, it looks like the Bainbridges are heading for the big D (and I don't mean Dallas) if he isn't traded or doesn't announce his retirement soon. Sources close to the couple have said that Bainbridge has, in fact, cheated and isn't willing to let the mistress go, and the current Mrs. Bainbridge isn't willing to concede to a divorce without some serious cash flow. As it's been stated before, the senior Mr. Bainbridge made sure his son was fully protected from any gold digging that might occur, and Mrs. Bainbridge is none too happy that no one is willing to pay her off.

Isn't marriage grand?

Ethan Davenport—Boston's resident Most Eligible Bachelor—is off the market. His college coed—who didn't graduate with her class this month—has been seen going in and out of his house nightly. Thanks to Mr. Davenport putting his address on Twitter, we're able to send our spies out whenever we want.

Easton Bennett has yet to acknowledge the recent birth of a son to his sometimes-girlfriend. In fact, he hasn't even been seen with her, but has been spotted going in and out of her apartment. I guess we're waiting for that pesky blood test to reveal the true identity of the father.

The BoRe Blogger

TWENTY-TWO

I'm standing against a rental van equipped with a wheelchair lift and a brand-new scooter inside. I'm not trying to buy Daisy's love, but trying to ease her burden. She struggles financially, something I didn't take into consideration until Boston University had graduation and she didn't invite me to attend. I tried not to let my feelings get hurt, but when I read the list of graduates and she wasn't there, I had to ask her why. It took some prodding and some definite hot-ass kisses to get her to spill. I played it off, acting like it didn't affect me, but the truth of the matter is that it does. I don't see her as a charity case. She's my friend...my girlfriend, in fact, and if I want to help her, I'm going to.

When Daisy steps out, her eyes widen. I know she's probably thinking that I bought this for her, and while that would definitely be a grand gesture, she's far too young to be driving around in a van.

"What's this?" Daisy asks, walking toward me.

Spreading my arms out wide, I say, "This is our mode of transportation today. However, there is a surprise in the back for your grandpa."

Her eyes narrow in skepticism as she leans in to look. The windows are darkened, limiting her line of sight. "What? I don't see anything," she says, stepping back and crossing her arms.

Pressing the button on my fob, the door slides open, revealing a custom black-and-red (of course) motor scooter. As much as I want to admire the craftsmanship of the decals, her expression is far more heartwarming. Her mouth drops open and there's a slight cry of surprise before she covers her mouth with her hand.

"We can't accept this," she says. I knew she was going to say that. Everyone always says that when you try to give them an expensive gift.

"Why not?" I want to hear her excuses, and if they're valid, I'll donate the scooter.

"Because it's too much."

That's definitely not a valid enough reason. I step forward and pull her into my arms, kissing her gently on her cheeks and finally her lips.

"Over the past month, I've seen a man come to life because he's doing what he loves—attending Renegades baseball games. I know I've made that happen, but I also think that your grandfather would probably like to get out by himself every now and again, maybe go to the store and get some things for himself. This thing is motorized and takes little effort. It's a gift, Daisy, one that you'll both benefit from. He'll be able to move around the house more freely and not depend so much on you or the nurses."

She nods, knowing I'm right.

"The van will still pick him up for games, so you won't have to worry about the T or anything like that, but all he has to do is get in the elevator and now he'll be able to do that by himself."

"Only if the elevator works," she says, wiping her tears away. I kiss her again and again, not caring who is watching from the street.

"The elevator will be working today. I made some calls and was assured that by the time we get back, the elevator will be fully functioning."

She gasps and steps back. "You did what?"

I shrug. It wasn't a big deal, at least not to me. However, her stance tells me I may have crossed the line. "What?"

"You can't go around making phone calls like that, Ethan. There are rules and...Well, you just can't do it."

I bite the inside of my cheek, trying to cool my temper. "You live in a housing unit that the state funds; you need working equipment. I made a call and it'll be working by the time we get back, otherwise they're in violation and you're not required to pay rent."

Daisy crosses her arms and looks down the street. I do what seems natural and pull her to me, enveloping her in my arms. "I'm only trying to help. I thought it'd be nice to have an elevator that actually works so when you're carrying groceries up, you're not killing yourself."

"I know. I'm sorry," she mumbles into my shirt. "I'm not used to anyone doing such nice things for us. I don't know how to take it."

I pull back, cupping her cheeks with my hands. "Get used to it, Daisy."

She stretches up on her toes, giving me a chaste kiss. "Where are we going today?"

"We are going to New York City to watch the Mets play."

Her mouth drops open and her eyes light up. "Seriously?"

"Would I lie?"

"No, but, oh my...My grandpa is going to be so freaking happy." She leaves me standing by the van as she heads to her door. "Wait, why not the Yankees?" she asks with a smile, before disappearing inside. I shake my fist at her before going to work on getting the scooter out of the van. That damn elevator better work today, because there's no way I can carry this up the stairs.

As far as road trips go, this is one of the best. The drive is just under four hours from Boston to New York City and John has made sure to pass the time easily for me. Stories of Daisy when she was a little girl have had me laughing the entire time. Each time I hear "Oh, Papa, no" I know it's going to be a doozy of a story.

"When Daisy was about ten, she had this crush on the neighbor boy. I think he was about three years older..."

I reach for Daisy's hand and give it a squeeze. She's been a trooper, letting her grandfather go on and on about her life growing up.

"Her grandma and I told her that he was too old for her and that he'd break her heart, but she wouldn't listen. Each day she'd wait for him to get home from practice or whatever he did after school, sitting on the front porch step watching each kid go by. When he'd go by on his bike, she'd run out there to say hi, and he'd talk to her until his mom started hollering for him.

"One day, he brought a girl home and little miss Daisy became so enraged she socked the girl right in her shoulder before she came running into the house, telling us that boys are stupid."

"Do you still think boys are stupid, Daisy?" I ask her, hoping my voice is low enough that her grandfather can't hear us in the backseat.

"No, she doesn't. She likes you, doesn't she?"

"Papa," she scolds as she turns around. "Ethan is a fine young gentleman and doesn't bring other girls home on his bike." We're both laughing by the time she ends her sentence.

"I can assure you, John, I won't be bringing any girls home on my bike."

Daisy is shaking her head and trying to control her laughter. I'm trying to stay focused on the road while I navigate to Citi Field. When the front office called to get me tickets, they offered me a luxury suite. They also suggested I invite the rest of the team, but that defeated the purpose of having some quality time with John and Daisy. Instead, we're behind home plate with all-we-can-eat food—another important part of sitting where we are. This is more for John, though, and our combined love for the game.

"John, do you think you'll want a shirt?" I ask, after showing the parking attendant my pass. He waves me on, leaving me to find my own spot. With the new scooter John has, we can park wherever we want and walk while he drives along beside us.

"And be a Mets fan for the day? Nah, I don't want to waste my money."

I don't blame him, but I'd rather be a Mets fan than a Yankees fan.

The moment we're parked and out of the van, John is getting himself out. Already, he's found some quick independence, and I'm sure to point that out to Daisy, who rolls her eyes. We have yet to tell him that the scooter is his to keep, because she's not sure how he'll react. I suggested we not tell him until he asks, or until I drop them off tonight and he's taking it up and I'm leaving without it. Either way, I'm not bringing that sucker home.

Daisy and I walk hand in hand, following John to the gates. He's like a little kid going to his first game, and I love that I'm a part of this. Daisy stops us mid-step and pulls me down, placing a sweet kiss on my lips. So many thoughts about heading back to the van run through my mind, except now wouldn't be the right time for a quickie.

"What's that for?" As if she needs a reason to kiss me. I'll stop and kiss her anytime, anywhere.

"The only way I can thank you for doing this for my grandfather."

"Your being here with me is thanks enough, Daisy." Looking into her eyes, I see a girl who has lost so much, but who is trying to hold on to what is important to her. I hope that when she looks at me, she sees a guy who is going to try to make sure she doesn't lose anymore.

"Come on," I say, pulling her forward. "Your grandfather is going to sell our tickets if we don't hurry up."

"What took you so long?" John asks when we reach him and his decked-out scooter. People are looking at him funny and a few have stopped to take pictures of it. A couple of kids come up to me, asking for my auto-graph when they see me standing with John, but security is quick to provide us an escort into the park. Once we're inside, only the fans behind the plate will have access to me. We're talking under about a hundred people, and I have a feeling they'll leave us alone.

I make John stop at the T-shirt stand. I know he's not a fan of the Mets, but he *is* a fan of baseball, and sometimes you need something to commem-orate your visit. The great Jackie Robinson played for the Brooklyn Dodgers whom the Mets replaced as New York's National League team back in the sixties. While Robinson never played here, the park is dedicated to him.

The stand is somewhat cramped, but people make way for the scooter. I'm praying he's not hitting anyone in the back of the heels with that thing. At least I haven't seen anyone try to beat him up yet. I follow him around while Daisy is off looking at the girly things, and I pick up whatever he puts down. I know he's not going to buy anything and that's why I'm here, to make sure today is the best day he's had in a long time.

"Well, I don't see anything I like," he says with his back facing me. I'm sensing that he's not exactly telling the truth, because everything that he's picked up and put back down again is all retro league wear—the throwback designs—from the earlier years. I'm not a Mets fan, but I do love the old stuff.

"I'll go grab Daisy and meet you by the entrance," I tell him, thankful he never turned around to see what I was holding in my hand. Part of me thinks that he already knows, but I'm hoping the element of surprise is in my favor today.

"Are you ready?" I ask Daisy, who is posing with a Mets shirt in front of the mirror. Thankfully, it's generic and only has their logo and not the name of one of their players.

"What are you buying?" she asks, while looking at me through the mirror as her eyes go from mine to the pile in my arm.

"Stuff your grandfather took off the rack and probably wished he could buy. He left the store empty-handed."

"You knew he would," she says with a smile as she turns around. "Can I get this?"

I hate that she feels that she has to ask and doesn't feel comfortable enough to put it in the pile I'm already holding. I've told her repeatedly that she can have anything she wants, anytime she wants. I know the words are easier for me to say than they are for her to believe or follow through with, but she has to trust that I'm being genuine here.

"You know you can."

"I thought I'd sleep in it," she says, stepping closer. She pulls her bottom lip between her teeth and has a wicked glint in her.

"You're evil."

"You love it."

"I do and I lo—" I quickly shut my mouth before those words sneak out. I have no doubt that I'm in love with her, but telling her in the middle of the Mets' team store isn't exactly how I see myself spilling the beans. I have no doubt it's going to happen, because every time I'm with her, especially when I know I won't see her for a while, the words are right there threatening to come out.

TWENTY-THREE

We're back to facing the Orioles and they're kicking our ass. I'm so sick of losing. I know our team is better than what the standings show, but damn if we can't prove them wrong. The number of fans in the stands is starting to dwindle. There are more important things going on right now for them to come and watch their hometown team lose, although the faithful are here telling us exactly what they think of us.

The one fan I can count on is Daisy, even though she doesn't stroke my ego or sugarcoat how poorly we're doing. She does tell me what I need to work on. I take her criticism seriously because she's usually saying the same shit my dad is. Her knowledge of baseball is a serious turn-on. She's like my own personal aphrodisiac.

It's the bottom of the fifth and I'm on deck. The score is Renegades zero and Orioles four. We need five freaking runs in order to win. It's harder than one might think, a comeback like this, but it can be done.

Bainbridge is currently on second, stuck in no-man's land unless one of us can single and move him at least to third. Kayden Cross went down swinging, giving us our first out of the inning. Preston Meyers is in a duel with the pitcher right now, hitting foul ball after foul ball and barely staying alive.

Baltimore is still using their starting pitcher, who hasn't slowed down and continues to throw heaters down the middle at ninety-eight miles per hour. One always hopes that by midgame the starting pitchers begin to wear out, allowing us to get the bat around more quickly, but it seems as though this one is just getting started.

Meyers hits a line drive toward the shortstop, freezing Bainbridge on second. The throw to first isn't in time to get Meyers, making him safe. The fans cheer, but the skipper for Baltimore comes out of the dugout, clearly not happy with the call. While the umpires get together to discuss it, I wander over to Meyers to chat for a minute.

"Nice hit."

He shakes his head, taking off his batting gloves and handing them to our first base coach, Shawn Smith.

"He's throwing heat, but it's garbage. His slider sucks right now. Wait for the fastball." His words are quick and rushed, as he's trying to keep our conversation to ourselves without their first baseman rushing off to tell his pitcher.

The instant replay airs on the Jumbotron, much to the delight of the fans. Meyers is safe by at least one full step, and the umpires agree after they review the footage over by the dugout. The home plate ump calls the game back into play and my music comes on.

I can hear John heckling the pitcher. It makes me smile that since the first time I made sure he could get to a game, he hasn't missed one yet, and has even taken to talking about my stats when I come over for lunch. I know Daisy's happy he's getting this opportunity and thanks me every chance she gets.

In two weeks she's meeting my parents. I know it's early, but my mom is right when she says you just know when you've found your "one." Since I've been with Daisy, my nervous twitch has lessened. So much so that even our general manager has asked about it, wondering if I needed to take a piss test to see what kind of drugs I'm on.

When I look at Daisy, I don't see a summer fling or someone I'm with just to pass the time. I see someone whom I can come home to every night and wake up with each morning. I see the woman that I want to spend all my free time with, and when we're not together, I count the hours until we are.

And now, when she's yelling at me to keep my eye on the ball and to swing through, instead of being mad at her heckling, I want to kiss her and thank her for being the support that I need.

Standing in the box, I stare down the pitcher, showing him my bat. I dig my right foot into the dirt and move some away with my left before resting the bat on my shoulder. His first two pitches are high and outside and well out of my strike zone. I step out of the box and readjust my batting gloves while the catcher jogs out to the mound. I can't imagine they're pitching around me with my batting average being less than stellar right now. I'm not a threat up here, and they're better off pitching to me. With my luck it could be in their favor and I'd hit into a double play.

As much as I want to look at Daisy right now, I don't. My focus needs to be on the game, my bat, and mostly the pitcher. Meyers's words are on auto-play through my head as I step back in, repeating my ritual.

The next pitch is high and inside, brushing me off the plate. The crowd surrounding me has a few choice words for the pitcher, who is stoic. It's the way he should be, no emotion. Maybe he felt like I was crowding the plate and is sending me a subtle reminder that this is his territory right now. What he's forgetting is that I own him with a count of three and zero. As far as I'm concerned, I'm about to take a walk to first base, loading the bases for Singleton.

The pitch is delivered, and the ball is the fucking meatball I've been waiting for all night. This is that moment when I can either stand here and take the strike—because that is what's expected of me and I'll still be ahead in the count—or I can swing for the fences.

If I swing, it has to be full on through the hips with a follow-through so hard that the bat smacks against my shoulder blades. I need to make him pay for giving me the fastball I love so much, the one right down the middle.

The motion of my bat is automatic, as if it knows it wants a piece of that white-leather, red-stitched ball flying toward us. My eyes follow the ball as it smacks hard against the grain of my Louisville Slugger. The deafening crack has the catcher saying, "Oh, shit." I let out a battle cry as the bat hits my shoulders before it slowly comes back around and hangs at my side as I watch the ball fly to dead center. The Orioles outfielders are running back, both left and center, wondering which one is going to catch it. Meyers and Bainbridge are tagged and ready to run on the catch; Bainbridge will score easily if it bounces off the wall.

The crowd is hushed as we all watch the ball sail through the air, no doubt each of us wondering if it has enough height to clear the wall. The center fielder crashes into the wall just as the ball clears the boundary. Everyone erupts as I drop the bat and take my required run around the bases, slapping hands with our first and third base coaches when I run by them.

After a home run, stepping on home plate is something different. Your team is there to meet you, to celebrate with you. When you turn to see the scoreboard, what was just a zero now reads three. We're now only down one run. We need to hold them so we can come back and win this thing.

We're pumped when we return to the dugout, cheering Singleton on. When he takes the first pitch and hits it out of the park into right field, the announcer is yelling, "Back-to-back home runs!" and now we're meeting him at home plate. That's when I glance at Daisy and John, who are both cheering, right along with everyone else in the stadium. She doesn't see me staring, giving me a brief moment to just look at her.

There's a soft glow about her, which could be the overhead lights, but I don't think it is. I think she looks happy, and I hope it's because of me.

We lose.

Singleton's home run was as close as we got. We gave up two more runs, losing 6–4. And now I'm sitting at a long table, dirty and sweaty, waiting for a press conference to start. Right now I'd like to go back to the time when I didn't have press access so I could be in the shower or resting in the whirlpool instead of here.

My name gets called, and I take a drink of water, waiting for the question.

"How did the home run feel tonight?"

Who comes up with these questions?

"Uh...I guess it felt good. I mean it brought in some runs and built some momentum."

The next question goes to Bainbridge and the following question to manager Diamond. I sit there, wondering why the hell I'm here. I can't provide an eloquent answer, and honestly, all the cameras make me slightly nervous.

"Ethan, are you looking forward to the All-Star break?"

"Yes," I say into the microphone. "It's a good time for us to regroup and have a little fun."

Diamond excuses Bainbridge and me from the press conference while he stays to finish up. Surely, they're going to attack him more than they will us. They know if they're not nice, we'll stop speaking. Diamond, on the other hand, doesn't have a choice. It's his job, whether he likes it or not.

The temperament in the clubhouse is somber. Everyone is quiet and a few of the guys are already gone. I don't blame them for bailing after the game. It's what I wanted to do. No one wants to hang out right now because we're all feeling the same. We're all tired of getting so close, only to lose.

I throw my shit into my locker and kick my stool across the room, lucky that only a few of my teammates are still here and that I didn't hit anyone with it.

"You're not the only one who's pissed," Jasper Jacobson, our catcher, says as he starts getting dressed. "We're on the same team here, Davenport. Sure, you brought in the runs, but it's a fucking team effort."

He's slamming shit around and muttering under his breath. I realize in this moment that I need to keep my mouth shut, because bringing up his stats probably wouldn't be a good idea right now. One of the runs tonight was on a passed ball that he let go through his legs, and I felt that the effort put in on his part was lacking.

Unfortunately, he sees me smirk and is now in my face.

"You have a problem, rookie?" he spits out, going chest-to-chest with me.

"I'm not a rookie," I say, stepping forward, showing him that I'm not going to back down from him or anyone else who wants a piece of me.

"You're a cocky son of a bitch, that's what you are. You think your shit don't stink, but let me tell you something, sophomore, punks like you are a dime a dozen."

I'm not even sure what his problem is. I kicked my stool across an empty room and it landed nowhere near him. He plays a different position, so it's not like he's backing me up. My batting average is better than his, and maybe that's why he's jealous. He could want to be in the third spot in the lineup and if that's the case, he needs to speak to Diamond about that.

"If we're a dime a dozen, you'd think we'd be all over the place. I don't know what your problem is, Jacobson, but it's not me."

"What the fuck is going on in here?" Diamond says as he walks in.

"Just talking, Skip," Jacobson says, waiting for Diamond to walk into his office. Once the door slams shut, his attention is back on me.

"You're my fucking problem." He puffs his chest out before storming away.

"What was that about?" Bainbridge asks after coming out of the bathroom.

I shake my head and grab my clothes. At this point, I'll change when I get home. I need to go pick up Daisy. I *need* Daisy.

"I kicked my stool across the floor and he jumped on my shit."

"I know you're frustrated and you expect us to win, but sometimes teams have to take some lumps. We're going to bounce back. We'll dominate. We'll be on top again." Bainbridge squeezes my shoulder as he passes by. I hear a faint knock on Diamond's door and wonder if Bainbridge will be around when we bounce back.

TWENTY-FOUR

Aside from the team's being well under five hundred, I'm doing remarkably well. The batting title is within my reach but I know that unless we make the postseason that will be an afterthought. At this point, we're not even close to making the postseason because the teams from Texas are fucking killing everyone right now. We can't even put together a winning streak, but we can sure as hell lose multiple games in a row.

The only bright spot right now is Daisy, whom I wish was living at my house. Even though I say that, I don't really want her to move in, at least not yet. It's far too soon to take a giant step like that. What sucks is having her in my arms, almost falling asleep, only to have to take her home to relieve the night nurse. I've offered to pay for a full-time live-in nurse but she balked at the idea, saying her grandfather is her problem, not mine. She doesn't understand that I want more time with her. My schedule really limits our quality time together. I suppose in the long run it doesn't really matter, since she's still taking classes—one more semester and then she'll graduate.

Typical of New England weather, one day we woke up and it was already freaking ninety out. This summer has been hotter than last year; I'm not complaining, just unprepared for the sweltering heat. I long for the days of hitting the beach or lake with my buddies to cool off after class.

Today, Daisy is skipping school and we're going to the cabin that Steve Bainbridge owns. He says it's nothing special, but it does have a small beach if we want to go swimming. I don't care if it means she can't see me for two days in a row because of homework. I don't have to work and I want to spend the day with her. She said I have to help her study, but since she's not a sex-ed major, I doubt I'll be very useful.

Right now, I'm counting the hot summer days until the All-Star break. I'm flying her and her grandfather to Cincinnati for the All-Star Game. It wasn't easy telling her, but there isn't anything she can do about it. Her grandpa loves baseball, and this is probably his only opportunity to see a game like this. She knows she can't win this battle, since I'll ask John if he wants to go and use it against her.

The All-Star break should be a time to rest and recuperate, but I'm playing, so I'll be part of the festivities the entire week. My parents will be there, along with my sister and my niece, and they'll be meeting Daisy and John for the first time. If I didn't feel strongly for her, the introductions wouldn't be happening. This is a big step for me and one I'm not taking lightly.

I'm going all-out for this trip to the lake. I ordered a picnic basket a few weeks ago in preparation for today and it's all packed with a blanket sitting on top. I have the wine chilled and food ready to go. Daisy should be waiting for me. I just need to grab everything and we'll be on our way.

So why am I stalling?

My palms are sweating and my heart is racing. I'm not sick, so the only thing I can attribute this to is that I want to tell Daisy that I love her. I don't even need her to say it back, but I need her to know how I feel, and I have a feeling that today needs to be the most romantic date that we've ever had.

With a deep breath, I pick up the basket and head to my SUV. As soon as I pull up in front of her apartment, I realize that I forgot to buy her some flowers, and it's too late to get some because she's there, leaning up against the wall, waiting for me.

She's in the car and leaning over the console before I can even get out and open the door for her. I hate when she does that, but I understand that she's in a hurry because she doesn't want me to get a ticket for parking in the no-parking zone. I know I'm pressing my luck when I park here, but it's worth it.

"Where are we going?" she asks, weaving her fingers with mine. The console gets in the way; I wish I had a truck with a bench seat or something so I could pull her close. Even though we're in the same car, she seems so far away at times.

"Well, since it's an off day and I have absolutely nothing to do today or tonight, I thought we'd go to the lake. Bainbridge owns a cabin with a private beach."

"Okay, two things," she says, turning in the seat to face me. "One: I don't have a swimsuit. Two: Will he and his wife be there?"

I don't have a suit either, and as nice as it is outside, I forgot that we needed them.

"So my plan isn't perfect."

She leans over the console and gives me a quick kiss, trying not to interrupt my driving.

"And no, they won't be there," I say, answering her second question. "I do, however, have some wine and food in the back, along with a blanket. I thought we could sit out and just enjoy the quiet and maybe skinny-dip."

"I'm *so* not going skinny-dipping."

"What?" I scoff. "Why not? It's private. No one will see us."

She turns and glares at me. "That's how you get infections and shit. I don't need a parasite invading me."

"I'd like to invade you," I say, wiggling my eyebrows at her.

Daisy shakes her head and tells me to watch the road. Every few seconds, her thumb rubs along mine and she lets out a heavy sigh. I don't know what's on her mind, but I have learned over the past month or so that sometimes it's better to wait her out rather than ask. More and more, she's been opening up about things, but if I prod she shuts down. Unfortunately, patience is not my strong suit.

Daisy startles awake when the terrain turns bumpy. I have to let go of her hand to navigate the small driveway. If this is Bainbridge's idea of keeping his in-laws away, he's doing a fine job of it. I'm about ready to turn around and say screw it.

"This is it?" she asks incredulously.

The way she asks the question mirrors my own thoughts. If we were expecting a grand home with large picture windows facing the lake, we were sadly mistaken.

I put my car in park and slowly exit. The slamming of Daisy's door makes me jump.

"What the fuck is this place?"

"Are you sure it's the right house?" she asks, as I nod. "What a shithole."

"You can say that again." I take her hand and walk us toward the shack that looms in front of us. This house is not a representation of a highly paid Major League Baseball player, but a bum who has fallen on hard times and can't afford the upkeep on his house.

"I don't even want to go in there," Daisy says, and I agree. By the looks of it, the walls will come tumbling down any minute.

"Fuck this bullshit," I mutter, but feel her hand tighten around my arm. I look down at her and see her green eyes shining from the sun.

"We still have a picnic and each other."

And just like that, what could've been a shitty day has turned around because she's so optimistic about everything.

"Stay here, don't move," I say, leaving her standing there in the middle of whatever this is that Bainbridge calls his yard while I run back to the car and grab our stuff.

I grab her hand and pull her along my side until we reach the water. I don't want to know what's growing in there and am thankful she isn't willing to chance it, either. I'm game for seeing her naked, but not in this water.

Daisy spreads our blanket out and kneels down to pull out the food. I stand back and watch her, wondering what it will be like once I tell her how I feel. How much will change? And what's our next step?

The way the sun is bouncing off her blond hair and kissing her skin tells me this is the moment.

"Daisy?"

"Huh?" she says, without looking at me, more focused on putting together plates of food for us.

"Look at me, please." When she does, I feel whole. "I love you, Daisy." I drop to my knees and pull her hands into mine. "I'm in love with you."

Her small intake of breath doesn't escape my notice and neither do the tiny tears watering her eyes.

"I love you, Ethan." Her lips crash into mine and she tries to crawl into my lap. I fall back on the blanket, thankfully, because who knows what the hell is on the ground.

Her mouth moves quickly and her hands push my shirt up. When she sits back, my throat tightens at the sight of her lifting her shirt over her head.

"I thought you didn't want to skinny-dip," I say stupidly. "You're afraid of an invasion or something."

"You can invade me," she says, repeating my words as she falls back down on top of me and rubs her perfect breasts against my still-clothed chest. The shit that comes out of her mouth turns me the fuck on. I grab her hips and rock her back and forth, creating some friction for both of us.

I sit up, cupping her face in my hands. She's still moving her hips, driving me insane. "Daisy, are you horny?"

"Yes," she says, breathlessly.

"Do you want to fuck outside?"

She pulls her bottom lip in between her teeth and nods. Her hands grip my shirt and she starts pulling it over my head. When I join in to help her, she moves her hands down and begins working on my shorts. Who the fuck knew three little words would incite this from her?

The moment I pull down the cup of her bra and take one of her breasts in my mouth, it happens. I feel the first raindrop, but ignore it. It's New England, after all; the weather will change again in a few minutes.

We kiss, our tongues moving together in heated passion. I don't know if I'll ever get enough of her, and I'm not sure I ever want to find out what my limit is. She pulls my dick out of my shorts and starts stroking. I have dreams of her sucking me off, but I'm not going to ask her. I know when she's ready to try, it'll be exactly how I've been imagining. My fingers slide into her shorts, dipping them inside her already wet pussy.

"Fucking hell, baby," I say as I pull my fingers out and lick them. She licks her lips in return before taking the opportunity to taste herself while I finger-fuck her. Daisy grinds against my hand, trying to get off as the sky opens up and starts to rain down on us. I know she's close and don't want to stop, but I also don't want to get fucking drenched out here, either.

Her blond hair is sticking to her face and neck as she leans her head back, letting the rain pelt her. It's the fucking hottest thing I've seen, and it's driving me nuts.

The sky around us turns dark and cracks as I scramble to pick her up. Her legs are wrapped around my waist with my dick tickling the inseam of her shorts, reminding me that the promised land is just beyond this flimsy fabric.

When I reach the car, I push her up against the side, not caring about the rain, and immediately get back to her pussy. Her head slams back against the window as she cries out, "Oh, fuck."

"Yes, that's what I'm about to do." I open the door and set her on the seat, opening my shorts before climbing in after her. Thunder sounds overhead and I can't think of a better way to spend a rainy afternoon.

I pull a condom out of my wallet and make quick use of it, sheathing myself while she strips off her shorts.

"Come ride my cock," I say huskily, pulling her to me with our mouths crashing against each other. She settles over me, sliding down slowly. I inch down the seat, giving her more leverage, and watch as she starts to move up and down slowly. Right now I'm very thankful I have a bigger car.

"Fuck, baby," I hiss out as she picks up speed. There's nothing hotter than watching her ride me.

"Ethan!" she screams out, the orgasm that has been building working her into a frenzy. I pull her close to me and weave our fingers together, feeling her rub her clit along my pelvis. When I thumb her clit, she slams our conjoined hands into the fogged window and her breathing become heavier.

"Yes, yes, oh yeah ... I ... oh God."

"I feel you, baby. Squeeze my dick. Make me come with you," I encourage her as we both find our release.

Daisy collapses against me, her chest heaving. I slowly pull out of her, missing the connection we share.

"Wow ... that was ..."

"Intense," I finish for her.

"Yeah, intense."

She looks away, avoiding eye contact with me. I move her wet hair behind her ear and pull her chin toward me.

"Daisy, I love you." I kiss her twice softly, until I seek out her tongue with mine and start round two.

BOSTON RENEGADES

A strong effort by Ethan Davenport and Branch Singleton fell short when the Orioles added two more runs and the Renegades were unable to come back.

With 33 wins and 42 losses, it doesn't look like the Renegades will make the postseason unless...

They have to turn things around. The bats need to be stronger and the guys need to utilize the pitch count. Study the pitcher and know who is going to be strong or who has the ability to hit the longball. Diamond needs to learn to play some small ball, get a base runner or two, and let Davenport and Singleton bring them home. With Jasper Jacobson batting fifth, he's a power hitter as well.

The bottom line here: we need base runners.

The pitching needs work. We can't have five or six strong innings from the starters, only for the bullpen to come in and give it up. Pitching coach Cole Fisk (yes, nephew of the great Carlton Fisk) needs to figure out what's up with this crew and fix it—fast.

WE WANT TO WIN!!!!

In case everyone is wondering, the "curse" is over! Stop using it as an excuse.

Only a few weeks left until the All-Star Game. The Renegades have three of their finest vying for a spot in the home run competition: Davenport, Meyers, and Singleton.

GOSSIP WIRE

Sources say that Jasper Jacobson is asking for a trade! I'll keep you updated when I find out more information.

Ethan Davenport and his college girlfriend are keeping things hot and heavy. The couple had full-on PDA at Tequila Rain, where the coed met him after the game. There's no speculation with these two; let's just hope they're using protection.

Steve Bainbridge has been seen with a mysterious brunette. My best guess is that this is the mistress we've heard so much about. Sources are telling me that from the look of things, he's not leaving her anytime soon.

The BoRe Blogger

TWENTY-FIVE

Darkness starts to fall, and the rain isn't letting up, continually pelting the top of my SUV. The sound is so soothing it lulled us to sleep. Daisy and I stay huddled together in the backseat. Her head is firmly planted in the crook of my neck and I'm staring out the window, wondering what kind of beast is going to come out once nightfall hits.

I am blown away by this shitty place. Not only does Bainbridge own this dump, but he sent me here on a date thinking this would be romantic. If we weren't locked in my car, I'd fear for our lives. Come to think of it, I do fear for our lives. Something is almost certainly going to come out of the woods and eat us alive.

"Hey, babe, where's your shirt?" I rub my hand up and down her arm, laughing because she now has goose bumps.

She brushes my hand away and snuggles deeper into my side. I'm going to be sore from sitting in this position, but it's totally worth it. I lean my head back, close my eyes, and wrap my arms around her a bit tighter. If she's not ready to move, who am I to make her? When we're together, she gets to live in a fantasy world where everything is okay and she's not taking care of her grandfather. No one her age should have to do that, but he's all she has. I admire her for her courage and for the love she has for him.

A deep howl causes me to open my eyes with a jolt. I sit up abruptly, scaring a sleeping Daisy.

"What was that?" she asks groggily.

"Um...I'm not sure, but we should go." I look down at her, clad in only her bra and panties. "Seriously, babe, where's your shirt?"

Her head turns slowly, and she reaches her hand up, her finger pointing out the window.

"It's outside?" I ask, confirming my fear.

She nods slowly. "Along with the food and wine."

"Shit, and my picnic basket." I'm proud of that basket, but I'll buy another one. Her shirt, though, is another story. I turn slightly, enough to knock her off my lap and reach into the back of my SUV. I know I have a spare shirt somewhere in the back, and while it'll be huge on her, it's better than getting out at my house with her half naked. And it's sure as hell better than getting out of this vehicle right now to go get the one she left outside.

"Please don't think less of me, but I'm not going to run out there and get our stuff, so put this on." I hand her one of my BoRe shirts and help her slip it on. As I suspected, it's huge and looks like a dress on her. She partially stands and shimmies back into her shorts while I climb up front and turn the car on. I crank the heat, because even though it's not cold, I'm chilled from thinking about what's outside watching us.

"Shit," Daisy says as she climbs up front, looking at her phone. "There's no service here." She moves her phone higher in the car, looking for a signal.

"What's wrong?" I look behind me, trying to determine if I can back up to get out of here, then remember how shitty the driveway is, and I know that I need to turn around. I don't know why I didn't think of this earlier. Oh, I know why. I was too busy professing my love and getting busy in my back-seat. This is a classic case of thinking with the wrong head.

"I…uh…I forgot to call the night nurse."

I look at her questioningly, but she doesn't meet my gaze. It seems odd that she wouldn't arrange for a night nurse, knowing that I have the day off and had planned for us to spend it together. Is it because I didn't ask about the night, too? I can see the worry on her face, so there's no point is making a big deal about it.

Once I get turned around and off the driveway, I'm driving faster than I should, but the thought of John being home alone without care worries me. It's not like Daisy to forget, and that worries me, too. As soon as we hit the interstate, I take her hand in mine. I need to touch her, especially when she's this close.

"Your grandpa will be fine," I tell her, trying to calm her nerves. She seems agitated, and that's the last thing I want. I push the speed limit and weave in and out of traffic, watching my mirrors for the blue lights that could be riding my tail.

The moment we exit the interstate, her leg starts to bounce. "We're almost there, babe."

"I know, thank you."

She knows she doesn't have to thank me; I'd do anything for her and her grandfather. Luck is on our side, and we hit every green light possible and there's very little traffic. Her seat belt is off before I pull up along the street.

"Thanks for today," she says as she places a peck on my cheek. She is out the door before I know what's happening. She runs through the rain, to the entrance, and punches in her code before disappearing behind the door. She didn't even look back and wave or anything. Hell, I don't know if I'll even see her later.

Driving the streets to my house, I'm trying to figure out how everything changed so fast. One minute we're freaking out together about the noises out-side and then she's in full panic mode about her grandfather. What strikes me as odd is that she didn't even call him. She could have called once we were on the road to make sure he was okay and we wouldn't have had to rush home. We could've even stopped to pick him up some dinner and watch a game together.

As soon as I pull up outside my house, I decide to call her. I need to make sure she's okay, as well as her grandpa. Daisy's phone rings...in my car. Her screen is glowing, the phone peeking out from under the seat. I hang up and reach down to pick it up.

Every sound around me stills.

All the blood rushes from my face.

My mouth goes dry.

My hand shakes as I hold her phone in my hand. It's locked, but her notifi-cations are lighting up her screen like the Fourth of July.

I swallow hard and close my eyes, praying that when I open them again what I'm looking at won't be what I think it is. Only it is. Tweet after tweet directed at @BoReRenBlog. As I try to read one, another one comes in, and then another. These are tweets to her from other people. I may not be the smartest when it comes to Twitter, but I know what the notifications mean.

Everything I thought I knew about Daisy is a lie.

Everything I hate about this blog, every complaint that I've made has all been for nothing, because she's the fucking blogger.

I slam my hand against my steering wheel repeatedly and bite the inside of my cheek hard. I will not cry over this dumb bitch. Pushing my shoulder against the car door, I step out into the rain. The weather is fucking perfect for my mood, and I can only hope it continues to rain so I don't have to leave my house tomorrow, because I plan to get fucking wasted tonight.

"Ethan," she calls out over the rain. I turn slowly to see the girl whom I professed my love to standing a few feet away, soaking wet. I look down at my hand, her phone still there and the notifications still coming in.

"I think you lost this." I toss her phone at her, wanting to keep my distance.

"Let me explain." She steps forward. Her chest is heaving, and she brushes her wet hair out of her face.

I shake my head. "I'm not sure there's anything you can say that's going to change things right now."

"Yes, there is," she says, stepping closer. I put my hand out, letting her know I want her to stay back. The resolve on my temper is teetering and I can feel myself about to explode. I feel sorry for anything in my house because it's about to be damaged. "I'm sorry I didn't tell you. I never thought we'd meet or even hit it off. The blog is a job from my sports journalism professor. You made it easy, at first, with the things you were doing. Once we started dating, I didn't know what to do. I need the job, but I need you, too."

"You knew how I felt about the blog, and you used me anyway. The first time we stopped talking you should've come clean. You should've fucking told me who the hell you are!" I growl in anger and frustration.

"I didn't—"

"You didn't what? Want to have to write about how you deceived me in your fucked-up blog?" I tug at the ends of my hair to keep from hitting something. I'm trying not to yell, because the last thing I want to do is draw attention from the neighbors. I'm actually thankful it's raining right now. The rain drowns out our voices and keeps people inside.

I feel bile rising when I look at her. She stands there, a shell of the girl I thought I knew. It breaks me to think she used me to gain knowledge of my teammates, my friends. I try to recall any time I gave her any information. I can't, but I let her into the clubhouse.

"I don't know what you want from me. Do you finally want your quote? Post this: the Boston Renegades third baseman told me to go to hell."

I instantly regret the words, but I refuse to take them back. I look at her and feel nothing but hatred. "Go back to your apartment and write about how many times I adjust my cup and how Bainbridge's marriage is falling apart. Go write about how fucking well I treated you, only for you to lie to my face day in and day out."

"You have no right!" she yells. "This is my job and I need it!"

"All you had to do was be honest with me. All you had to do was give me a chance with the truth, but you didn't."

"What am I supposed to do now?"

I shake my head and start walking up my stairs. "Not my problem, Daisy. I don't care what the fuck you do as long as you don't do it around me."

"I gave you everything," she says, climbing the steps next to me. "You took everything away from me." Under the porch light I can see her red eyes, letting me know she's crying even though any tears she has are mixing with the rain.

I let her words sink in, allowing the rage to build. "Are you talking about your virginity?"

When she doesn't answer, I feel the rage burning deeper in the pit of my stomach. "You've got to be fucking kidding me! You freely gave yourself to me, so don't act like I forced you into anything. Go home, Daisy." I don't give her a chance to respond before unlocking the door and stepping into my house. I slam the door once I'm inside, locking it behind me. She stands on my porch, her shadow visible through the glass.

How could she ruin everything like that?

My lamp is the first thing to go. It flies through the air, slamming against the wall. The lightbulb pops and breaks into a million pieces.

There's a knock on my door. It's her. Her dark figure looms on my porch. Unwilling to give up even though there is nothing left. I ignore her and walk into the kitchen, reaching into the cabinet and pulling out a bottle of tequila.

The liquid burns as it travels down my throat. I stand there, drinking, until half the bottle is gone. With the lack of food in my system, it doesn't take any time for the alcohol to start working. My eyes blur, but that doesn't limit me from throwing the bottle toward my front door. I hope she's still standing there.

I hope she's still there...

TWENTY-SIX

It's been four weeks since shit went down with Daisy, and I'm still not over it. I'm obsessed with everything she does, and I troll the web waiting for her to upload a new blog post. I don't know what I'm looking for, but it's something. She tried to call me once. Just once and gave up. Not that I blame her; she *should* give up. What she did was wrong on so many levels, not to mention the pain she's caused me for no reason. She should've come clean the first time we went to dinner. Thinking back to that night, she freaking tweeted about me being with someone while we were together. I even tweeted her back. Who does this kind of shit to people?

The All-Star Game is tomorrow. I shouldn't be going. I should've been replaced by now, but I'm a fan favorite, so I'm packing my bags so I can get to the airport and fly to Cincinnati. Daisy and John are supposed to be there, along with my parents. We were supposed to have some time for all of us to spend together, but that is not going to happen.

I'm not that much of a dick to take this away from John. If it were just Daisy, I would've canceled the trip, but John hasn't done anything wrong, and he deserves this. The car service will meet them at the airport when they land and take them to the hotel. They'll be treated to an all-expenses-paid trip, which is probably an experience of a lifetime for John.

I have no hard feelings toward John, but not Daisy. She's been at every home game, and for the first time in months I find myself looking forward to away games. Those are the nights that are easier because I don't have to look at her or hear her voice. Those are the nights when I bat well. Those are the nights when I sleep longer than a few hours without getting up to check my Twitter app to see what she's said or to read her stupid blog. I hate that I actually want to read what she has to say. She's yet to mention me or the two of us breaking up.

Home games suck.

Homes games mean I have to see her, because my eyes betray my wishes and seek her out against my will. My brain, however, can't stand her. Those two vital organs are not communicating, and it's pissing me off. I won't even talk about my heart, because it's so fucked up it's not even functioning correctly. There's a pain there that the whirlpool can't fix and physical therapy can't make go away.

To make matters worse, we lost to the fucking Yankees yesterday.

I finally understand why guys are so shut off with their emotions. It's because their douchebag friends make fun of what they're feeling. One hint of emotion and they're asking you when your period is due. This is why guys need chick friends, even though they come with problems, too. The biggest problem is usually the fact that you end up screwing each other, but that's beside the point. The point is I need a chick friend right now, and the only one I can talk to is three thousand miles away playing doctor and can't drop her shit to tend to me. I'd never expect her to do that anyway.

The only highlight of the coming week is that my family will be with me. I'll get to spend some quality time with my niece. She's the one girl in my life that can make everything go away. To be a toddler right now would be heaven. I'd have no worries and everyone would love me because I'm fucking cute.

This flight is different from others. The team didn't send us on our chartered plane so Singleton, Meyers, and I flew commercial, but we made sure to fly first class. There is no way the three of us can sit together in a row of three. We all do too much man-spreading. It's odd flying without our usual flight attendants, though. They already know what we like and what we drink.

Singleton is sitting next to me, beside the aisle. I'm trying not to listen to his conversation, but am forced to since I forgot my headphones. It's not easy to zone out, even if I am seeing Daisy's face in the clouds. I'm such an idiot for letting myself fall for her. I was better off just having one-night stands and my regular hookups with Sarah. Those are safe and no feelings are ever involved.

That's exactly what Singleton is doing now. He's trying to join the mile-high club with this airline. I have no doubt he'll get his membership wings before this flight is over. Maybe that's what I need, to adopt his carefree "I don't give a fuck" attitude. It seems to work for him most of the time.

The flight to Cincinnati is short, but walking through the airport is another challenge. I think this is why teams fly the players on commercial airlines—to build up the hype of All-Star week—and it's working. There's a massive number of kids in the baggage claim area accompanied by parents, all carrying posters, balls, bats, hats, and whatever else they've brought to have signed. Officials from MLB are here to gather our belongings and take us to the hotel, but I can't imagine we're getting there any time soon.

News cameras shine bright lights on us as we sign the paraphernalia they brought and pose with the kids here. A lot of these people won't be at the game. It's hard to get tickets and most of them are bought up by corporations. It's annoying because the game should be about the fans, and it's not that way anymore.

The MLB reps finally step in and build a wall around the various players in the baggage terminal so we can get out of here and over to the hotel. My parents are there waiting, but I won't see them until I get to the field. That's when I'll see Daisy, too. She has a pass to every day at the park and I can't imagine she'll let John miss anything.

The madness at the hotel is as crazy as the airport, if not more so. People are lined up outside, snapping pictures with their cell phones and yelling out their phone numbers. I find it silly, actually, that they think we're going to randomly remember a ten-digit number and dial it later. I know it's done for attention, but there are other ways you can become a slump-buster if that's your goal.

As soon as I step into the hotel, I immediately feel the void from Daisy not being with me. She was supposed to meet me here, and as I see all the other wives and girlfriends of the players in town, it makes me question how I got so deep so fast. She's just another girl—that's what I keep telling myself, at least—just another girl who can be easily replaced.

I'm lost in my thoughts until I hear the screeching of a three-year-old calling out my name. I bend down in time to scoop my littlest BoRe fan up into my arms and she wraps hers tightly around my neck. Shea is, without a doubt, the best medicine to cure a broken heart. Her innocence and views on the world around her are so pure and lighthearted. Just don't take away her stuffed Boar. She'll cut you deep if you touch that.

My mom squeezes into my side, knowing I'm not going to put Shea down until I have to, and then barely steps away so I can hug my dad.

"Where's Shana?"

"On the phone with Mike," my mom says with a slight sigh. Red flags go up instantly, and I make a note to ask her about it later. Mike has been gone an awfully long time; I don't think he's Special Forces, so I'm not sure why he hasn't come home yet.

"Unc, you play today?"

"I do. Shall we go to the ballpark?"

"I ready, see?" she says, pointing to her BoRe shirt and hat. In true Shea fashion, she is decked out from head to toe in BoRe gear, including her socks.

"We're going to meet you there," Mom says, as she kisses me on the cheek and reaches for Shea. "We are going to do a little sightseeing before everything starts tonight and give you some time to spend with your girlfriend." I don't correct her, even though I know I should. This isn't the time, and definitely not the place, considering reporters are lurking around.

I reluctantly hand Shea over and tell my parents I'll see them later as I make my way to my room. And since I don't care to run into my ex-girlfriend, I catch the first player shuttle available to the park; at least there I can hide.

The lights are on at Great American Ball Park and the sea of red is all around. It's a good thing that's a color I like. The camaraderie is what makes the home run contest fun, and while we're trying to win, we're also easily impressed with how far the longball can be hit.

I have no chance of winning, not with the likes of Albert Pujols in the lineup. The man is a freaking monster despite his age. I've heard a few of the wives refer to him as fine wine, although I'm pretty sure they're not talking about his batting average. Singleton has a chance to win, though, and I'd like to make it to the second round if possible.

Families are all sitting in the same section. It's funny to watch the mothers of members of rival teams chat like they're old pals from a knitting club. Tomorrow it will be American League versus National League—the line will be drawn in the sand. The winning league will have home-field advantage in the World Series. For the longest time, the AL dominated the All-Star Game, until recently, when the NL started making a comeback.

Spotting my parents is easy because Shea is standing on my dad's legs cheering and likely blocking the people behind them. I tried to get them front-row seats, but I'm still a "nobody" and destined to stay that way unless I get my batting average under control. The only thing going for me right now is my defense. Don't hit the ball my way if you're planning on making it to first, because chances are it won't happen.

Noticeably absent from their seats are Daisy and John. I'm trying not to let it piss me off, but it does. I went out of my way to pay for their trip, and she hasn't even bothered to bring him. This is his one opportunity to see an All-Star Game and she's making him watch it from home.

It's a good thing I left my phone in the clubhouse, because right now I'd tweet her, not text, and ask her why she bailed like this. *This* week was about her grandfather, not us. If I was willing to put everything aside to make sure he had a good time, so should she. Hell, I'm not even the one who lied and built a mountain of deception. That's all her. I'm just the one who doesn't want to put up with her bullshit drama.

TWENTY-SEVEN

The second I have my bags I'm hailing a cab. Everything about this past month, and more important, these past two days, has been complete bull-shit. Daisy and John never showed up. They never checked into the hotel, never used their airline tickets, and certainly never claimed their seats next to my parents. You would think that I've at least earned a fucking phone call regarding the matter at hand, but no. It's been radio silence from the blogger who is hell-bent on being a bitch to me.

My leg bounces in the backseat of the cab while the driver prattles on about my stats and the All-Star Game, where I played two of the worst innings of my life. I was a fucking joke, sitting there wondering why the fuck I give a shit about this woman who clearly wants nothing to do with me. When I found out who she was, I should've written her off instead of making sure she and her grandfather still had the things that I promised them.

I think that's what pisses me off the most. I don't want to look like the fucking bad guy here when that shouldn't be the case. I would *never* take back something I've already offered, especially a gift like this. *She* is to blame, not me. John is dependent on her and would've been there if he'd been given the choice.

The cabbie stops in front of her apartment, and I throw a couple of twenties toward him. In hindsight, I should've gone home to drop my shit off, but with my attitude being what it is right now, driving would not be in my best interest. The way Boston traffic is at this time of day, I'd likely have a major case of road rage, and that wouldn't be pretty.

I press Daisy's buzzer and wait for her or John to answer. There's a good chance she's not here, but John should be home. I wait five, maybe ten seconds and press again before stepping back and looking up to the third floor to see if anyone is up there, even though she doesn't have a window facing the street. The front door opens when a group of kids come out, and I use this to my advantage and walk in. I take the steps two at a time until I reach her floor. The hall is quiet, which means that if I start pounding on her door, her neighbors will hear.

"Daisy?" I knock quietly and call out her name. I hear faint footsteps, but there's no sound of the television coming from her apartment. I can't imagine John is out with one of his nurses, but who knows? Apparently I've been kept in the dark about a lot of stuff, so that wouldn't surprise me.

The dead bolts click and the door opens as far as the chain will allow it. Daisy doesn't look at me, instead keeping her eyes to the ground.

"Want to explain yourself?" I ask, my tone harsh and demanding.

Her head moves slowly, until her red-rimmed eyes are steady on mine. She's been crying, and for the life of me I can't imagine why. It's not as if she was betrayed like I was.

"I'm sorry we couldn't make it—"

"You're sorry?" I cut her off, finding it hard to believe anything that comes out of her mouth. For all I know, when she heard the buzzer, she probably thought it was me and started cutting an onion.

"Hey, Robinson, three days," a stout lady says as she walks by and yells at Daisy. I watch her walk to another apartment and yell the same thing before taking the stairs to the next floor. When I look back at Daisy, she has fresh tears streaming down her face.

"What is she talking about?"

"It's nothing. What do you want?" She tries to act tough, but her voice is weak and doesn't scare me.

"Well, for starters I want to know where the hell you've been and what that lady is talking about."

Daisy tries to crack a smile, but to no avail.

"Go home, Ethan. Just go home and pretend you never met me." She tries to close the door, but I put my hand out to stop her. The door falls open, the chain giving way due to the age of the wood. I shake my head and wonder who is going to fix that for her.

"What's going on?"

She shakes her head. "Nothing, please go."

"Where's your grandpa? I want to talk to him." I invite myself in, side-stepping her small frame and dropping my bags by the door. When I step into the small living room, he's not there, and there are a bunch of boxes stacked against the wall.

"You're moving?" I ask her, or maybe the wall. It doesn't matter, because the question is rhetorical. "Why?" I ask, turning to face her. "And where's John?"

When she doesn't answer me, I go to her. As much as it pains me to admit this, I love this girl, even though I don't trust her. Her hand attempts to move a piece of paper out of my line of sight, but I'm too fast for her. I pick it up and read it, and in an instant my heart is sitting in my stomach.

"When?" I ask, unable to read another word.

"Monday night. I was packing and he wanted to help. I told him to stay in his chair and I'd bring his clothes to him to pick out, but he didn't listen. He got up and started walking down the hall. I tried to get him to go back to his chair, but he said he was fine so I let him help me pack. I went to the bathroom to grab my stuff and when I came back he was bent over the bed. I called 9-1-1, but he was already gone."

I pull her into my arms without hesitation and let my own tears fall. She's left with no one. John was it for her, and even though she knew he wouldn't be around forever, I think she thought it'd be longer than it was.

"Daisy, I'm so sorry."

She steps out of my grasp and wipes her tears, but I don't bother to wipe mine. She needs to see that I care about her and her grandfather.

"Can I do anything for you?"

She shakes her head. "Just leave, please."

"Daisy?" My voice trails off. Her eyes are sharp and to the point.

"Get out. You've done enough." She steps away from me, putting her head down.

Her words shoot me straight through the heart, breaking off what little life I had left. I nod and brush past her, stopping only to pick up my bags and leave. I walk out her door without looking back. If ever there was a relationship that's over—it's this one.

I decide to walk to my house. I'm far too agitated to get in the back of some cab and listen to the guy tell me his theory on why we suck or what I need to do to get better. Everyone is a fucking coach, player, and personal life coach, even when they're driving cars around for minimum wage.

Cars honk and women pull over, asking if I need a ride home. I know I'm going to be on the front page of the paper tomorrow with some jacked-up headline about how I can't afford a car. One thing is certain: I won't be on the BoRe Blog, because she's not walking with me, so her "source" can't tell her anything.

As soon as I hit my block, I see a shadow sitting on my steps. For one brief moment, I think it's Daisy and that she's here to apologize. Only it can't be her because she would've seen me walking down the street, and I highly doubt she can afford a cab right now. The closer I get, the easier it is to make out the features of the other woman I know so well: Sarah.

I pause at the bottom of my steps and look at her. "What are you doing here?" I ask, realizing that I'm more than happy to see her.

She shrugs. "Your mom called, said she thought you could use a friend. I had a break from classes so I thought I'd fly out and spend some time here, maybe look for a job or something."

"I'm happy you're here." I climb the stairs and set my bag down next to her. I pull her into my arms and hold her, feeling my body sigh.

"Do you want to talk about it?"

No. Yes. Never, because guys don't do that type of shit. "I don't know."

"Come on," she says, picking up her bag and standing by the door. I do the same, pulling out my keys and unlocking the door. Thankfully, my maid has been here, so the broken lamp and tequila bottle have long been cleaned up and my place no longer smells like the floor of a dive bar.

"I see you haven't changed the place much."

I shake my head. "The color suits me." The grays and whites fit my personality to a tee right now.

"Right." Sarah takes her stuff down to the extra bedroom before returning to the living room. She goes to the kitchen, grabs two beers, and comes to sit next to me. Like a pro, she twists both tops off and hands one to me.

"Spill," she says, and I do. I tell her about how Daisy is the blogger and how I've fallen for her but can't trust her. I tell Sarah how much I love her and that I saw Daisy living in my house and being here when I come home from a long road trip. I talk about John and his love for baseball and how I brought him to the games, only to find out that he died the night before they were supposed to leave for the All-Star Game. I tell Sarah that Daisy is alone and that her family is gone and that I went there angry and left more heartbroken than ever because, despite being alone, she still doesn't want me.

Sarah lets me talk all night while she holds my hand, comforting me when by all accounts she should be angry that I've chosen another woman over her.

"Are you ready?"

Sarah stands in the doorway to my bathroom, watching me fumble with my tie. She's dressed in a knee-length black dress while I'm in a black suit with a red dress shirt. Sarah used her connections at the hospital to find out which funeral home is in charge of John's service, called them, and found out the funeral details. I know I could've called Daisy to ask her, but my gut told me she wouldn't answer.

"Almost." I stare at myself in the mirror as I prepare for what is likely to be the most awkward event of my life. The Renegades sent a large spray of flowers for the service, as well as a donation to help fund Daisy's last days of school. I didn't ask for that, but I am glad it happened. I also paid for next year's tickets so Daisy doesn't lose them. I don't know if she'll ever attend another game, but her seats will be there waiting for her regardless.

Sarah is still here, but she's leaving in two days to head back to Seattle and school. I'm going to miss having her around. Everything with her is easy; I wish things could be this way all the time. After our long talk the other night, I'm no clearer than I was before she got here. The only thing I can positively say is that Daisy and I happened at the wrong time in both of our lives.

"The car's here," Sarah says, breaking my reverie. I follow her out, opening the front door for her, and then the car door once we reach it. A few of the other guys will be there today, as well as the driver who was gracious enough to pick John up for the games. The service is a simple graveside ceremony, according to the funeral director Sarah spoke with.

I look out the black-tinted windows, feeling like a piece of me is missing.

At this point, I'm not sure how many pieces are left for Daisy to take. Over the past few days, things have been sort of a blur. I go to work, play the game, and come home to find Sarah studying in my living room. We have a late dinner, talk, and go to bed.

During each game, I'm looking behind the visitor dugout for Daisy, figuring she'd try to hold on to the recent memories of being here with her grandfather, but her seats remain empty. During one game, I freaked out when someone seat-hopped and took hers. I had the usher remove them and send them back to their nosebleeds. I didn't think it was right, and I clearly overstepped my position with the team, but I don't care.

"We're here," Sarah says as she grabs my hand. I quickly let go, not wanting Daisy to see us holding hands. It means something different to me, but it won't to Daisy. It doesn't matter that we're not together. She doesn't need to think I've moved on. I haven't and I don't want to.

Sarah grabs the crook of my arm as we walk up the steep hill. My teammates Kidd, Branch, and Cross all follow behind me, along with Ryan Stone and his wife, Hadley Carter. I nod to Ryan, silently thanking him for attending. He didn't know John and didn't need to take time out of his day, or Hadley's busy schedule, but he's here to honor a lifelong fan. That speaks volumes for our organization.

The Boston Renegades sit two rows behind Daisy. She doesn't turn to see who is arriving; she keeps her focus on the casket in front of her. To the left stands the spray of flowers that the team sent with the words "#1 Fan" on the sash.

A few more people arrive, sitting in front of us and blocking my view of Daisy. When the minister arrives, he rests his hand on Daisy's shoulder, making me wonder if this is the same man who presided over her parents' and grandmother's funerals after they passed. Do you keep someone like this in your contacts just in case?

The minister starts with words of wisdom and love, telling us that love is about forgiveness. Sarah pinches me, reminding me that she said the same thing the other night. I'd like to stand up and remind everyone it's easy to say the word *forgiveness* but much harder to actually commit to the act when something causes you so much pain. I want to go back to the day we met and have her tell me that she's the damn blogger and let me make a decision about whether or not to see her based on that. It's easy to say now that I would because I'm in love with her, but that night at the burger place, maybe not.

I can honestly say, though, that she fascinated me enough the night I met her that I would've tried to find out what makes her tick. She's had me on a string from the first time I saw her.

The minister asks if anyone would like to speak. I clear my throat and stand. As I walk past Daisy, I catch a slight intake of breath come from her. I offer her a smile, only to have her turn around and look behind her. When she faces forward, tears are streaming down her face—whether they're fresh or not, I can't tell. I *should* be sitting by her side through all of this. All she had to do was ask.

"I had the privilege of meeting John a few months ago, and I'm sad to say I haven't known him long enough. He was a true fan, not only of the game of baseball but of my personal game. He had the ability to turn what I would consider a fair game into a good game, highlighting the hidden stats of my teammates and myself.

"My short time with John will not be for naught. I'll take with me, and cherish, everything he taught me about life, love, and baseball."

I hesitate for a moment, seeking Daisy's request to sit by her, but she still doesn't make eye contact with me. Her head is down and her fingers fiddle with the tissue in her hands. When I sit down, Sarah reaches for my hand and I let her take it. I have nothing to lose at this point.

A few other people get up and speak, most of them older. They recount stories from Daisy's childhood with her parents and her grandmother, and promise to be there for her. I want to stand up and ask who is going to open their house to her because she has to move now. Where does she have to go?

When the service is over and everyone is leaving, I remain seated. "I'll meet you in the car," I tell Sarah, who kisses me on my cheek before she leaves, handing me the ball that I put in her purse earlier. I don't want to cause any more pain for Daisy, but I have something for John.

I go to his casket and set the signed ball from the current roster on top of it. I don't know if it'll make it inside, but I hope so.

"It didn't take you long to move on."

Her voice catches me off guard. I breathe in deeply and remind myself that she's hurting, and it's easy to assume that Sarah and I are together. I decide it's best that I sit down next to her so she can hear me clearly without tuning me out.

"That's Sarah, my ex. You know about her because I told you everything about our relationship. When you didn't show up in Cincinnati, my mom knew something was up and called her. She was sitting on my steps when I came back from your apartment."

"Oh yes, she's your road-trip hookup."

"That's not fair, Daisy. I know you're hurting right now, but Sarah isn't to blame and neither am I."

"You went to her apartment in Seattle?" Her broken voice tears me up on the inside. I lean forward, resting my elbows on my knees and turn my head so I'm looking at her.

"I don't know why you're bringing this up now, but yes, I did. You and I had stopped talking. I was pissed."

"Did you sleep with her?"

I shake my head. "No, but we did some other stuff until I said your name and she walked out on me. I spent the rest of the night telling my ex that I was in love with this beautiful, smart, and crazy girl with an adorable accent who knew how to put me in my place."

A sob overtakes her body. I try to reach for her but she shies away. Instead, I pull her hand into mine and sit back. This should've been my spot from the get-go, but she refuses to allow me back in.

"Daisy, I realize this may not be the best time, but I need to say this to you. I want to figure things out between us because I'm in love with you. If you don't love me, let me know, but if you do and want us to have a future, you know where to find me."

I stand up and kiss her on her forehead, lingering there as long as possible before I leave her to say a private good-bye to her grandfather.

TWENTY-EIGHT

EDavenport @TheRealEthanD—1 hour
@BoReRenBlog I miss you

It's been a month since I saw Daisy, and I have a feeling that was my last time. Each home game, I walk out of the dugout looking for her, only to find her seats empty. They remain vacant during the game, diminishing any hope I have of ever seeing her again.

When I left her at the cemetery, I thought for sure she'd call or show up. I even left my door unlocked a few times, hoping I'd come home from a road trip to find her living there. It's been a letdown each and every time. I've tried calling her. For a while her phone went to voice mail after four or five rings until one day the call didn't even go through. I don't know if she changed her number because she's sick of me calling or what.

The only thing that hasn't changed is her blog. It's still up and running, reminding the team of just how poorly we're doing this year. I've kept her secret from the team. I figure if she wants to tell everyone that she's the BoRe Blogger, she can do that when she's ready. It's not my news to share.

We're in the middle of a long home stand, ten games until we hit the road again. The Cleveland Indians are in town, and after my last at bat, we're leading three to nothing. I thought that after the funeral my batting average would continue to suffer, but it hasn't. I'm currently batting .320, the highest in the American League, but not in the majors. A couple of guys in the National League are still kicking my ass. Also kicking my ass is my nervous tic. It's back with a vengeance since Daisy and I broke up. Who knew she was the cure, and now that she's gone, it's something I have to continue to live with.

One thing I have learned from Daisy is that she was accurate in her assumptions. I spent hours poring over her blog, reading the shit that she was writing, only to find out most of it is true. Cooper Bailey *is* coming to Boston, and soon. No one knows what his position will be, as there's still no word on what's going on with Bainbridge.

Jasper Jacobson is currently up to bat. The rumors about him not being happy in Boston are true, which makes things a bit awkward in the clubhouse. He wants a trade, but Stone hasn't done anything about it yet. There's speculation that Jacobson might be involved with Bainbridge's wife, but no one's talking.

Jacobson is facing a full count and the fans are rallying behind him. We're all standing in support. We need a win; after our last two games being losses, we need some happy. He swings and connects with the ball, sending the right fielder to the warning track. We lean back and pray as the right fielder jumps, missing the ball by an inch. We run out and meet him at home plate, slapping him on the back and trying to show him that we're still his team despite everything going on with his personal life.

With no outs, all we have to do is add more runs. Bryce Mackenzie is up next, with Travis Kidd on deck.

"Someone's dogging ya," Kidd says as he nods behind me. I can hear my name being called, but I don't want to look because he's likely up to something. The fact that my name is being called means nothing, since the kids are always trying to get us to sign things, give them a bat during the game, or even look at them. It was a thrill when it happened to me as a kid, so I know what it's like to get attention from your favorite player, let alone any player.

"Just a fan, I'm assuming," I say, shrugging him off and focusing on Mackenzie's at bat.

He shakes his head and starts laughing. "A super fan," he says, nodding behind me again. "You might want to turn around."

"You might want to pay attention to the game. Mackenzie could hit a foul ball and smack you in the tallywacker."

"Jesus, Davenport, just turn the hell around."

I roll my eyes and finally give in, but only halfheartedly. I look over my left shoulder and see no one calling me and over my right to find the same thing.

"Don't know what you're talking about."

Kidd swings the bat a few times before he stops because Mackenzie has a hit and is now on first base. "Turn all the way around, Davenport. Stop being a bitch."

I do as he says, and I'm met with a pair of green eyes that I have burned into my memory. She's sitting behind our dugout in the center seat. She stands and points to her shirt. The front of it says, "I'm sorry." I can't help the stupid-ass grin that is plastered all over my face.

I lean forward, resting my hands on the edge of the dugout. "Are you busy after the game?"

"No," Daisy says with a smile.

"You are now," I say, not caring that I'm probably jumping the gun and assuming she wants to see me. It's not a guess; I know she does. "Stay right there and I'll come get you when the game is over."

Before I know it, we're on the Jumbotron with hearts all around our picture. She covers her face and I turn back to the game, only to turn around and wave my hat at the section she's in. They roar with cheers and start chanting my name.

We win, nine to one. I had a few more hits and some RBIs to add to our run count. Every Renegades player had at least one hit. It's odd when that happens, but we take it and run with it when it does. As soon as I enter the clubhouse, the reporters are there. They call my name and, instead of me going to them, they come over to me and shove their microphones into my face as soon as I sit down.

"Ethan, you made a pretty big display of affection today during the game. Do you care to tell us about your girlfriend?"

"Yeah, sure," I say, running my hand through my hair. "I've been in love with her for as long as I can remember. She means everything to me." Suddenly their microphones are even more in my face.

"What's her name?"

"Baseball!"

I wish I had a camera at this exact moment so I can capture their expressions as they all deadpan at my answer. They're stupid if they think I'm going to say anything about Daisy. We have a long road ahead of us and the last thing we need is the media hounding us. I do enough stupid shit that brings us plenty of attention. We don't need any more.

The reporters don't like me much after that answer, not that I can blame them. Kidd punches me in the shoulder and winks at me.

"Gettin' laid tonight?"

I start to undress, hoping that if I ignore him, he'll go away, but he doesn't. It's not in his nature to just let something like this be brushed under the rug. He elbows me, and I make the mistake of looking at him. His tongue is doing things I can't even describe to his cheek.

"Not gonna happen," I say, bursting his bubble.

"Why not?"

"Because we have a lot of unresolved issues, and jumping into the sack isn't how you fix things."

Kidd looks at me like I have two heads. "You're a fucking pussy. You better turn in your man card. I think I'm embarrassed to know you." He shakes his head and stalks off to the showers. It would be easy to be like him, but that's not who I am. I tried to be the one-night-stand guy and it wasn't for me. Yeah, sex with no attachments is great, but sex with someone that you really care about is *so* worth it.

After I shower, I walk out of the clubhouse and back toward the dugout. The lights are still on and people are cleaning the stadium. Daisy still sits in the same spot she was in earlier, right where I asked her to stay. I sit down in the empty seat beside her and look out over the field.

"The reporters asked about you tonight. They asked me to tell them about my girlfriend."

"What'd you tell them?"

"That I was in love with her."

Her head turns and the light catches her eyes just right, making them sparkle.

"Oh, yeah?"

I nod. "Yeah, and they asked for her name. I told them her name is baseball."

Daisy's lips morph into the biggest smile I've seen in a long time. "That's the best answer ever."

"I know," I say, proud of myself for the quick thinking. "What are you doing here?"

"I got your tweet."

I sent her a tweet before the game started, telling her that I missed her. It was a last-ditch effort to reach her and to show her that I'm serious. I know I don't owe her anything, but I feel something for her that I can't let go. Call me a psycho stalker or a sociopath, but I want to be with her, or at least have her in my life.

"I'm pretty good at tweeting."

"Yes, you are," she says.

We sit in silence, watching the grounds crew cover the field and preserve the infield for tomorrow's game. They'll be here first thing in the morning to get it ready. They'll mow, edge, and make sure everything is in place before they cover it up again before batting practice. It's a tedious job, but they're damn good at it.

"I don't deserve to have you in my life."

"I know," I say, agreeing with her. Anyone else would've walked away, never looking back. But they'd be fools to walk away from someone like Daisy.

"I should've told you about my job when we first met."

"Yes, you should have, but why don't you tell me now?"

Daisy sighs, rubbing her hands over her bare thighs. It was ninety out today and the night air is the perfect temperature.

"When you arrived in Boston, my professor thought it would be a good idea for someone in class to cover you. Sort of like a fan blog about you, but I had the idea to do the whole team. He gave the job to me because I have season tickets, or at least I did. He offered to pay me, plus I could do whatever I wanted with ad space. I needed the money so I took the job, thinking I'd never meet you or any of the other guys.

"At first, you made it easy. The stupid things you were doing were tabloid fodder and I was having so much fun. Then you'd tweet me and I could tell you were getting pissed, so I started writing about the other guys as well. Tips were coming in like crazy. I'd get tweets about who was in the bar hooking up, who's cheating, what wife just spent an obscene amount at the store... The more I posted, the more hits I received, which meant more ad traffic, and that meant more money in my account and better food on our table.

"The first night we had dinner, someone in the restaurant tweeted me about you being on a date. I thought for sure you figured it out by the time I sat down, but you never said anything, except for me to call your agent. Believe me, I have... He's not very nice."

I have to laugh at her last statement because it's true: he's a dick.

"The day you surprised me in the library I was uploading a new post. And when we fought, I saw it as an opportunity to escape what was coming."

"What was that?" I ask.

"Heartache."

She broke my heart.

"But I couldn't stay away, and it wasn't because of some story, but because I was... still am... in love with you. I never used you, Ethan. I didn't have to. There were enough people surrounding all of you that were willing to give up a story. Bainbridge's wife is one of them. She e-mails me on a daily basis. It's sad, really." Her voice trails off, and I start to question why I'm not angry with her now that she's coming clean. This is the story I've been waiting for and I should be yelling, but I'm not.

"I'm sorry I wasn't honest with you. That is my biggest regret. After everything you've done and were doing for my grandpa... there were so many times I wanted to tell you, but I just couldn't find the words."

"That night in the car, when you said you forgot to call a night nurse, what was that about?"

"I had forgotten to cancel the post and freaked out. You would've wondered about all the notifications or asked me why I was fiddling with my phone so much. I couldn't turn my phone off because my grandpa might have called."

I would've taken her phone away if she were messing with it while we were together. Our time was valuable and limited. The last thing we needed were interruptions.

"How did you know I went to Sarah's in Seattle? You never posted about it."

"Steve's wife. She tells me everything."

And Steve heard it in the clubhouse and told his wife? I'm not buying it.

"I don't think Bainbridge would've told her."

Daisy looks at me. "He didn't. Jacobson did."

"Interesting."

"Honestly, Ethan, sometimes you have these blinders on. You need to take them off and look around. There's a lot of shit going down in your clubhouse."

I know she's right, but sometimes you want to keep the blinders on so you don't lose who you are or start thinking about the shit your teammates are doing. Sometimes it's better not to know.

"There are things I tweeted to you as a blogger, about you as the person I fell in love with. I'm trying to wrap my head around that. There are days when I think it's no big deal, but other times it freaks me the fuck out."

"I know. I'm sorry. I wish I could take it all back, but I can't."

I sigh and lean forward, looking at her from an angle.

"Where do we go from here, Daisy? What do you want?"

I know it's an open-ended question and the answers could be endless. I have no doubt she'd ask for more time with her parents and grandparents if she could, or even world peace at this point. I hope she knows I'm asking about us and giving her the choice.

"What I want is you, if you're willing to have me, flaws and all. Where we go? I don't know, but I'm flexible."

We're not meant to be perfect in this world, and yes, I know she fucked up, but under her circumstances, I get it. I might have gone about things differently, but I understand why she did what she did.

"It's what I want, too," I tell her, as I pull her into a kiss, loving the feel of her lips against mine once again. She melts into me and pushes her fingers through my hair. I tug gently at her lip before our tongues meet and fireworks go off around us. I pull away and watch the night sky light up with red, blue, and white lights.

"I think someone is helping us celebrate."

"I think we ought to take this someplace else," I tell her, pulling her to her feet.

"Dinner would be good."

I look at her questioningly and she shrugs. "We can do dinner."

We start up the stairs hand in hand, until we reach the top. "There's just one thing, though."

"What's that?"

"I want to make sure we're clear on one thing."

"Okay," she says, drawing out the word.

"I don't care about the blog. In fact, I want you to keep it going as long as you stop posting how many times I adjust myself."

"Does that mean I have to stop counting?" she asks with an evil gleam in her eye.

"No, just think of it as me thinking about you."

"I like that."

I push her hair behind her ear and sigh lightly.

"Also know that I am, without a doubt, truly in love with you. I love you, Daisy." I cup her cheek with my hand and kiss her until the fireworks start again. The people of Boston are going to start wondering what's going on at Lowery Field tonight if we don't get the hell out of here.

TWENTY-NINE

"Hey, babe," I say as I walk into the house. From where I stand, I can see her trying to hang some kind of garland on one of the shelves of our floor-to-ceiling bookshelf. Our house is fully decorated, down to a huge-ass tree with white lights and all the Christmas decorations we could find. There is garland wrapped with more of the same white lights that are on the tree and red bows on every available surface, as well as tied around the pillars that separate the living area from the hallway. There's a mountain of presents under the tree, too. None of them are for me, though; I know because I've checked.

My parents, sister, brother-in-law, and Shea arrive tomorrow to celebrate Christmas with us. Daisy is nervous about meeting everyone. I'd say I get it, but she talks to my mom on the phone more than I do. My mom already loves Daisy.

Daisy moved in with me two weeks after we got back together. It wasn't a rash decision, but one I took very seriously. She wasn't comfortable moving without helping with expenses, which I thought was ludicrous, but I understood where she was coming from. She pays the utilities and cooks. I pay, happily, for everything else.

She's also done with school, but won't be looking for a job until February when I report for spring training. We want to spend as much time as possible together before the season starts. Her graduation is in May and we'll be having a huge party for her.

The Boston Renegades didn't make the postseason, which isn't surprising. I don't know where we ended up in the standings, but if I wanted to know, all I'd have to do is ask my resident blogger. It took a bit of getting used to, but I now fully support her job as the BoRe Blogger. She knows I won't provide her with any dirt, though. I also haven't told anyone that she's the blogger, keeping her secret so the other wives don't give her shit. Every so often, for the remainder of the season, I had to remind Daisy to write something about me so that she didn't seem biased. And just because she's my girlfriend doesn't mean she went easy on me.

"I'm in here," she says, clearly forgetting that I can see her.

"Do you want some help?" I ask, walking up behind her on the stepladder. I place my hands on her hips and kiss her shoulder.

"I think I got it." She stretches up on her tippy toes to set the garland on a hook that I could've easily reached, but she's fiercely independent and I don't want to piss her off. Once the garland is hanging, she turns in my hands and jumps into my arms. Her lips find mine briefly before pulling away.

"How was your meeting?" she asks.

"Um...I wasn't exactly at a meeting." Her face falls as the lie sinks in. When she tries to get out of my arms I hang on tighter. "Hold on, let me explain. I had to tell you I had a meeting so you wouldn't ask to come with me. I went to pick up a present for you."

"Why didn't you just say you were going shopping?"

I shrug. "I don't know, because I'm a dumb guy?" I walk us over to the couch and set her down, kissing her nose before letting her go. "Stay here." I walk around the half wall and grab one of the two boxes I picked up for her today. Neither are Christmas gifts—those are all under the tree, professionally wrapped by the amazing women in the department stores.

Her eyes widen when she sees how big the box is. I have a feeling she knows what this is, even though I had it wrapped.

"This is a 'just because' gift." I sit down next to her and hold the box on my lap. "I think you're amazing and love you so much. I can't wait for you to succeed in your career and this is to help you along."

I slide the box over to her lap, watching her eyes light up as she tears into the paper. I know for a fact that her Christmases have been so different since her grandmother passed away, and since this is her first without her grandpa, I'm trying to make it special—which is *one* of the reasons why my parents are coming. My mom plans to show her how the Davenports celebrate.

"Oh, my God, Ethan…This is too much. I can't." She tries to hand me the MacBook Air, but I push it back toward her.

"You're going to need it when you start working, and I'm tired of hearing you complain about that crappy Acer you bought." I lean in and kiss her cheek. "Besides, I've seen how much you love mine. Now we can be twins."

When Daisy looks at me, her eyes are full of tears. "I love you so much, Ethan."

"I love you, too. Meeting you has been the best thing that's ever happened to me."

She looks at me quizzically. "Really? What about being drafted?"

I take the laptop from her and put it on the floor, pulling her in to me so we're lying down on the couch. I reach for the remote and turn down the lights before turning on some soft music. The white lights from our first Christmas tree twinkle, casting a luminous glow over the living room.

"I told you before, meeting you was kismet. I meant it then and I mean it now. We were destined to be together."

Daisy wraps her arm around mine and presses her back into my chest. I love lying with her like this, where neither of us can move away from each other.

"Sometimes you sound like a girl."

"I know. I can't help it. You bring out my girly side."

Trailing my fingers up and down her arms, I know I have to be careful or she'll fall asleep here. It's happened so many times, and while I don't care, I have another present for her.

"Daisy?"

"Hmm?" she says, close to sleep. I sit up slightly and roll her over to face me. I can't resist the small pout on her lips and lean down to kiss it away. She deepens the kiss, but I pull away, leaving both of us breathless.

My fingers ghost down the side of her face as she looks at me with her vibrant green eyes. "You're so beautiful." I tell her this every day. I never want her to think that I don't find her the most beautiful woman I've ever seen. "I'm so lucky to have you in my life. I think we need to make this permanent."

"We live together, Ethan."

"I want to share everything with you, Daisy." She sits up, matching my position. "I know I'm not doing this right and it's not how I planned this out in my head, but some things are best left unplanned, right?"

She nods, pulling her bottom lip between her teeth.

"I wish I had the opportunity to ask your dad or grandfather for permission, but I think your grandpa would be okay with this question…" I roll over her legs and onto my knee. She moves so she's facing me. I pull the ring that I picked up earlier out of my pocket. I'd put it in my pocket, hoping to move it to my nightstand so I could propose in the morning, but right now feels right, and I don't want to wait.

"Daisy, when I look at you I see my future. I see you as my wife, partner, and cheerleader. I see you as the one who will keep me grounded and be the first to remind me that I'm being stupid. I want to be there when your career takes off and hold your hand when we find out we're starting a family. I want you to be the first one I kiss when I finally win a batting title or the World

Series. Most important, I just want to be with you. Daisy, will you marry me?" I hold the platinum band with a three-carat solitaire surrounded by diamonds between my fingers.

By the time I finish my speech, her mouth is covered and she's crying and so am I. "Yes, Ethan. Oh, my God, yes!"

I take her hand and slip the ring on before pulling her into my arms. Our lips meet and our kiss deepens as I set her back onto the couch. I pull her shirt off and mine quickly follows, building a pile in the middle of the floor. With a flick of my thumb, her bra is off and my mouth waters at the thought of sucking on her breasts.

"You're breathtaking," I tell her as I stand and kick off my shoes and pants. She copies me, tossing the rest of her clothes onto the floor. My erection bounces against my stomach when I take off my boxers, causing her to laugh.

"I'll show you," I say, as I climb on top of her, centering myself. I look into her eyes. I see nothing but love and lust in her green orbs. I place my hands on the arm of the couch and push into her, watching her mouth drop open. She squirms underneath me, digging her nails into my back.

"Ethan," she mewls, bringing her knees up over my hips. I have never felt so connected to someone as I do with her. Each thrust brings out a moan from her, spurring me on. As much as I want to go slowly, that will have to wait for when we go to bed, because Daisy is rocking her hips against mine, pushing me closer to the edge...an edge that I'm willing to fall over every time with her.

"Merry Christmas!" my mom yells as she enters the house. She runs right to Daisy and pulls her into her arms before she comes to give me a hug. I already know how I'm going to rate in this family now that my mom has met Daisy.

Shea, though, loves her unc and comes running into the house and into my arms, followed by Shana and Mike.

My plan was to pick them up, but they called us from their rental car saying they were here and to just unlock the door. I know my mom wanted a grand entrance that wasn't awkward for Daisy. I step outside with Mike to help my dad with the luggage. We hug, and he loads my arms full of suitcases.

"Are you moving in?"

He scoffs. "No, these are presents."

I look at him questioningly. "What's in my closet then?" I've been receiving Shea's Santa presents for months now.

"These are for you, Daisy, Shana, and Mike. Any excuse to shop…that woman will do it," he says as he reaches for more.

As soon as I step into the house, my mom is standing in front of me. "Ethan, she's beautiful and lovely. I just love her."

"I love her too, Mom," I say, kissing her on the cheek and winking at Daisy, who is blushing like crazy.

I carry all the bags to the extra bedroom, where Mike and Shana will stay with Shea. My parents are going to sleep on the couch that pulls out into a bed. I never thought I'd host everyone at my place or I would've bought something bigger. Maybe that's something Daisy and I need to look at once the holidays are over.

Before I know what's happening, my mom has the eggnog open and has poured everyone a glass. She holds her glass high in the air and clears her throat. "I'm a blessed woman," she starts with tears already in her eyes. "I have the best family and I'm so happy to bring this beautiful young woman into our lives."

"Forever," I add with a smirk.

Both Mom's and Shana's mouths drop open, and Daisy looks at me, smiling.

"Ethan?" Mom's voice is happy, yet scolding.

I shrug and hold up Daisy's hand, much to the cheerful delight of everyone in the room. "Daisy and I are getting married."

"When?" Mom asks.

We had talked about a date into the wee hours of the morning the night I proposed, finally settling on one that would work for both of us. "We know it's short notice, but we're going to get married in February before I report for spring training. We don't want anything big, and Daisy wants to get married on the beach. So we thought we'd all take a trip to the Keys and have us a little party."

"Are you pregnant?" Shana blurts out. Both Mike and my dad glare at her. She shrugs. It's an honest question.

"No, I'm not pregnant. There's just nothing keeping us waiting."

"Here's to my son and his beautiful bride. I'll be very happy to spend some time down south in the winter." My dad laughs as he gives us a toast.

Mom comes over and pulls us into a hug, congratulating us. Shana and Mike are next, followed by my dad. It doesn't escape my notice that he hugs Daisy for a long time, and when he pulls away, she's wiping tears. I look at her, but she shakes her head, leaving me to talk to my family while she disappears down the hall.

"I'll be right back." I hand Mom my glass and follow Daisy down the hall, finding her in the bathroom.

"Are you okay?" I rub her back while she dabs a tissue to her eyes.

"Yes. Your dad said something that made me cry."

"What?"

Daisy turns, resting her hip against the sink. "He said he'd happily walk me down the aisle if I felt like I couldn't do it myself."

In this instance I feel my throat swell up with emotion. "Wow, what'd you say?"

"I told him I'd think about it."

"You do whatever you're comfortable with, babe." I kiss her chastely and wish I could close the door and have my wicked way with her, but we can't. In fact, we won't be able to be together as long as everyone is here.

When we come out of the bathroom, my mother and sister are putting more presents out and Shea is picking up every one they put down, trying to read the names. I go and scoop her up and bring her over to the couch so she can get to know Daisy.

"Daisy is going to be my wife. That will make her your aunt."

"What do I name her?" Shea shrugs.

"How about Auntie?"

Shea shakes her head. "Maybe I call her Flower."

Daisy and I both look at each other and laugh, which causes Shea to laugh. It's not long until my mom is calling Daisy and Shana into the kitchen to cook dinner, and Mike and my dad are relaxing in the living room. I stand back, looking at my family, and realize I don't think I could be any luckier if I tried.

My life is complete.

BOSTON RENEGADES

It's time for preseason.

Our Boston Renegades are gearing up for another season. The Grapefruit League will start in a few days, ending April 2, when the BoRes return home to open up at Lowery Field.

An off-season trade sent Jasper Jacobson to the Toronto Blue Jays in exchange for future draft picks and the Renegades will welcome Cooper Bailey to the roster. The BoRes also added some much-needed pitching.

After much speculation, Bainbridge returns to the Renegades for another season.

Here's to another season of Renegades baseball! Bring on 2016!

GOSSIP WIRE

I'm sorry to all the women of Boston...

Ethan Davenport has wed his girlfriend, Daisy Robinson, in an intimate ceremony at dusk on the beach in Key West. It's rumored that Ethan's father walked Ms. Robinson down the aisle, while his niece served as flower girl. Travis Kidd is rumored to have been the best man. No word on the official bridal party at press time.

The BoRe Blogger

BOSTON RENEGADES

BATTING LINEUP

Kayden Cross—First base

Preston Meyers—Right field

Ethan Davenport—Third base

Branch Singleton—Designated hitter

Jasper Jacobson—Catcher

Bryce Mackenzie—Second base

Travis Kidd—Left field

Easton Bennett—Shortstop

Steve Bainbridge—Center field

ACKNOWLEDGMENTS

My dedication speaks for itself, Dad, when I say thank you for introducing me to the vast world of sports. Our shared love goes beyond baseball, and I love how we can sit on the couch and watch everything together: baseball, basketball, auto racing, tennis, and even golf. You taught me to not only appreciate sports, but to have knowledge of the game, and that is something I've been able to pass along to my girls.

To my usual crew, as always, thank you for everything that you do to help bring each idea to life. Yvette, Traci, Georgette, Tammy—you guys put up with a lot of harebrained ideas and I appreciate it. Amy, Audrey, Kelli, Tammy, and Veronica—you guys work so hard to make sure everyone knows about my stories; thank you. To Susan—thank you for putting everything aside to read *Third Base*.

To my family—as always, I appreciate everything you do.

Is it spring training yet?

Cooper Bailey just got his first real shot at being a Major League ballplayer. It's the dream of a lifetime—so why can't he get his mind off Ainsley Burke? With his career on the line, Cooper can't afford to lose the one thing that made his game so good: his *heart . . .*

A preview of

Home Run

follows.

COOPER

I dive into the swimming pool and stay under as long as I can before I begin to stroke. Swimming is my way of loosening up my sore muscles to keep them from getting strained. I can't afford to get injured during the preseason or not to be in the best shape of my career. Everyone is watching me. They're waiting for me to come out and hit the shit out of the ball or to fuck up. The critics out there are wagering on whether I can make it in the majors or not. They say Stone kept me in the minors for a reason, and now I have to prove them wrong. Their opinions shouldn't matter, but they do.

With each lap I complete, my mind becomes clearer. My body cuts through the lukewarm water, creating a path so I can glide easily into my next stroke. This is the only time I have to myself before I'm "on." Before I'm officially Cooper Bailey, Boston Renegade. I know it's going to be different, with a lot more expectations, and for that I'm ready. I'm ready for what today is going to bring, with a whirlwind of activities, and I want to be my best. I want to stand out among my peers.

After the first day of conditioning, I thought the guys like Davenport, Meyers, and Cross wouldn't talk to me again. However, they have, and we continue to go through our workouts together. They're making me feel welcome, and I've even been razzed by Kidd with some off-the-cuff one-liners that had me bent over gasping for air because I was laughing so hard. But there are still some guys in the clubhouse that give me sideways glances. I get it. I just hope they know I have no control over who gets the starting spot—that is determined by the performances of Bainbridge and me, and the decision is in the hands of Cal Diamond.

I know in a semi-perfect world, Bainbridge and I would split the spot, but that doesn't work for me. There are goals I want to achieve, accolades I want to receive, and you can't earn those if you're sitting the bench for half the season. Part-time players don't earn batting titles or the Gold Glove. And if I'm sitting the bench, I can kiss my Rookie of the Year nomination good-bye. I'm sure Bainbridge feels like he's in a similar boat: perform or get benched. The difference is he's been there before. He's received the awards. It's time to let the young ones take over.

I finish my laps and head back to the apartment. I'm sharing it with a couple of the other rookies, both of whom are just out of college. Technically this is my second year, but it's my first in the majors. The guys I'm living with are straight out of college trying to make the forty-man roster. Last year, I wasn't even invited to spring training due to a late-season muscle tear that left me sidelined. My arm is good to go now. I've been working my tail off to make sure something like that doesn't happen again.

As I climb the steps back to my place, I pause and look around the courtyard. This place is nice, nothing fancy, and it's cheap. It's what we can afford. We each got signing bonuses—I received mine last year—but that doesn't means we're rolling in the cash like the other guys, so we live on the inexpensive side.

After I get ready, the guys, Brock Wilder and Frankie Guerra, pile into my car, and we head to our training facility. There's a coach bus waiting for us when we arrive. The other Renegades are all dressed similarly in khaki shorts and our red polo shirts and ball caps. We don't look much like baseball players, more like golfers.

I take a seat next to the window and pretend I'm interested in something in the parking lot. From my experience on team buses when I was a freshman in college, I know it's best not to make eye contact with anyone. The last thing I want to see on their face is a look of disgust when I'm still trying to find my footing.

The seat next to me is taken, and a quick glance sends me into a partial panic attack. I shouldn't be scared or even nervous to sit next to Steve Bainbridge, but I am. When it comes down to my love for the game, he is one of the best. I've modeled some of my skills after him, and here I am gunning for his job.

"I thought I'd introduce myself," he says, extending his hand to shake mine. His grip is firm, strong, really, and meant to send me a message. Message received but not processed. What's that saying: keep your friends close, but your enemies closer? I'll be his best damn friend if that's what I have to do. I'm not afraid to be underhanded in order to get what I want.

"It's nice to meet you," I say to him with pure honesty. Two years ago, I'd have been lining up for his autograph. By the end of spring training, he'll be asking for mine.

If I was expecting a conversation on the way to the zoo, I'm sorely mistaken. Bainbridge stands and moves to the back of the bus. Travis Kidd fills the seat vacated by Bainbridge almost immediately.

"His bark is worse than his bite."

"Okay?" I shake my head and focus on the scenery outside. Everything here is green and lush, unlike Boston. In New England, it's cold, dreary, gray, and gross. I long for the dry heat of Arizona where I can play ball every day of the year unless it's raining.

"It means he's really a nice guy once you get to know him."

"I'm sure he is."

Kidd doesn't say anything after that, riding next to me in silence. From what I've heard, and, believe me, rumors travel fast in the clubhouse, Kidd is a major partier in the off-season, and doesn't hold back much during the season, either. My dad has read articles about him, cautioning me against that type of behavior. He's reminded me that my image is everything, and once the public sees you doing something stupid, it's hard to come back from that. Keep my nose clean, that's what I'm supposed to do.

"Hey, Rook, tonight a bunch of us are hitting the bar. We have late practice tomorrow. You should come." I'm surprised by the invite from Kidd but happy as well.

I shake my head slightly. "I don't do bars during the season."

He laughs and slaps his hand down on his leg. "There will be lots of women."

"I don't do women, either." The second the words are out of my mouth, I regret them. His face pales before he starts to nod.

"I get it—"

"No, it's not like that," I say, interrupting him. "What I mean is, I don't date or anything like that. I'm focused on my career right now. Shit's hard enough, and I'm trying to make the roster. I need to keep my priorities straight."

"I was that way, too, my rookie year, until about midway through the year and we were in a slump so I had to drown my sorrows. Once those floodgates open, man, you can't stop them."

"Let's hope we don't hit any slumps." My goal, like everyone else's on this bus, is to win. Our team, as a whole, needs to put up high scores, outpitch the other team, run the bases harder, and challenge the opposing players to get us out. Make them work for their victory and hand them nothing.

Last year, the Renegades didn't even make the wild card, and they were projected to. The season was a letdown, and I half expected to be called up much earlier. Sports analysts have said the Renegades tanked last year because Cal Diamond was supposedly sick and not truly focused on the game. Others say we're too young and need some veterans. If the latter is true, it explains why guys like Bainbridge are still around but doesn't give much explanation as to why I'm here. They could've easily traded me and secured future draft picks if they're looking to keep veterans.

The guys start hooting and hollering when we pull into the zoo parking lot. Yellow school buses and lines of kids surround us. Kids aren't my favorite things in the world, but I can smile, sign autographs, and act like I'm having a good time to do my part and make the organization look good.

As we file off, the kids start pointing. A few scream when Singleton, Davenport, and Bainbridge step off the bus. Steve walks right up to them and starts shaking their hands. It takes me a minute to realize what he's doing. *This* is why he's a fan favorite. *This* is what I need to emulate in order to be successful on both sides of the fence.

I start shaking hands. Most of the kids don't know who I am, and I'm okay with that. I answer their quick questions and even ask a few back, letting them know that I'm as interested in them and that I care.

We're ushered inside the zoo and met by staff. My eyes immediately fall on the woman who seems to be in charge. She standing in front of a group of people all dressed in different shades of khaki green. I have never seen someone so poised and self-assured; it's mesmerizing how she commands the attention of everyone around her. Her smile brightens up an already sunny day, and I find myself stepping closer so I can get a better look at her.

"Good morning. My name is Ainsley Burke, and I want to thank you all for coming out today. The third graders that you met on your way in are from underprivileged schools, and coming to the zoo is something they usually only have the chance to experience once a year on field trips like this. At noon, we'll meet at the cafeteria, where we'll have lunch before finishing the second half of the tour. There are about one hundred kids here today, and you'll be in groups of five. That puts two players with each group."

Her name is Ainsley. I say it over and over again in my head as I stand here staring at her. She smiles at me, but her eyes move away quickly as she watches my teammates filter to their locations to meet the children. The activity around me is a vision of blurry bodies while she stays crystal clear. The only thing missing is the epically cheesy music that either signifies a connection or our untimely doom.

"Bailey!"

I snap out of the trance I'm in to look for the source of my name-calling. Davenport is waving his hand in the air, beckoning me over. I step toward him, but not before looking back at Ainsley. That's when I see it. She's watching me, and when our eyes meet, she blushes and runs her hand over her blond ponytail. Is it an automatic response that her head tilts down as she tries to hide the grin on her face?

"Dude!" Davenport says when I reach him.

"What?" I ask, feigning indifference, but on the inside, I'm bustling with excitement. What I'm feeling isn't foreign. I've liked women before, even dated a few in college, but never did I have the physical urge to stare at someone, to memorize them before they faded away. Something must be wrong with me.

"You were eye-fucking her like there's no tomorrow."

My brows furrow at his comment, and he looks at me oddly.

"Are you a bat boy?" he asks, whispering in my ear.

"What?" I choke out. "You know I play center field."

He shakes his head. "You know," Davenport says, waggling his eyebrows and pointing down to his crotch. No, I actually don't know.

I shake my head. "Umm, no, man, that ship sailed back in high school."

Davenport wipes his forehead and lets out an exaggerated "phew" before glancing over in the direction that Ms. Ainsley Burke is standing. She's talking to some other woman, a teacher maybe, and when she looks in my direction, she smiles.

"Well, I think she wants your juice packer." A hand is slammed down on my shoulder as Kidd steps next to me. Davenport starts laughing while I try to contain myself.

"What did you say?"

Kidd shrugs and continues to look at Ainsley. "You know your cooch lover. She wants to ride the jerk boner. Just don't do her in the cheap seats," he says, patting me on the shoulder before whistling at someone to get their attention.

"What the hell did he just say?"

Ethan shakes his head. "The one thing you need to learn about Travis is that he has this whole array of slang words for everything sexual. Cheap seats means having sex on the floor."

"Ah," I say, pretending to understand. "And bat boy?"

"Virgin, man. And if you are, don't you dare let Kidd find out. You'll never live it down, and you'll become his new favorite hobby."

Before I can respond, the kids start filing in. I'm sure they were told not to run, but you can see them speed walking to get to their player. Davenport and I are with three girls and two boys, all of whom seem very excited to be here. I was excited, too, until we had to leave and I could no longer openly gawk at Ainsley.

ABOUT THE AUTHOR

Heidi McLaughlin is a *New York Times* and *USA Today* best-selling author. Originally from Portland, Oregon, and raised in the Pacific Northwest, she now lives in picturesque Vermont with her husband and two daughters. Also renting space in their home is an overhyper beagle/Jack Russell, Buttercup, and a Highland Westie/mini schnauzer, JiLL, and her brother, Racicot.

When she isn't writing one of the many stories planned for release, you'll find Heidi sitting courtside during either daughter's basketball games.